Chasing the Stars

VIRGINIE GRIMALDI

TRANSLATED BY ADRIANA HUNTER

REVIEW

First published in Great Britain in 2019 by
HEADLINE PUBLISHING GROUP

1

Cataloguing in Publication Data is available from the British Library

ISBN 978 1 4722 6534 0

Cover credit © Librairie Générale Française

Typeset in 12.5/15.5 pt Baskerville MT Std by Jouve (UK), Milton Keynes

Printed and bound in Great Britain by Clays Ltd, Elcograf S.p.A.

Headline's policy is to use papers that are natural, renewable and recyclable products and made from wood grown in well-managed forests and other controlled sources. The logging and manufacturing processes are expected to conform to the environmental regulations of the country of origin.

HEADLINE PUBLISHING GROUP
An Hachette UK Company
Carmelite House
50 Victoria Embankment
London EC4Y 0DZ

www.headline.co.uk
www.hachette.co.uk

For my mother

A mother is the truest friend we have, when trials heavy and sudden fall upon us; when adversity takes the place of prosperity; when friends desert us; when trouble thickens around us, still will she cling to us, and endeavour by her kind precepts and counsels to dissipate the clouds of darkness, and cause peace to return to our hearts
– Washington Irving

Anna

'Anna, can you come and see me when you finish your shift? I need a word.'

I tie my apron round my waist and do one last check of the tables before the first customer arrives. I know what Tony's going to say; I overheard him talking to someone yesterday. It's high time.

In the last three months L'Auberge Blanche has worked its way up to the top of the ratings for restaurants in Toulouse. We were busy enough already; now, it's packed. I barely have time to clear a table before someone else sits down. I'm the only waitress and Tony can't help out unless he has nothing else to do.

Last Monday I was just taking a crème brûlée to table six when my head began to spin, my eyesight went foggy and my legs turned to jelly. The dessert landed on the customer's head and I landed up in my boss's office.

At first he just shouted. I'm used to it – it meant he was worried. He once confided that he has *situs inversus*: he said his heart is on the left side of his body and his liver on the right. His communication skills are obviously the wrong way round, too.

1

'What the bloody hell were you doing?'

'Bloody fainting, that's what.'

'Well, why would you do that?'

'To liven things up a bit – what a question! I mean, it is a bit quiet this evening, isn't it?'

He relinquished his anger with a great sigh then moved on to the empathetic phase.

'Right, are you okay?'

'I'm a bit better. I'll go back out.'

'No, leave it, I'll take care of things this evening. But you're back on tomorrow, okay?'

'Have I ever missed a single shift?'

He smiled. This was my moment.

'I'm tired, Tony. I'm about to turn forty – I can't keep this up. It would be great if you took on someone else.'

'I know, I know, you've said that before. I'll see what I can do.'

He picked up his phone and called Estelle, his mistress, to tell her he'd like to be inside her knickers right now. I deduced that our conversation was over. My neighbour Paul says I should change jobs. He's taken over his daddy's chain of shops and obviously thinks jobs are delivered by storks who've gone in a new direction since the baby market was nabbed by gooseberry bushes.

The truth is, there's nothing else I can do. I did go to college, though; I've got an accountancy and management diploma. I found out I was pregnant on the last day of exams, Mathias was earning a decent living, so we decided I'd stay at home with Chloe. When she started nursery school three years later, I applied for dozens of jobs in accounts and admin. I got only one interview, during the course of which I realised everything about me was wrong: I had no experience, I'd given myself three years off to play with a baby and I had the impertinence to answer 'no' to the question 'Is there someone to look after your child in an emergency?' I couldn't compete with the countless seasoned, uber-qualified applicants whose priorities hadn't come out of their wombs.

So I accepted an offer of work from Tony, a friend of Mathias's who runs a restaurant. For the first seven years I just did the lunchtime shift, which meant I could spend time with my daughters. Until I had no choice but to do evenings as well.

I've just wound down the metal shutters when Tony shouts for me. I go back in and sit down opposite him.

'You know I really like you, Anna.'

Situs inversus. This isn't looking good.

'How long have you been working here? Ten years?'

'Fourteen.'

'Fourteen! Time does fly. I still remember your interview, you were so—'

'Cut to the chase, Tony.'

He rubs his temples with the tips of his fingers and sighs.

'Estelle's been made redundant and I want to take her on.'

3

'Ah! That's a relief, I thought you were going to give me bad news. I have to say, I'm not sure it's the brain-wave of the century as far as your wife's concerned, but, well, that's your problem. When's she starting?'

He shakes his head.

'I want to take her on *instead of you*, Anna.'

The information takes several seconds to wend its way to my brain.

'What do you mean, *instead of me*? You can't do that!'

'I know I don't have any reason to fire you. Mind you, there's always something if you look hard enough, but I wouldn't do that to you – you don't deserve it. I've got a proposal for you: let's do this amicably, come to an agreement. I'll give you a little envelope as a thank-you.'

I don't know how long I sit there not reacting. Long enough to think about all the bills I already can't pay. And to picture the fridge even emptier than it already is. And to realise there'll be more visits from the bailiffs. And to imagine the look on my daughters' faces when I tell them their mum's lost her job.

'So what do you say?'

I push back my chair and stand up.

'Go fuck yourself, Tony.'

The Chloe Chronicles

First of all, I want to thank you for all your comments.
When I started this blog a year ago, I never thought
so many of you would read the ramblings of a
'hypersensitive' seventeen-year-old. Thanks ♥

I adjusted my beanie and took a last glance in the mirror.
Perfect. Hiding behind foundation and lipstick, I was
ready to take on the day.

I put my headphones on as I raced downstairs. The
front door was still broken and the wind was blasting into
the stairwell. If only it would blow away the smell of piss.

Lily was already at the bus stop. She waved at me, but
I ignored her and kept walking. I wouldn't be getting on
the bus with her this morning.

Why bother going to school? My future's all mapped
out. In three months I'll get a merit in my exams and I'll
enrol at uni to do Literature. And I'll never set foot in the
place. Uni – at worst, you have to pay for it; at best, it
doesn't pay to go.

Mum got another registered letter yesterday. She hid it

under her trousers in the drawer with all the others, but I'm not stupid. As well as her waitressing job, she does ironing for neighbours. I can't go on living off her so I'll start work next year.

I watched the estate come to life as I walked through it. There's a smell of hope about the place in the mornings. Maybe today would be the day everything changed. A chance meeting. An idea. A solution. A fresh start.

Every morning I mentally sketch out my dreams in pencil. And every evening I rub them out.

I waved hello to people – we've been living here five years so I know everyone. There was Leila taking Asia and Elias to school. Madame Lopez drinking coffee at her window. Ahmed going over to his car. Marcel walking his two chihuahuas. Nina running to catch the bus. Jordan struggling to get his scooter to start. And Ludmila having a fag by the front door of block D.

'I was waiting for you,' she said, opening the door.

She lives in a studio flat on the seventh floor. It was the first time I'd been here. She pointed to the sofa bed for me to sit on.

'Malik promised me you were reliable,' she said, taking a packet from under the coffee table. 'Are you?'

'Yes, I'm reliable.'

'Who do you usually buy from?'

'I've never bought any – this is the first time. I just smoke my friends' stuff.'

'Okay. Let's see the ring.'

6

I handed her the gold ring and she inspected it as if she knew what she was looking at.

'It's worth a ten, okay?'

I gave this confident nod so she couldn't tell I don't know what 'a ten' is. She held up a little brown cube, wrapped it in foil and slipped it into my hand.

'If anyone asks, say Jo sold it to you.'

I put the packet into my backpack with all my school-books then headed for the door. I was just about to close it behind me when Ludmila called, 'Hey, wasn't that you what won the writing competition last year?'

I pretended not to hear her and closed the door.

Lily

3 March

Dear Marcel,

Saturday was my twelfth bday and my
godmother gave me a diary: you! She's really nice,
probs to make up for her beaver teeth, but that was
way out of line. First of all, I've never seen the
point of keeping a diary, and I've got enough
homework anyway. Plus, she chose you, with your
gross pink cover with all the hearts. All that's
missing are a few sequins!

I wasn't planning on using you – I left you in the
kitchen in the hope Mum or Chloe would chuck
you out with the junk mail – but this thing just
happened to me and I really need to tell someone,
but I can't tell anyone. So I've coloured all over
your cover with a red marker, I've put a padlock on
you (better safe than a sorry state) and I've found
you a perfect hiding place, but I'm not telling
where. (If you're reading this, Chloe, stop right
now or I'll tell Mum you've been nicking her bras.)

So, your name's Marcel. I hope you like it. It's coz you're red like Marcel Musson, the baldie on the first floor.

I don't know if I'll write in you very much. If it's anything like my spot cream, I'll forget at least two thirds of the time, but I'll give it a go.

So here goes.

I had a stomach ache on the bus this morning. I didn't even manage to finish my cereal at bfast, which was weird, but I thought that was because of our English test. I don't know all the irregular verbs and it was stressing me out. Except that after the test my stomach still hurt. So I thought it must have been yesterday's supper. Me and Chloe reheated this stew Mum brought home from the restaurant, and it was so rank.

It was basketball in PE today. I screamed at Theo to pass me the ball for, like, ten minutes, and she finally did, just when I was tying my hair back up. The ball hit me right on the nose and it started bleeding, so the teacher told me to get off the court.

I was sitting on the side with my head tipped back and toilet paper in my nostrils (there wasn't any cotton wool) when I heard chuckling behind me. It was some older boys and a girl sitting a few rows up. They were all looking at me. This little dark-haired boy with a face like a toilet asked me if the ball hit me on the arse. I was, like, no, just my nose. They all laughed and kept staring at my bum, and then I got it. That explained the stomach ache – Mum's told me about the whole period thing a few times. It had to happen the day I was wearing my white trackie bottoms.

I backed over to the door and slipped along the wall to the changing rooms. There was blood everywhere. I didn't know there'd be so much – my knickers were like a crime scene. I did my best to clean them up, and put a few sheets of toilet paper inside to protect them, but it was soon obvious that wasn't going to be enough so I flattened the toilet roll and put the whole thing in my knickers.

I walked around like a crab the whole day, with my coat tied round my waist. I don't think anyone noticed anything. I need to ask Mum to buy some pads.

See ya soon, Marcel
Lily x

PS What if it's not my period but a cerebral haemorrhage (from when the ball hit me) coming out the bottom end, and I'll be dead tomorrow?

Anna

Every morning is the same: I start by saying, 'No TV,' try to get a conversation going but hit a brick wall of silence and end up convincing myself that if we're all staring at the same screen at least we're looking in the same direction.

Lily's pouring milk into her bowl, captivated by a cartoon.

'Can you get real cereal next time, Mum?'

'Turn that down, please. Isn't that real, then?'

She tears herself away from the screen for a moment and trains her green marble eyes on me.

'You know it's not – it's not a brand. It's like eating polystyrene! You have to get the ones on the middle shelf. The stuff on the bottom's scuzzy.'

I don't have time to answer. Chloe pops her head round the door, lobs us a 'See ya!' and disappears. I catch her just as she's heading down the stairs.

'Can you come and sit with us for a few minutes, Chloe?'

She turns round with a sigh. She must have applied her foundation with a spray-gun.

'Not hungry.'

11

'I know, you never are. But you can still come and spend a bit of time with us, can't you? Breakfast is the only time we get to see each other.'

'Whose fault is that?' she spits out, glowering at me, before thundering down the stairs.

I'm still standing like a lemon on the landing when the entry phone rings. I don't answer it – I'm not expecting anyone and nine times out of ten it's someone trying to sell me roller blinds or give me the low-down on Jehovah.

Two minutes later someone knocks at our door. I tiptoe over to the peephole. There's a man outside who looks about as welcome as a colonoscopy. I already know how this scene plays out, but I don't have a choice. I open the door.

'Madame Moulineau? Good morning, I'm a bailiff, my name's Monsieur Fox. May I come in?'

It's a rhetorical question: he's inside my flat before he gets to the question mark. He looks through a file and takes out a sheet of paper. I close the living-room door so Lily can't hear.

'I'm very pleased to have caught you. I imagine you haven't received my messages?'

'Yes, I have. I'm so sorry, I—'

'Well, then, you know why I'm here,' he interrupts. 'I'm now handing over in person the legal order for you to pay the sum of 5,225 euros to Cefitis.'

I take the document and the pen he's offering me, read it on the diagonal, lean against the wall and sign it.

'Can I ask you something, Monsieur Fox?' I ask, handing back the piece of paper.

'Please do.'

'If I haven't managed to honour several monthly payments, do you really think I'm going be in a position to pay 5,225 euros in one go?'

He shrugs his shoulder pads and attempts a sympathetic smile.

'I'm very sorry. The creditor has been patient, but you haven't honoured the terms of the agreement.'

'I promise, I'm doing my best! I've been paying a hundred euros a month for years to pay off this loan, except for three occasions when I couldn't. *Really* couldn't. They can't ask for the whole repayment just like that!'

'They can. Cefitis offered you a repayment schedule to manage your late payments, but you only kept to it for a short time. I could have offered you an arrangement, but you never replied to me. Unfortunately, it's now too late for any discussion.'

I want to protest, to beg. And swear I'm not lying, and tell him that I'm trying to honour the terms of this sodding repayment schedule, this one, and those from all the other creditors; that everything I earn goes into paying off my debts; that I sometimes manage to keep my head above water for months but in the end there's always a wave that knocks me back down. The fan belt goes on the car, or it's the washing machine, a school trip for Lily, or Chloe's gone up another bra size. Some people like surprises, but I can't wait for the day when I don't have any. I want to tell him I didn't spend this money on a week in the sun or on jewellery. And if I hadn't been really hard pushed, I'd never have borrowed at such a bonkers interest rate in the first place. I'd like to tell him so many things, but all I can manage is to give a little whimper and dissolve into tears.

The bailiff is embarrassed; I'm embarrassed for making him embarrassed. While I try to pull myself together he gives a little cough and reaches one hand towards my shoulder before remembering I'm not his friend and riffling through his papers.

'I'm so sorry,' he eventually says.

'What if I can't pay? What happens then?'

He sighs.

'We'll have to take you to court to recover the debt by any means at our disposal. Believe me, I know from experience that the case would be accepted.'

'Seizing my assets?' I squeak.

'For example, yes.'

'Well, that's perfect – there's the solution! My car's nearly twenty years old, the windows and third gear don't work. We must be able to get thirty euros for that, then we'll only need 5,195. I could sublet my flat – a three-bedroom apartment in a high-rise building with a dodgy lift must be worth a bit. What would you . . .'

I don't have time to finish my sentence: the living-room door opens to reveal Lily, with milk all round her mouth. She frowns when she sees the tears on my cheeks.

'What's the matter?'

'It's nothing,' I say, wiping my face with the back of my hand.

She tilts her chin at the bailiff. She appears to have heard everything.

'Why are you crying? Is it because of Monsieur Wolf?'

'Monsieur Fox,' he corrects. 'I was about to leave. May I wish you good day.'

He opens the door and gives me one last look before making for the stairs. Before I've completely closed the door Lily slips her head through it and yells, 'You're not all that fantastic, Mr Fox, you know!'

Then she pulls on her puffa jacket and backpack, and she, too, disappears.

The Chloe Chronicles

Thursday's the best day to skip school. Lily finishes at five and Mum doesn't come home between shifts in the afternoon – she goes to see Nanny. I have the flat to myself; I'm nobody's daughter or sister. I can do what I like and invite who I like.

I've been going out with Kevin for six days. I think I'm in love with him. He's kind. He works at the bakery just down from the estate, and he always looks pleased to see me when I go to buy bread on the way home from school. He's not very good-looking, but I don't trust hot guys any more.

Our relationship started last Friday. I asked for the usual baguette and I could see him out the back, putting some pastries in the oven. He smiled at me and gestured for me to wait for him outside. He came out a few minutes later with a cigarette clamped in his mouth.

'Hey, I'm Kevin.'

'I'm Chloe.'

He had blue eyes and flour on his cheek.

'Do you live round here?'

'Block C.'

'I like seeing you every evening.'

I looked away; I could feel my cheeks flushing. I always feel awkward when people pay me compliments. It's like they're giving me a present that's too expensive.

He took my chin between his fingers and lifted my face gently.

'I get off at eight. Will you come and wait for me?'

At eight o'clock I'd showered, done my hair and make-up, tried on three outfits, left Lily watching TV – making her promise not to tell Mum a thing – and I was standing outside the bakery.

At eleven o'clock, just before Mum got home, I snuck into bed, thinking back over the evening: the sandwiches Kevin had made, the bench by the pond, his thigh next to mine, his mouth on mine, his voice whispering that I'm beautiful, his freezing hands worming their way under my jumper, his hips pressing against me. I said no when he suggested getting into his car, and I could tell he was disappointed. He sat there smoking in silence, frown-ing, so I snuggled up to him and put my hand in his boxers. He was nice all evening after that.

When I told him this morning that I was alone in the flat for the afternoon, he immediately agreed to come over. I gave him the entry code and he came round at two. He didn't have any flour on him; it's his day off. He handed me a little bag with fresh choux pastries in it.

We sat on the sofa, listening to a romantic playlist on my phone. I put my head on his shoulder and took his hand. He stroked my palm with his thumb. He looked so huggable, Kevin did. Not like the boys I've known before, who were only interested in one thing and it was always take, take, take with no give. That little gesture, his thumb just touching my hand, might seem trivial, but maybe it meant he was the one. Maybe he was *really* interested in me. Maybe he would shower me with love and affection; maybe we'd make plans together and I would matter. Well, I was going to show him he mattered, too. He can't have that many opportunities to meet people, working at the bakery. I turned to look at him and reached my lips towards him. He sat back up, which meant I had to as well, and slapped his hands on his thighs.

'So, you going to show me your bedroom, then?'

Lily

16 March

Dear Marcel,

I hope you're okay and you're not too annoyed with me for hiding you behind the radiator. I thought Mum had switched it off.

Seeing as you ask, I'm doing fine. At the start of the year I didn't have a problem with Manon and Juliette. Everybody loves them, first of all because they're twins (buy one, get one free). Plus, their dad's cousin is neighbours with Kev Adams's mum's hairdresser, and everyone loves Kev Adams, except for the geeks who do Latin and Greek – and who wants to be loved by people who do Latin and Greek?

Personally, I didn't really care about them either way, but that stopped when they noticed my existence. It was all because I put myself up for election as class student rep. No one told me Manon wanted to be the only one. I only got one vote, and that wasn't even mine (thank you, Clelia), so I didn't

understand when the twins started being all nasty.
Okay, they didn't exactly invent waterboarding, they
just tripped me up a couple of times and chucked
bread at me in the canteen, but it was better when
they didn't know I was there at all.

I told my sister about it during the Christmas
holidays, not to be a snitch (I'm not a snitch), but
because she'd heard about it from Nahima's
brother (and he *is* a snitch). I made her swear on
Beyoncé not to tell anyone, and she promised but
then nabbed the twins as they came out of school –
poor Beyoncé. She told them I was vulnerable and
they were hurting me and they should try thinking
what it was like for her, they'd do the same if it was
one of them . . . The twins went bright red,
burying their faces in their scarves and nodding
their heads. Juliette promised to leave me alone,
Manon said she was really sorry. The next
morning the whole class was calling me 'Snitch'
(I'm not a snitch). That's the first and last time I'm
telling my sister a secret.

Sorry, Marcel, I had to go and change pens; it
stopped working. Right, I need to be quick because
my favourite show is about to start.

The twins eased off a bit for a few weeks, I don't
know why, and I wasn't about to ask them. Until
this morning, in Chemistry. We had to work in
pairs on an experiment and Max came and stood

next to me where Clelia usually would be. The thing is, Max is Manon's boyfriend – it's not like you can help noticing; they spend every breaktime eating each other's faces, like those fish that clean the inside of the tank. So, anyway, I turned round, and Manon was sending me daggers. I gave her this little smile, like, 'don't worry, I won't touch,' but seeing as she gave me the finger, she must have thought I was winding her up.

At breaktime me and Clelia were lying on the ground in the playground and the twins came over and asked me if I had a problem. I said no, because I didn't, and Manon was, like, 'Well, I do have a problem and it's called Lily.' I said that was really funny coz my name's Lily, too, and she scowled at me, so I tried to explain that I'm really not interested in Max because I don't have this ambition to be in a relationship when I'm not even a teenager but mostly because the guy's got the worst breath ever, like, it shouldn't be allowed, I mean, does he eat rotten-cabbage sandwiches for breakfast? So she didn't need to worry. Juliette gave a little laugh, Manon snapped at her to shut it, then she crouched down on a level with me, brought her face up to mine (close enough so I could tell that rotten cabbage gets passed on in saliva like glandular fever) and whispered that I'm nothing but a little tart, like my sister.

I don't know what I was thinking – maybe it was because of the report on llamas that I watched at the weekend – but I spat right in her face. Juliette grabbed my hair, Clelia grabbed Juliette's hair, Manon grabbed Clelia's hair and I grabbed Manon's hair, and we stayed like that, not moving, until the bell went, and then we went off to Geography.

I don't know what she meant about Chloe. I get to see first hand that my sister's a bitch, but she's not a tart.

Have a great evening, Marcel!

Lily x

PS I'm not a snitch.

Anna

'It's green, Mum!' Lily yells.

I put the car into first and flash her a smile in the rear-view mirror, then sink back into my thoughts. I did the maths a while ago. To clear all my debts, I'd need 12,689 euros. It made me cry. For several months now, since I realised I'll never dig myself out of this, since my stomach's been producing ulcers and sleep's been producing nightmares, I've turned into an ostrich. What's the point of confronting an enemy if you know it's going to knock you flat?

I stopped thinking the day the monthly payments on the credit agreements my ex and I had taken out together became impossible to cover on my own and I tried to salvage the situation by agreeing to a loan with interest payments worth more than the capital. I stopped looking at my bank account, where every refused payment and every cent overdrawn is cranked up with exorbitant charges. I stopped opening envelopes. I stopped answering calls from unknown numbers. For months, I've been living with part of my life anaesthetised. It's painful waking up in the morning. It costs 12,689 euros.

'We're here!' Lily shrieks.

I park the car outside my father's house, the windscreen wipers valiantly battling the deluge. Sitting on the passenger seat, Chloe's been lost in her phone since we left the flat.

'We're here, Chloe.'

'Wa-hey.'

'Please try, Chloe, your grandpa loves seeing you.'

She shrugs and unclicks her seatbelt. Her chin's wobbling.

'What's the matter, sweetheart?'

'Nothing,' she says, clearly struggling to hold back her tears.

'Are you sure?' I prod, stroking her cheek.

'Stop it, Mum. I said it's nothing.'

She gets out of the car, slams the door and goes to join Lily on her way to the front door, shielding her hair under her bag.

My father and my stepmother, Jeannette, give us four kisses each, just in case we didn't notice the first two. They're smiling so broadly we can see their wisdom teeth.

'We couldn't wait for you to get here. We've got something to show you!' my father says excitedly.

Standing next to him, Jeannette claps her hands. The last time I saw them in this state, they'd just had their respective nicknames tattooed on their chests: Pops and Poppet.

My father opens the French windows and leads us into the garden.

24

'Follow me.'

'Pops, it's raining!' Chloe protests.

'Just a few drops,' Jeannette retorts, nudging us outside.

At the corner of the house, my father signals to us to stop.

'Are you ready?'

'Yes!' Lily exclaims.

'Wait,' Jeannette intervenes. 'Shall we let them guess?'

He agrees, beside himself. Pops and Poppet do love a game.

'Have you bought a dog?' Chloe asks listlessly.

'A tiger?' Lily suggests steadily.

'A new car?'

'You're getting warm, Anna,' Jeannette says. 'But bigger than a car.'

'A space rocket?' Lily offers.

'A campervan?'

My father blinks. He lets us walk on and spreads his arms with a 'Ta-daaaa!'

Beyond him is an imposing white vehicle. He puts his arm around Jeannette's shoulders and she purrs.

'We decided to treat ourselves for our retirement. We're planning to go to Italy this summer. It's not new, but it's only just ten years old. We couldn't let such a bargain slip through our fingers. Go in, have a look around!'

He unlocks the door and gets us to climb into their campervan, but not before asking us to take off our shoes.

It's small but functional inside. There's a bedroom

with a double bed, storage space everywhere, a living area with a bench seat that can be used as a bed, a kitchenette and even a shower cubicle, where I can just about fit half a leg.

Standing outside, drenched by the rain, Pops and Poppet wait for our reactions. I nod encouragingly at the girls, hoping they get the message, before making my opening gambit:

'It's absolutely wonderful, you're going to have such a great time in here!'

'And these curtains are gorgeous!' Chloe picks up the baton, stroking the fabric, with its big yellow flowers.

Lily glances around the van looking for inspiration, then her face lights up.

'It's practical,' she says. 'It's so small you can cook a meal while you're having a poo!'

When we go through to the living room for coffee after a gargantuan lunch Chloe slinks off to the study to be by herself. Her mood yoyoed all through the meal, and her phone was holding the string. Every time she looked at it her eyes filled with either tears or twinkling stars. Adolescence has unstable weather.

When I go to find her she's sitting on some cushions reading *Wuthering Heights.*

'How are you doing?'

'Good,' she says, not looking up from the book.

I sit down next to her.

'You can talk to me, you know.'

She shrugs.

'Do you know that, Chloe?'

'I know, Mum, but . . .'

'But what?'

'Nothing.'

'What is it, sweetheart?'

'Nothing. It's fine, Mum. Can I just have a hug?'

Of course you can have a hug, my big girl. I open my arms and she nestles into them, her head in the crook of my neck and her hair tickling my nose. She's been nicking my perfume again.

Chloe's always liked me cuddling her. When she was little she could only get to sleep right up next to me. Every evening when I went to bed I'd find her in our bed. It drove her father mad. I would grumble, but I savoured that closeness, knowing it would be short-lived. She still sometimes comes into my bed at night, claiming she's had a nightmare or has a stomach ache. I've stopped complaining. I move aside the duvet and let her sleep in the warm space I've just been in, not admitting that she doesn't need to come up with an excuse.

She pulls away gently and rakes her fingers through her hair before going back to her book. I get up slowly.

'You know I'm here if you need to talk.'

I step out of the study and close the door behind me. It's almost completely closed when I hear Chloe's voice.

'When you're not working.'

Anna

I arrive at the restaurant every morning hoping Tony will have realised his proposal isn't acceptable. And I leave every evening hoping he'll be struck down with amnesia in the night.

He doesn't forget. And doesn't capitulate.

'So, have you changed your mind?' he asks, standing behind the bar and watching me push the mop between the tables.

'Nope, Tony, I still haven't.'

'Why don't you want to?'

'I've told you a hundred times: I'll never find another job at thirty-seven.'

'But there's too much for you to do here, you've said so yourself. Anyway, I can see you've been getting tired recently. You get out of breath so easily and you never stop complaining.'

The mop stops dead.

'Don't take the piss,' I say, turning to face him. 'Don't go looking for reasons to fire me. You won't find any – everyone knows how good I am at this. I do two people's

28

work all by myself, and if I'm tired it's because you refuse to take anyone else on!'

He pours himself a glass of cognac and downs it in one.

'I won't do that to you, I'm legit. Otherwise, I wouldn't have offered you the deal. I really like Estelle, you know, it's not just the sex.'

'I don't want to know,' I tell him, trying not to picture them.

He lays his hands flat on the counter and looks at me.

'She's a good woman,' he says in a softer voice. 'I'd really like to work with her. She's agreed to it so long as I take on her sister as well.'

'Her sister? You mean there'll be two of them waitressing?'

'That's the plan.'

Without a word I go back to cleaning the floor, doing my best to ignore the mop, which is begging to be hurled over the bar.

'Anna, are you refusing to do this because of my wife?'

'Pardon?'

'Is this a feminist solidarity thing? Or are you jealous?'

I let go of the mop handle and stride angrily over to my boss.

'Do you think everything revolves around you, Tony? You can sleep with Estelle as much as you like, you know. You can even have her, her sister, her grandfather and her hamster, if it turns you on – I don't give a stuff. This may go way over your head, but right now I'm thinking about myself, my daughters, my future and my bank balance. I'm not saying no because of anything to do with you but for my own reasons. So please stop talking about it. I won't agree to it.'

He pours himself another glass and sips it in silence. I pick the mop back up to finish cleaning the floor. As I work my way round, my anger dissipates, soon replaced with exhaustion. I'm reduced to an empty husk by the time I nip round the back of the bar to get my handbag. He hasn't moved.

'Goodnight, Tony. See you tomorrow.'

'Anna, is there *nothing* that'll make you change your mind?' he persists.

I can feel my hackles rising, my fighting spirit ready to lash out. Instead, I turn to him and hear myself say:

'Well, there might be something . . .'

The Chloe Chronicles

Kevin doesn't love me any more. Well, he didn't actually say that – he claimed I'm too good for him and he doesn't deserve me. I've been past the bakery at least ten times, hoping to see him, to talk to him. Considering what we had together, I'd have liked more than a text with a typo – 'its over'. I saw him on his break, but only from a distance. Lea's clearly *not* too good for him.

I thought things over as I sat in the lobby of my building waiting for the postwoman.

I don't understand. I've made a list: I've been out with seven boys in my life. The first four dumped me because I wouldn't sleep with them. The last three dumped me as soon as I did sleep with them. But I thought that was what they expected; the messages were loud and clear, not at all subliminal. When I give them what they want, why do they stop wanting it?

Every time I think, this is it. They're affectionate and considerate, they say 'we' and talk about the future. How can I help falling in love?

Ines says I should wait, let them stew in their own juice, give them time to get to know me. Marion says I must be rubbish in bed and there are YouTube tutorials to help you get it right. Charlotte reckons they're all pigs. But I don't know. Maybe men are like Cinderella: they change after falling in love.

The local postwoman's usually Sonia, who I used to do synchronised swimming with in primary school. She's always happy to hand the post over to me instead of putting it in the box. It wasn't her today but a young guy with curly hair. He leaned his bike against the wall and gazed at the dozens of names, looking baffled.

'If it's any help,' I said, getting up, 'I can take anything you have for Moulineau.'

'I'll be fine. I'll find them, thanks.'

'Come on . . . I'm expecting an urgent letter and I've forgotten my key.'

He shook his head.

'I'm not sure I'm allowed to do that.'

I gave him my most persuasive smile and promised him Moulineau really is my name. He asked to see my ID, and I showed him.

'Okay, so I'm not exactly a Moulineau,' I explained. 'My parents are divorced, but it's my mum's name.'

He looked at the picture, then at me, then at the picture, then at me.

'You're prettier in real life.'

I smiled, and this time it wasn't forced.

He rummaged in his bag, took out two letters and

handed them to me. I kept the one with the school logo on it and slipped the other one in the box.

I was heading towards the stairs when he called out to me.

'Hey, Moulineau! How do you feel about meeting up some time?'

His name's Lucas, he's twenty-one and he's just got his job as a postman through his mother, who works at the post office. He plays guitar in a band and I'm going to the cinema with him on Wednesday afternoon.

I didn't take the lift but ran up the stairs so my heart had a good reason to beat so hard. Mum had left for work an hour ago; her perfume still hung in the air in the flat. I shut myself in my bedroom, said hi to the picture of Dad that's always on my bedside table (the one where I'm two years old and he's holding me in his arms), lay down on my bed and imagined how it will go on Wednesday. I hope we watch something romantic.

Lily

21 March

Dear Marcel,

I'm really sorry I haven't written for a few days, but I had the flu. OMG, at one point I had such a high temperature I didn't want to risk sitting on plastic chairs. Don't worry, I'm better now, but in the morning I still sound like Morgan Freeman.

There was a strike at school today. The staff went off and strutted their stuff in the streets and because Chloe *was* at her school, Mum wanted me to go to see Pops, but spending time with sixty-year-olds, well, thanks a bunch, but I'm not an antique. So I ended up going to Clelia's. Her dad said he was happy to look after us, but he basically watched TV the whole time.

I love going to Clelia's house, partly coz she's got this adorable dog called Rocky but mainly coz she has rats. Rats are well cool. Everyone thinks they're dirty but, actually, they're clean, and plus, they're mega intelligent. I watched this programme which said they don't even need a reward to come and help other rats in distress. Maybe I'd like people better if they were more like rats.

Clelia's rats are called Prattle and Drat. She thought they were both female, but seeing as Prattle's had seven babies, either Drat's a male or you can get pregnant by eating carrots (hope not). I'd have liked to have one but, boohoo (no, not the website), I had to say no. Once, when I was little, we saw a mouse on the stairs. My mum screamed so loudly I was basically deaf for a few minutes, then she shot downstairs like she was on skis. That's why I go to Clelia's whenever I can. We put Prattle and Drat on our shoulders and go out for walks, and they reach up to give us kisses, resting their little paws on our lips. It's so cute.

When I came home to work on my presentation on the northern lights, Chloe was shut away in her room, listening to music. She didn't answer when I knocked and didn't come out to have the macaroni cheese Mum made before going to work.

I'm going to bed now coz, I don't know about you, but I'm pooped. I'll brush my teeth tomorrow. I hope Mum won't notice when she comes in to give me a kiss after her shift.

Night, night, Marcel
Lily x

PS My feet are cold so I blew the hairdryer over
my sheets, but by the time I'd put it away they were
freezing again.

Anna

I'm unemployed. I've been saying that over and over since I got up this morning, as if to convince myself. It's nearly midday. I went back to bed after Chloe and Lily left for school. It's a long time since I've lazed in bed, taken my time. It was nice, but I mustn't get a taste for it. Starting this afternoon, I'm going to look for a new job. When I've found one, and only then, I'll talk to the girls. No point worrying them. I'm stressing enough for the three of us.

Tony didn't accept my proposition straight away. He laughed at first, until he realised I meant it: either he gave in, or I stayed on. He didn't talk to me for two days and then, yesterday evening, he handed me an envelope.

'You did say you'd prefer cash, didn't you?'

There were notes in every colour – it was like being the banker in Monopoly. I followed him into his office, we signed the mutually agreed termination of contract and he provided me with all the necessary documents.

'Today was your last day,' he said. 'I'll let you off your notice.'

'I don't know if we can . . .'

'Come on, Anna, with what I've just given you, surely you're not going to be a pain?'

I looked away, a lump in my throat. It was the last time I'd be in this place. I hadn't even had time to say goodbye to the regulars, to André and Josiane, who'd been coming for the table near the window every Wednesday for ten years; to Bertrand, Jamel and Dylan, who had the 'express' menu every lunchtime and always left a few coins along with their luncheon vouchers; to Marlene, who came and sipped a coffee every evening to delay being alone by a few minutes.

'Right, well, thanks, Tony. It was tough, but I liked working here, you know.'

I thought I saw a sheen in his eyes. He turned away towards the door.

'I know. You've worked well. Right, that's enough of that, I need to close up. My wife'll be wondering where I've got to.'

It was cold outside. Tony started bolting the door, then he planted an awkward kiss on my cheek.

'I hope you find something good.'

I didn't manage a reply. I went over to my car, giving my tears strict instructions to go back where they came from.

In the car, I counted the money.

Not what it takes to buy a chateau but enough to pay off all my debts and, if I tighten my belt, to keep the bailiffs away for two or three months. If I'm lucky, perhaps I'll find something better paid so I actually earn more than we spend. At the end of the day, I thought as I drove off, maybe leaving this job is a good thing.

The anxiety has set in since then. What if it takes months to find work? What if I don't find any? What if we end up on the street?

I haul myself out of bed before these negative thoughts get the better of me. I take out the earplugs that I rammed in this morning when the man in the flat upstairs thought he was the lovechild of Mariah Carey and a werewolf and come out of my bedroom.

I close the glass door to the balcony with a sigh. Lily always leaves it open, rain or shine, as if the simple act of clicking the handle back in place has been erased from her brain. Last night's dirty plates are still on the coffee table. If I clear them up, the girls will go on thinking it's my job. If I leave them, the place will be due for demolition within a month. I wander into the toilet, and I'm just promising myself I'll find a way to get them to contribute to the household chores when a very white, unfamiliar bum appears in front of me. There's a naked man peeing in my toilet.

'AAAAAAAAAAAAAAAAAAAAAAAAAAAAA AAH!'

'AAAAAAAAAAAAAAAAAAAAAAAAAAAAA AAAAAAAAAAAAAAAAAAH!' the bum replies.

Still screaming, I close the door and hold the handle shut to stop him coming out. I'm frantically wondering how I can contact the police, what with my phone being in the bedroom, when Chloe comes running, her hair all over the place.

'Stay away, Chloe, there's a naked man in the toilet!'

She blushes.

I get it.

'Chloe? What are you doing here? Why aren't you at school?'

No reply. Do I really need one, given that my daughter's wearing nothing but her knickers?

I open the door to the toilet and the bum immediately hares off to Chloe's room. Two minutes later it's covered itself up and left the flat.

I wait alone for a while, trying to steady the shaking in my hands and to assimilate the painful information: my daughter's not five years old any more. Then I go into her room.

'Are you planning to explain yourself?'

She's lying on her unmade bed, staring at the ceiling. Her cheeks are wet with tears.

'Talk to me, Chloe. Is he your boyfriend? For how long? Didn't you have school today?'

I go over to her and sit down next to her. She throws herself into my arms, her body wracked with sobs. I push her away firmly.

'You must talk to me, Chloe. How long have you been sleeping with this boy? What are you doing home?'

She wipes her tears, sits against the wall, brings her bent knees up to her chest and looks right into my eyes.

'What about you? What are you doing home?'

The Chloe Chronicles

Lucas has stopped answering my messages. I promised him I didn't know my mum was at home and it won't happen again, but he's ghosted me.

I waited out on the balcony for him to come with the post, but he's been sent to another area because Sonia's back at work. Obviously, I would go to see him, but I'm grounded. Mum only lets me go to school and on to the balcony – it's a nightmare. And she's here the whole time now, too. I practically have to ask permission to go to the toilet. I wish I could fast-forward three months, three weeks and a day, when I'll be eighteen, an adult.

It's the first time in my life I've been kept in like this. It's hard, but there's worse: Mum doesn't trust me any more. I've disappointed her.

She asked me loads of questions – she wanted to know everything – and then she started going through my stuff. And if you look hard enough . . . you find.

When she found the box of condoms, she went white.

When she found the packet of pills, she went red.

When she came across the weed, she walked straight out of the room.

I went to find her later, in the evening. She was watching TV with Lily. Her eyes were red. I said I was really sorry. She opened her arms and I burrowed into them. She stroked my head and I could hear her heart thumping quickly.

'Talk to me, sweetheart,' she whispered. 'Tell me what's wrong. How can I help?'

I didn't answer. I don't know what's wrong. I don't know how she can help. I just started to cry, helplessly, for a long time.

Later, Mum came to kiss me goodnight in bed. She said she had to do something, she couldn't let me destroy myself like this. She also said it probably wasn't a solution, but she was going to punish me, to protect me.

'You can't stop me going out,' I said.

'Yes, I can, Chloe. I'm your mother. You're not an adult yet. I absolutely can stop you going out.'

I was so angry my stomach felt all tight.

'Do you want me to kill myself, is that it?'

I saw the fear in her eyes, but she kissed my forehead and left my room. I cried myself to sleep, holding the picture of Dad.

Lily

25 March

Dear Marcel,
   Just now on the news they said it was National
Procrastination Day. So I'll write to you tomorrow.
   Love
   Lily x

Anna

Chloe's headteacher is called Martin Martin. While I wait for him outside his office I wonder what his parents were thinking when they chose his name. There are two possible options: either they didn't like their son or they both had stammers.

'Do come in, Madame Moulineau.'

A fifty-something man holds the door open for me. I shake his hand and sit in the chair he gestures to.

'I'm pleased to meet you at last,' he says, also sitting down.

'At last?'

'Yes, I've been wanting to see you for some time. This is about Chloe, isn't it?'

I get an unpleasant feeling, the sort that's usually followed by bad news. I tell the headmaster about my concerns and he listens attentively, his hands clasped under his chin. Chloe's latest reports have been excellent, with the teachers praising her work as well as her behaviour. I've often thought how lucky I am to have such an easy child. She adapts to the world around her like a chameleon, tackling it with ease and curiosity. But

44

for some time now the chameleon seems to have been stuck on the same colour – and it's quite a dark colour. I feel helpless. Perhaps the head or one of the teachers has noticed something?

Martin Martin nods several times and straightens his glasses.

'Have you not received my letters?' he asks.

'Your letters?'

'Right. I *was* surprised that you hadn't replied, but Chloe told me you work long hours. I've written to you several times. Your daughter's been absent from school a good deal recently. She's completely lost her motivation. I've spoken to her on a number of occasions to try to understand, and she insists everything's fine. Has something happened that might explain this change in her behaviour?'

His words bounce back off my brain.

'Are you sure you're talking about my daughter? Chloe Leroy?'

He's sure. Over the course of half an hour he lists her absences and insolent outbursts, he shows me absence notes with my signature on them, he tells me about my daughter – my sweet, sensitive Chloe – and it feels like he's describing a stranger. A stranger who's about to mess up her whole life.

My horror must be written all over my face; Martin Martin hands me a tissue. I take the whole packet.

It's empty (and so are my reserves of tears) by the

time he sees me to the door and wishes me the best of luck.

I drive aimlessly for several minutes. Today wasn't meant to be like this. I was planning a nice supper with the girls to celebrate the end of our worries: Monsieur Fox has granted me a meeting next week to settle my debts. I should be feeling light and easy, not like a dead weight. How did I not see what was going on? I thought Chloe never hid anything from me. She must feel so alone. She must be in such a bad place. Without thinking, I pull the car up on to the pavement and take out my phone.

He answers after three rings.

'Hi, it's Anna.'

'Hello, Anna, it's good to hear from you. How are you?'

His soft voice brings back a thousand memories. I clear my throat.

'Not great. Chloe's having some problems. I need to talk about it.'

'Yes, of course. Fire away.'

I tell him: the tears, the silences, the absences, the lies, the boys, school. The only thing I omit is the cannabis. I just can't bring myself to say it out loud.

'These are cries for help. She's not in a good way. She must feel alone, what with me working too much and you being in Marseille.'

'You mustn't feel guilty, Anna, you're doing your best.

And so am I. I Skype them at least once a week and have them down to stay as often as possible.'

'They haven't seen you for more than a year.'

He doesn't say anything for several seconds.

'I know, I know. It breaks my heart,' he says eventually. 'My mother's too tired at the moment – I can't have them at her house. If only I could afford the journey . . . I miss them terribly, you know.'

His voice cracks. He takes a shuddery deep breath.

'I sometimes regret moving so far away,' he goes on. 'I probably should have thought it through first, but it was a question of survival. I couldn't stick around, knowing you didn't want me any more.'

'Okay, I'm hanging up now, Mathias.'

My heart rate is accelerating, my hands are growing clammy. I know these symptoms only too well.

'Anna, just one word from you and I'll drop everything here.'

'All I'm asking is that you try to see your daughters. They shouldn't have to pay the price for all this.'

'Neither should we.'

'I need to go. Bye, Mathias.'

His voice is still coming out of the phone when I hang up. My ears buzz and there's a prickly feeling in my jaw. I close my eyes and inhale quickly, then exhale slowly, just as the psychiatrist taught me after my first panic attack. Short inhalation. Long exhalation. Short inhalation. Long exhalation. My heart slows down. Short inhalation. Long exhalation. The shaking steadies. Short inhalation. Long exhalation. Short inhalation. Long exhalation. The threat's gone.

I'm feeling ready to drive off when the phone rings. Unknown number. I answer.

'Madame Moulineau?'

'Yes.'

'Hello, I'm Martine Laroche, I'm in charge of pastoral care at Émile-Zola Middle School. We need you to get here as soon as possible, there's a problem with Lily.'

Lily

30 March

Liebe Marcel,
   Wie geht's? (I had German this morning.) I'm
pretty okay, except that Mum really sucks now
that she's at home the whole time. Maybe she
was like this before but, as we didn't see her so
much, we didn't notice it so much. That's just
maths.
   Okay, so she's kind, but she's always telling me
to clear the table and make my bed and open my
shutters and flush the toilet. It's like she thinks I'm
Cinderella! And now she's got this idea I'm being
bullied at school, and all because of the stupidest
little thing.
   I'll tell you what happened and you can say what
you think.
   It all started in Geography. Me and Clelia were
doing our presentation on the northern lights and
the teacher was looking happy with it – well, that's
a guess because he looks the same when he's happy

49

and when he's angry. He didn't fall asleep, so that's a good sign.

We'd worked really hard, but gotta say we were lucky with the subject. Even Mum and Chloe said it was sweet – not like Juliette and Manon, who had to research the tundra. We'd done a PowerPoint, everyone was well into it, and then Manon said it was too easy to get a good mark with a subject like that. Monsieur Vanier said he'd only be marking the quality of the work and he wouldn't be influenced by the subject, but Juliette muttered that 'Ooh, what a coincidence – the little snitch got the best subject' (I'm not a snitch). I don't know why, I felt like she was really picking on me, and I said it was better to be a snitch than jealous. And then Manon said, seeing as I've got a face like a guinea pig, there was nothing to be jealous of, and I said I'd rather have a face like a guinea pig than a face like a gondola. The teacher told us to stop, we finished our presentation and went off to Maths. And that's when it happened. I didn't see it coming, I just felt someone pulling my hair from behind.

When Mum came to get me from Madame Laroche's office she had that face she gets when she's going to sneeze. Tbh, Manon did a proper job – must remember to ask what make her scissors are. Clelia says it's original, it's like a fringe at the back of my head. It doesn't really bother me; it'll grow back. But Mum's convinced I'm being bullied and it's really serious and we can't leave it at that, and she can't stop kissing me and giving me weird nicknames (I mean, do I look like a pumpkin?)

Manon's got to have a disciplinary hearing. I hope she doesn't get expelled.

So what do you think, Marcel? I'm going to close you and throw you up in the air. If you're open when you land, then you agree with me. If you're closed, then you agree with Mum.

Okay, so you were closed. I knew you were a snitch.

Lily (no kiss)

PS But I do still like you.

Anna

My grandmother's waiting for me in her room, as she does every Thursday. She's put some blusher on her cheeks and is wearing her favourite perfume. She's laid out two glasses and a bottle of lemonade on a tray. I bend down to kiss her.

'How are you, my little Annie?' she asks.

'I'm fine, Nanny. How about you?'

She screws up her eyes and stares at me until I confess. I can't hide anything from her: she's a lie detector.

I sit at the foot of her bed and describe the chaotic week I've just had, dumping all this baggage I can't carry alone at her feet.

'I feel they need me,' I tell her, 'but I don't know how to help them. If I followed my heart, I'd drop everything and take them miles away from here.'

She puts down her glass and dabs her mouth with a napkin.

'Well, then, do it.'

'How do you mean?'

'Follow your heart for once. Listen to your instincts. You want to get away, so get away. It might not be the solution, but can you think of another?'

'But I can't, Nanny!'

She sweeps aside my objection.

'What's stopping you? If it's money, just take what your boss gave you. You've got the whole rest of your life to pay off your debts. I don't have much, but I could help you a bit, too.'

I peer at her face, waiting for her to congratulate herself for the joke she's playing.

'Don't you look at me like that,' she grumbles. 'I'm not going to attack you!'

I shake my head, laughing.

'I can't just up and leave, Nanny. It's not only the money, there's the girls' education, and I need to find work. In other words, it's impossible. Anyway, I wouldn't even know where to go . . .'

'I'm sure you'd think of somewhere. Didn't you say something about the northern lights?' she asks with a wink.

'Enough! End of conversation! Do you want to go for a little walk?'

'I'd love to. I've had enough of these four walls.'

I get up, take the handles of her wheelchair and push her through the corridors of the retirement home where she's been living since she lost the use of her legs. The garden has been recolonised by green after several months of brown. Little clusters of elderly people are making the most of the spring sunshine.

'It goes by very quickly, you know,' Nanny whispers.

'Why do you say that?'

'Because I love you, Annie.'

My throat constricts. I love you, too, my darling Nanny. I love you so much that it's torture every time I come to visit you. I love you so much that I can't bear to watch you gradually fade away or to think it won't be long before you're gone altogether. I love you so much that I cry at night till my eyes burn. I scream on the inside to think of all the years when you could stand up, when you were strong, stronger than grief and stronger than cancer, when you were young, all the years when you looked after me, when you were my refuge, my pillar, my everything.

I swallow my pain and put on a smile.

'Can I ask you something, Annie?' she says brightly.

'I'm all ears, Nanny.'

'If you ever go and see the northern lights, could you do me a favour?'

The Chloe Chronicles

Ines told me that she saw Mum coming out of the head-master's office the other day. She was crying. I banned her from the kitchen this evening and cooked the chicken dish with olives that she likes. The three of us ate together – Mum, Lily and me – with no TV and no phones. There were lots of silences, but we did talk, too. About the sort of job Mum would like to find, Lily's new haircut, the northern lights, some bikes that were stolen from the cellar and how my sauce had turned out more like a purée. When we got to dessert, I thought it was the right time to announce my news.

'I'm leaving school.'

Lily stopped blowing on her yoghurt to warm it up. Mum put down her spoon.

'What do you mean, leaving school?' she said. 'Don't you want to go to university?'

'No, I'd rather stop now. The canteen at the nurs-ery school are hiring. Ines's mum can pull some strings for me.'

'What about your exams?'

I shrugged, but I couldn't look up from the table.

'There's no point. Anyway, I need to work. I need to earn some money.'

Mum didn't say another word. She left the kitchen without finishing her yoghurt. I knew she'd be disappointed, but she'll understand one day. I'm doing this for her. My personal dream is to go and live in Australia, like Dad did when he was young. I've spent hours researching it. I've even started putting together an application for a working holiday visa so I can fly off as soon as I turn eighteen. I could get a job as a waitress in a restaurant – they love 'Frenchies' there. It would be amazing to earn a living and learn English at the same time. Maybe I could even have a career there and pay for my family to fly over and see me.

But I can't leave Mum.

Someone needs to help her pay the bills. She's trying to hide it from us, but I can see she can't cope. Now that she's unemployed, I need to get on with it. It's better for one person to sacrifice themselves than for three to go under.

Mum came back into the kitchen quite quickly. We hadn't moved. She stood right under the light with her arms crossed. I'd never noticed how deep the bags are under her eyes. She waited till we looked up and then, in this I'm-the-mother-here voice, she said:

'Go and pack your bags. We're leaving.'

Anna

Monsieur Fox was not impressed when I postponed our meeting. I claimed a family emergency, which wasn't a complete lie, and promised to get back in touch as soon as possible.

The pastoral-care woman from Lily's school was easy to convince. She accepted that I couldn't let my daughter stay under such circumstances and gave me all the relevant paperwork.

Chloe's headmaster quizzed me at length. I improvised. Martin Martin remained sceptical but admitted that he had no way of stopping me going through with my plan.

My grandmother congratulated me. It's a long time since I've seen that sparkle in her eye, and it got even brighter when she explained the favour she wants of me.

Dad and Jeannette, who I thought would be the easiest to win over, took a whole hour of persuading. In the end, the argument that got the better of them was the same one that made my mind up:

'Dad, I have a choice, for once in my life. I can use this money to pay my debts. Or I can use it to help my daughters.'

Lily

Dear Marcel,

I think this is it. This time, Mum's really lost the plot. I'm writing to you on the passenger seat of my grandpa's campervan somewhere in Germany.

She's been driving the whole time since this morning. We only stopped for a sandwich at a service station. There were policemen in uniforms, and I almost ran over to them to ask for help, but I don't know how to say 'SOS' in German, so I ate my sandwich in French.

When she told us to pack last night, I thought she wanted us to go and stay with our dad. I was furious. I don't have anything to say to that southern poo head; it's bad enough having to talk to him on Skype. So when she said we needed to take warm clothes I was relieved. I hassled her to tell us where we're going (I don't mind doing what she asks, but I don't want to be the butt of this joke, thank you very much), and she said we

58

were going to see the northern lights in Scandinavia. Like I said, she's totally lost it. I'm sure it's coz of my presentation. Good thing it wasn't about black holes.

We stopped off to say goodbye to Nanny this morning. She gave Mum a box. Apparently, there's an urn inside it and her husband's in there. Nanny promised she'd scatter him in the far north of Norway, on Cape I-can't-remember-what, because they went there together, but she could never face doing it, and now she can't anyway, coz of her legs. So she's asked Mum to do it for her. I never knew great-grandad, but he must have been really tiny to fit in there.

Then we went to see Pops and he showed us how the van works. I didn't really get it all, except for the stuff about the toilet. There's a tank that we have to empty when it's full. I'm telling you now I'd rather 'go' out of the window going flat out down the motorway than empty that gizmo.

Seeing as I can't be sure I'll come back alive, I'm going to use the time to write my will and you can give it to the undertakers if needed.

I, the undersigned, Lily, being of sound body and mind,

Bequeath my collection of rocks and minerals to Clelia. I know she'll take good care of it.

Bequeath my purple Brazilian bracelet to Prattle and my green Brazilian bracelet to Drat.

Bequeath my dictionary to Manon and my body lotion to Juliette.

Bequeath my *Diary of a Wimpy Kid* books to my mother, if she's still alive.

Bequeath my baby teeth to my sister, if she's still alive.

Do not want my father to come to my funeral.

Would like the photo of me with Brownie (the dog we had when I was little) on my grave. Definitely not a recent photo, because even though I couldn't care less that I have this Playmobil haircut, I am less scary with long hair.

So, Marcel, I hope this won't be the last time I write to you, but if it is, I've liked knowing you, you've been a nice diary. OMG, can't believe it! Mum's just put on a Celine Dion CD!

See you, Marcel

Or maybe not. ♥

Lily

PS I really need to learn to say 'SOS' in every language.

The Chloe Chronicles

I thought we'd just be going for a little trip, we'd be gone a couple of days and then pick life up again where we left off. But when Mum said we were going to Scandinavia I realised she'd left her common sense at home.

That was confirmed when we crossed the border into Germany and I got a message telling me I didn't have an international phone contract. Mum reassured me, saying *she* had one. I was busy installing Facebook, Instagram, Twitter, Snapchat and the app for my blog on her phone when she shattered all my dreams.

'Ten minutes a day, and no more.'

'What do you mean?'

'What I mean is the aim of this trip is to spend time together, discover new places and different cultures, not have your nose glued to a screen.'

We'd been behind the same lorry for a good hour. On our right there were trees and on our left . . . trees, so as far as new places were concerned, we really were discovering some amazing stuff. Not.

Lily poked her index finger at her temple. If even *she* thinks Mum's gone mad, it's serious.

I tried to negotiate.

'An hour?'

'Ten minutes.'

'Two hours?'

'Stop it, Chloe.'

'But, Mum, you couldn't live without oxygen, could you? Well, it's the same for me with my phone.'

She chuckled, and so did Lily. After a long battle I manage to secure half an hour. I may just about survive.

Towards the end of the afternoon we arrived in Cologne and my mum decided we'd spend the night there. We got settled into a campsite on the banks of the Rhine and she insisted we went and visited the city. I was well up for that: there were bound to be cybercafés in Cologne.

The woman at the campsite lent us bikes and told us how to get there, promising us it wasn't far. We biked along the river for over an hour, not counting the stops Mum insisted we made, allegedly to admire the scenery. As if we hadn't noticed, she'd gone as red as her jumper and her breathing sounded like a vacuum cleaner. Lily and I deliberately pedalled quickly. It was a good laugh.

We locked up the bikes and strayed randomly through the streets till it got dark. The city lit up, and it was beautiful. It was still early so we bought pretzels to see us through till suppertime. Lily insisted on having a bottle of water but once she had one she refused to open it, saying she'd rather keep it as a souvenir. That really surprised Mum.

Lily shrugged, as if we were simpletons.

'Well, duh . . . it's eau de Cologne!' she said.

At least my sister hasn't changed.

We stopped by a cathedral, which my mum wanted to visit, until she found out how many steps there were to climb. In front of it there was a weird-shaped bridge, the Hohenzollern Bridge. It looked as if someone had put three arches on a normal bridge. People were walking across it, so we did, too, and we noticed it was covered in padlocks put there by couples.

Mum suggested we put one there with all our initials on it so there was something to show we'd been there.

'Are you really happy to kill the fish?' Lily asked, horrified. 'You've seen what people do – they throw the key into the river. And you think fish can digest metal, do you?'

I nodded in agreement. We could just hold on to the key and spare the fish . . . and Lily.

The man selling them only sold them in pairs.

We borrowed a marker pen from an English couple and wrote all three of our initials and the date on the first padlock. On the second one I wrote 'You + Me'. That would work with anyone.

The bike ride back was worse than on the way there. I don't know who invented those saddles, but they must have been in a bad mood. We were knackered when we got back to the campervan. We gobbled down some pasta and went to bed, with Lily and me on the double bed and Mum on the bench seat. I waited a long time, till I heard Mum's breathing settle into a regular rhythm. She was asleep at last. Very carefully, making as little noise as possible, I slipped out of bed.

Anna

It took me a while to get to sleep. The mattress on the banquette is narrow and hard, and my body is neither of those. One of us was going to suffer. A warm breath on my cheek dragged me awake and I opened my eyes to see a face so close to mine I couldn't identify it.

I screamed. The face screamed. Lily screamed.

The face leapt back and in the half-light I recognised my daughter.

'Chloe, what the hell are you doing?'

'Nothing, I wanted to give you a hug,' she mumbled, holding one hand behind her back.

'What's in your hand?'

'Nothing.'

I glanced under my pillow: nothing there.

'Give me back my phone.'

'But Mum . . .'

'Chloe, give me back my phone right now! And if you try to take it again, you won't have it at all.'

She sulkily handed over the offending article and went back to bed. I'd just closed my eyes again when I heard

Lily whisper, 'You really think she was born yesterday, don't you?'

The rest of the night passed without incident.

We're woken by the cold at seven in the morning. After all that bicycling last night we were hot and sweaty and I didn't think to put the heating on. What with the stiff legs and the goose pimples, my body's proving a little sensitive this morning.

I set up the table and chairs in the sun. The girls don't emerge from under the duvet until breakfast is laid out. We eat in silence, looking out over the Rhine. The sun glitters on the water and warms our frozen bodies a little, and the familiar taste of coffee soothes me. For the first time since we left home, I think it might have been a good decision.

If I'd thought it through, I would have changed my mind. I'm not the adventurous type. I don't like surprises, I need to think of every eventuality, have everything organised. I get stressed by the unknown, completely paralysed when things are out of my control. I've shut myself away in a reassuring bubble: the same places, the same people, the same routes. And I systematically turn down anything outside that perimeter: a cousin's wedding at the other end of the country, a party in a restaurant I don't know, a meeting on the far side of Toulouse, a trip abroad . . . don't even go there (well, it's me who doesn't even go there!). I always come up with good excuses: I'm not free, I'm overtired, the girls haven't seen me for ages, France is so gorgeous there's no need to go anywhere else. Everyone believes I'm indoorsy, a homebody, old before my time. I often manage to convince myself but, deep down, I know.

I was eighteen when I had my first panic attack. I was driving at night on the Paris ring road, on the way home from a friend's party. The traffic slowed and then stopped altogether. First there was a fizzing in my fingers. Hot flushes. Choking. I opened the window and turned up the radio. My jaw tensed, my heart started beating hard, so hard and so fast I thought it would stop. I could hardly breathe and my head was spinning. I pulled on to the hard shoulder. I couldn't understand what was going on; I thought I was going to die there, all alone. I pushed back the seat and closed my eyes, hoping it wouldn't be painful. Everything around me was hazy, as if it wasn't real. I was shaking and I couldn't even hear the passing cars; all I could hear was my heart. It went on for what seemed like an age. Very gradually, I felt my heart rate slow, my breathing settle and my body relax. I started shivering, but I didn't wait any longer; I sat back up at the wheel and drove home. My father and Jeannette were asleep and I went to bed without a sound.

It started again in the night. And in the days to come.

The doctor sent me to see a psychiatrist who diagnosed panic attacks with agoraphobia. He prescribed me pills that I took for several months, as well as telling me I should sign up for cognitive behavioural therapy. I had to face up to my fears, to confront them so I could get used to them and be desensitised. I managed three sessions. When I told my psychiatrist I wanted to stop the therapy he admitted that the process of provoking panic attacks often proved painful. And it really was. But it wasn't as bad as giving up hope. It's reassuring to know there's an effective treatment method, for if and when the waves just get too high. If I apply the method and it doesn't work, then I no longer have a lifebelt.

By staying in my bubble, I was limiting the risks. I kept on going to the same places, seeing the same people and travelling the same routes. Until this decision. I didn't think it over. I didn't think about myself. My girls needed to get out, so I burst the bubble.

Lily

5 April

Dear Marcel,

I hope you're okay. I'm fine, except that I want to sleep but I can't. It's my turn on duty. It's four o'clock in the morning, or something like that, and I thought it would be nice to write to you in peace, but Mum and Chloe whinged because the light was stopping them sleeping. So I've attached a torch to my forehead by winding Sellotape round my head, and I'm hiding under the duvet next to Chloe. I just mustn't move my head too much or I can't see what I'm writing, but it's working okay.

Get this: we're in Hamburg, and that's in Germany. Mum found us a camper space by the port and we went for a walk around town – no bikes this time. It wasn't bad. We saw a big lake with swans, warehouses down by the water, big boats and houses like I've never seen. I found a pretty pebble as a souvenir, but it started to rain so we came back.

Mum wanted to empty the toilet-tank thingy, but she couldn't do it. Chloe and me pinched our noses and watched her through the window. We could hear her swearing. The man in the next campervan came to help her. She didn't want him to, I think she was embarrassed – I wonder why! He laughed so hard, but in the end he did manage to persuade her, and afterwards we had to go and have a drink with him as a thank you because – well, you could say he really got us out of the s**t!

There's actually a whole group of French people travelling together, and he's the organiser. His name's Julien. His son was there, too, Noah. He's about my age. I tried to talk to him, but he didn't answer, he just sat there rocking. His dad explained that he doesn't talk and he takes a bit of time to get to know new people. Oh, and there was a dog, too, Jojo, so adorable. I played with him.

And then we went to bed. I don't know how long I slept for, but I was woken up by whispering. It was coming from outside. You can hear everything through the walls of a van – they might as well not be there. Then there was, like, a little scratching sound and a knock on the door. I was getting scared. but I remembered that programme when the psychiatrist said fear's like an animal that you have to tame, so I told it to go back to its bed and it did as it was told. I tried to wake Chloe, but when she's asleep it's like she's been unplugged. As for Mum, OMG, I think she dies every night and comes back to life in the morning. I had only myself to rely on, so I stepped over Chloe to get out of bed and then I saw the door open and someone come into the van. I jumped down, grabbed the first thing I could get my hands on and dived at the enemy, screaming, 'BANZAI!' (I saw that in a film) and bashing him with the saucepan. The enemy ran away, Mum and Chloe jumped out of bed (like toast popping out of a toaster) and our neighbour Julien appeared a few minutes later. He told us there were a lot of thefts from campervans and it's best to have an alarm as protection, and that's also why they travel in a group. We decided that we'd take turns to keep watch tonight and fit an alarm tomorrow. So it's my turn and I'm tired, which is why I'm writing to you to stay awake (but don't worry, I'm not just using you).

Okay, then, Marcel, I'm going to make the most of everyone being asleep to do something about my secret (I can't tell you what it is, I'm too worried Mum'll read this). Have a good night.

Lily x

PS I've tried to take the Sellotape off my head, but it really pulls on my hair. It's horrible. So I'm going to leave it as it is.

The Chloe Chronicles

I'm 'hypersensitive'. The nurse at school told me that because I'd just fainted after cutting my hand. It felt as if she'd just found the missing link, as if she'd given me something I'd lost. That was it: I was hypersensitive.

Later, I was identified as 'gifted', which often goes hand in hand with hypersensitivity. I spent hours reading descriptions and testimonies online. I ticked every box.

I experience everything to the power of ten. I'm teeming with emotions, buzzing with feelings.

I often cry. When I'm sad, happy or angry.

I forget myself because I think about other people.

I'm so full of empathy and I understand other people so well that I'm easily influenced. I'm completely incapable of having a clear-cut opinion.

I don't like myself. But that doesn't matter so long as there are other people to love me.

I'm always judging myself. Harshly.

My brain never rests; my imagination's like a war machine. When I watch a film I wonder what the actors are doing right at that moment, and when I use things like a toothbrush or a tin-opener I think about the people who invented them and what their lives are like.

I'm always hypervigilant. I jump if I come across Mum in the corridor and scream if Lily comes into the bathroom without knocking.

When I hear something on the news I always imagine being the victim. I experience the events as if I was really there.

I see things so clearly. Too clearly.

But that has its good sides, too.

I'm a good friend. I'm understanding and not judgemental.

I'm quick to question myself.

I see the little details lots of people don't really notice.

My happiness is to the power of ten. A sunbeam, the smell of lilac or Christmas lights give me these great surges of joy.

Mum's always liked the way I rave about things. Apparently, when I was little, every car journey with me was a happy, noisy event. I internalise more now, but the fireworks are still there. So after we'd driven for ages through forests, walked a little way then climbed some steps and arrived, I just couldn't help myself.

'Woooooooow!'

The sea was there in front of us, unfolding in a thousand shades of blue, while the tall white cliffs under our feet stood close by, as if they were dipping their toes in the water. I'd never seen anything so beautiful.

Mum said we were at Møns Klint. I haven't seen her smile like that for a long time.

We weren't alone – there were a few tourists – but I blocked out their voices so that all I could hear was the birdsong and the music of the water. There was a chill wind, but the sun was fighting it valiantly. I could have stayed there for hours, feeling it caressing my face.

A little later we went down to sea level and walked over the grey pebbles. Lily picked up at least ten. The cliffs looked even bigger from down there. I felt like a grain of sand lost in all that vastness.

We went back to the campervan in silence. Even our words had been blown away. Mum got back behind the wheel and the trees flitted past for a long time while I floated in a bubble of happiness. A ringing sound jolted me out of it. The messenger notification on Mum's phone. She nodded at me to mean I could look at it. It was Kevin, the baker guy.

'Hi Chloe how's things? Can I talk 2 u at yours?'

You know those surges of happiness I was talking about just now? Well, I got one of those. I thought for a good ten minutes about how I should reply, typed my message and sent it. I *knew* he was a good guy.

Anna

'Mum, do you know anything about Apollinaire?'

Lily peers at me as she waits for an answer.

The problem with doing things on a whim is you don't anticipate the microdetails. For example, I couldn't have guessed how complicated it would be home-schooling my daughters.

For two hours every morning, we do schoolwork. For two hours every morning, Chloe protests that she's not going to take her exams anyway, and Lily plays with pens as if they were dolls.

Today – and the rain may have something to do with this – the girls are more or less concentrating. Chloe has only fallen asleep twice in Gide's *The Counterfeiters* and, so far, Lily has only asked a few time-killing questions.

'I know a bit about him,' I say, sitting down next to her. 'I studied him at school.'

'He was blind, wasn't he?'

'Why do you ask?'

She slides her book in front of me and points to a line.

'He says, "It's high time we relit the stars," but the stars *are* lit up. He needs a new optician!'

'Well, it's like when people talk about chasing stars. They're not really talking about the stars up in the sky, and neither is Apollinaire,' Chloe says with a sigh.

Lily stares at her, wide-eyed.

'Really? Because there are stars somewhere else, are there? You grown-ups are so weird.'

I'm revving up to attempt an explanation when I'm saved by the bell. Well, the ringtone, actually.

'Hello?'

'Good morning, Madame Moulineau, it's Madame Barrière here, at the Post Office bank. You and I had a meeting scheduled for half an hour ago, and I waited for you . . .'

I do this every time I'm in the wrong: I turn into a little girl.

'Oh poo! I'm so sorry, I completely forgot!'

'I thought you must have. We really do need to meet to discuss your account. I've had a cancellation for eleven o'clock tomorrow.'

'I won't be able to make that. Would it be possible to discuss this on the phone?'

'How about Thursday at two o'clock?'

Chloe glances at me questioningly. I can't go telling my financial adviser – who must have my name up on her screen in big red letters – that I've treated myself to a nice little trip. I climb on the girls' bed, draw the curtain and drop my voice.

'I'm really very sorry, I can't d—'

76

'I see. Fine,' she interrupts. 'Madame Moulineau, you've been overdrawn for more than thirty consecutive days and your salary hasn't been paid in this month. You do need to find a solution, don't you?'

I nod: I'm five years old.

'Absolutely, I'm going to find one. I've lost my job, but I'll be getting benefits until I find a new one. I'm doing my best, you know.'

'So you're not in work?'

Five-year-olds talk too much.

'Not at the moment, but . . .'

'Listen, given your circumstances, I have no choice but to refuse all debits from your account until you have the funds. You must understand that . . .'

I've stopped listening. I don't know what I was hoping when we left. As if my debts could have evaporated just because I was going away. As if my worries could stay where I'd left them. I had an opportunity to pay all my bills and start from square one again. All of a sudden – sitting on the thin mattress, shut up in a campervan in the rain, so far away from my bubble – I feel lost. What have I done? My pulse goes through the roof, my breathing accelerates, I count the flowers on the curtain, but none of it's enough to divert my attention. All I want is to start up the engine and drive all the way back. Go home. Back to my comfort zone.

'Good day, Madame Moulineau.'

'Thank you. You have a nice day, too.'

I hang up shakily and lie down on the bed to try to relax. Short inhalation. Long exhalation. Short inhalation. Long exhalation. Metallic noise under the bed. Short inhalation. Long exhalation. My heart rate slows. Metallic noise under the bed. Short inhalation. Long exhalation. Succession of metallic noises under the bed. That's all we need – for this thing to break down.

I get up, and my legs are still wobbly. Chloe has fallen asleep with her head on her book. Lily's drawing. I crane my ear closer to the bed to identify the source of the metallic noise. There it is again. I lift up the mattress and a board with a handle on it reveals a storage space I hadn't noticed. I open it and then: black hole.

Lily

8 April

Dear Marcel,

We're in the poo! No, I don't mean the toilet thingy again, but Mum's found out my secret. I did have a great hiding place, though, and Chloe was a pretty good accomplice, but now it's all over. And plus, Mum was so frightened she fell and knocked her face against the edge of the bed, splitting her lip open so wide it looks like Moses has been through it. We ended up in Copenhagen hospital and she's now got a dressing that's going to stick her lip together again like superglue. I'd have preferred it if they'd stuck her two lips together, because I can't tell you the interrogation I've just had.

I had to explain that he's a domestic rat, totally different to the ones you find in bins, and he's clean and won't do any harm. She asked me how I'd managed to hide him for so long and I admitted that I get him out as soon as she's busy with something and he sleeps in the bed with us at night, but she didn't seem very pleased about that. She wanted me to get rid of him and I said, 'Over my dead body,' and there was no way I was getting rid of Mathias. Her eyes popped out of her head like lollipops and she asked if she'd heard me right, if my rat really did have the same name as my dad. She was shocked. But it makes perfect sense. Don't they say rats leave a sinking ship?

A bit later she agreed that I can keep Mathias on condition that I don't get him out in public and I'm careful to keep him out of her way. I picked him up and held him out to her to stroke, but she screamed at me not to make her change her mind.

So, Marcel, we had a narrow escape, didn't we? I really liked having a secret, but I have to say I'm glad I can keep Mathias's cage out of his hiding place and let him out more often.

Also, we walked around Copenhagen, and it was pretty, even though it kept peeing down with rain (luckily, there were lots of sunny bits, too). When I'm a grown-up I'd like to have a colourful house like they have here. Chloe really wanted to go to the Tivoli Gardens, which is kind of half an amusement park and half just a park. Mum wasn't too keen because it's expensive, but in the end she said, 'Oh, who gives a damn about that!' and we

went. It's like there's alternating sunshine and
showers in Mum's head, too.

It's a real shame you didn't see the place,
Marcel – you'd have wet yourself (and that
would've made your paper all crinkly). We went on
the big wheel and it was so cool, but when we got
to the top Mum went totally white. She said she
was fine but we could see she wasn't fine at all. And
she obviously wasn't, because she ended up lying
on the floor of the pod with her legs in the air,
breathing like she was about to go free diving.
When it came to the rollercoaster, she said she'd
rather stay on the ground and take pictures (they're
all wobbly).

We walked for ages and Chloe's feet were sore –
mind you, she was wearing heels. She'd even
straightened her hair, and then she whinged
because it was raining. In Denmark they eat very
early. The restaurants all fill up at six o'clock, and
it made us hungry so we bought some smørrebrød
(like open sandwiches with all sorts of toppings; I
had one with cheese and one with fish), and then
went back to the campervan. Mathias was happy. I
swear he wagged his tail. The French group from
the other day were around again, but we didn't eat
with them.

Mum had left her phone on the table and it was
flashing. She said Dad had called and I pretended I

didn't hear, but Chloe wanted to call him back so I went to have a shower.

Gotta go, it's time to turn the light out.

Lily xx

PS My left nostril was blocked so I lay on my right side and that made it unblock . . . but then my right one got blocked. I'm going to sleep sitting up.

The Chloe Chronicles

A little message for my readers before I start.
I love reading all your comments and seeing how
much you like following my adventures! Even though
some things you say are hurtful, I'm touched by how many
of you understand me and don't judge me. To people who
want to see pictures of me, it's not going to happen. Some
people have recognised me because of our names,
but I'd like this blog to stay anonymous.
Thanks for being there ♥

Dad hadn't called for three weeks. It was good to talk to him, even though it always feels weird. At first it's like talking to a stranger and then I gradually get used to his voice again and I could talk to him for hours. Every time we hang up I have a lump in my throat. I miss him. I wish I could see him more often, but it's complicated. His flat's too small so we have to go to Gran's house, but it's too tiring for her. I hope one day Dad will earn enough to get a place where we can see him as much as we'd like.

As usual, Lily didn't want to talk to him. She's got a

problem with him; she says he abandoned us. But she knows it was actually Mum who left him. He'd have been happier staying with us. Me, too.

'Are you all right, my angel?' he asked.

I like it when he calls me 'my angel'. It makes me feel like calling him 'my darling Daddy', but I can't seem to do it.

I told him about our trip, without mentioning why we left – I don't need him moralising at me. I was worried he'd be angry, but he wasn't at all; in fact, he seemed happy and asked loads of questions.

'What a brilliant idea of Mum's!' he said. 'Travelling's a great way to broaden the mind. You'll both grow up a lot.'

He paused and then almost whispered, 'I'd have loved to have come with you.'

My throat went very tight, but I didn't let it show. I could see Mum was watching me. She'd been washing the same glass for ten minutes.

I'm trying not to resent Mum any more. She must have had her reasons for leaving him – maybe she stopped loving him, maybe she wasn't happy. But I've seen Dad cry and listened to him admitting how sad he was. I'll never forget the first time we went to Marseille for a weekend, six years ago. We hadn't seen him for a month, we hadn't even said goodbye to him. He was waiting for us on the platform and I didn't recognise him straight away. His eyes were lifeless. He hugged me so tight that my heart went all small. I could feel him sobbing. I hated Mum.

'I'll let you get on, my angel. Can I speak to Lily?'

'She's in the shower, but she sends a big hug.'

Before handing the phone back to Mum I checked to see if I'd had a reply from Kevin. I hadn't.

Anna

'Mum, you have to stop. I'm going to be sick.'

Lily just manages to get the words out in a strangulated voice. We're on Øresundsbron, the bridge that links Denmark to Sweden, and there's only a narrow hard shoulder to stop on. Not wide enough for the campervan.

'Try to hold it in. I'll pull over after the bridge. If you can't, do it in the toilet.'

She doesn't answer. Her hands are clamped over her mouth.

'It was the tunnel that made her sick,' Chloe says.

Lily confirms this with a nod.

'And you're driving weirdly,' Chloe adds. 'You keep putting your foot on the accelerator and then taking it off, so it's jerky. It's turned her stomach.'

Another nod from Lily.

Slightly offended, I keep my foot on the pedal until we're back on terra firma. When the safety barrier runs out, I slow down and park up on the hard shoulder. Lily opens the door, jumps down and runs off into the grass. I cut the engine and go after her.

After a few minutes breathing fresh Swedish air she has her voice back.

'Didn't you have pedals in the old days, when you did your driving test?'

She's feeling better.

We get back into the van to press on to our next stopping point. Chloe's still sitting in the same place, gazing blankly ahead. Probably stressed from talking to her father yesterday.

We've hardly got going before the campervan starts lurching. The girls turn to look at me, perfectly synchronised.

'I *haven't* taken my foot off the pedal!'

A few seconds later it splutters again. Lily giggles. I'm seriously questioning whether my right foot is working properly when we start grinding to a halt. I just have time to pull over again before it stalls.

'What's going on?' Lily asks.

'Well, what do you think?' Chloe snaps.

'Hey, what the hell! Who pulled your bell?'

'Don't you talk to me like that, moron.'

'You're the moron.'

'No, you are!'

'No, you are!'

'Okay, that's enough of that,' I intervene, trying to start up the engine for the third time. 'No one's a moron.'

'Well, Lily's not all there,' Chloe mutters.

'You're the one who's not all there,' Lily retorts.

'No, you are!'

I turn round to look at my squabbling daughters.

'If you don't stop right now, I'll chuck you out and carry on without you.'

'And you'll be pushing the van, will you?' Chloe asks, arching one eyebrow.

Lily sniggers. I ignore them and try the ignition again.

The engine turns over but doesn't fire up. We've broken down on a road in Sweden with no clue as to how close the nearest town might be. I try to keep my breathing under control so I can think straight.

'Try calling Pops,' Lily suggests. 'He might know why it's stopped working.'

Good idea. I grab my phone and call my father. One ring. Two rings. Three rings. Four rings.

'Hello, you've got through to Pops and Poppet. Please leave a message and we'll get back to you . . . or not!'

Their two voices stop talking, and now it's my turn. I hang up. For several minutes – between two further attempts to start the engine – I think about how to get out of this. Chloe comes up with an idea.

'Have you got Julien's number?'

'Julien?'

'Yes, you know, the guy who organises the group we've only bumped into *three times*! They can't be far away – we saw them yesterday. Do you have his mobile number?'

'I do, yes, but it would be awkward calling him to come and help us out.'

'So you'd rather we stayed here for the rest of our lives and ended up being eaten by Swedish bears?' Lily cries. 'Is that it?'

If I wasn't so stressed, I'd laugh. I look through my contacts for his name and make the call. Julien replies straight away. They're in Malmö, less than half an hour away. He's just sorting out a problem with a parking space and he'll be right with us, promise!

An hour later Julien's van pulls up behind us and he climbs out and comes over.

'Someone needs to tell him lumberjack shirts have had their day,' Chloe says.

'You've had your day,' Lily retorts.

'Girls, I don't want any more of this,' I say, opening the door just as Julien draws level with us.

He reaches out his hand to me.

'You were right to call me. I'm the campervan-whisperer!'

Chloe's sigh is clearly audible through the open door. Julien climbs in and sits at the wheel with a 'hi' to the girls. Only seconds later, he finds the cause of our break-down.

I daren't look at the girls. To be honest, I daren't look at anything . . . except my shoes. I did hear a beep when we set off earlier, but I never thought to check the fuel gauge. I was convinced a full tank would last longer.

Back from the service station with a can of petrol,

Julien gives the camper a much needed drink and it comes back to life. The girls cheer when the engine purrs.

'Thank you so much,' I say. 'I don't know how we'd have managed without you.'

He brushes aside the compliment sheepishly.

'Do you still not want to travel with us?' he asks. 'Travelling in groups avoids exactly this sort of setback.'

'That's very kind, but the point of this road trip is for the three of us to get to know each other again. I'm sure we'll keep bumping into you.'

'Well, it's up to you,' he says with a shrug. 'I was the same, my first time. I wanted to do the trip alone with my son, but I don't regret deciding to look for travelling companions online. It actually helps you to be alone. We only get together in the evenings. I take care of the parking bookings and the others just take up their spaces when they get there. During the day we each do our own thing. We can have supper together and talk about what we've been up to, which adds a lot to the whole experience, but that's not compulsory. And anyway, I'd feel more comfortable knowing you're not alone.'

'Me, too. I wouldn't be so frightened,' Lily says, having listened attentively to his little presentation. 'What with breakdowns and burglaries and things, I'm not exactly chilled.'

'Out of the mouths of babes . . .' Julien whispers with a smile.

I'm just wondering whether it would be a good idea to accept the offer when he brings out his clincher.

'And we have a themed evening once a week. This week it's karaoke in my van. I've got a fantastic deck. I love karaoke, especially Elvis!'

Chloe's eyes bulge with disbelief.

'Right, well, maybe we'll carry on on our own,' Lily mumbles.

I thank him wholeheartedly again for helping us out, close the door and get back on the road, hoping my decision won't make our campervan a heartbreak hotel.

Lily

12 April

Dear Marcel,

Sorry for not asking how you are, but I need to tell you what's going on right now. You'll get why it's a priority.

Right, are you sitting down?

Sure?

Okay.

Mum is wailing into a microphone like she wants to snap her vocal cords.

What *I* want is to turn her over to the authorities, but I don't really know who, and I don't speak Ikea anyway. So I'm leaving my eardrums to die a long, sad death.

Hang on a sec, and I'll tell you how we ended up here.

It all started last night. It was three in the morning and I was woken by a pneumatic drill. It turned out to be Mum snoring, so I did this thing I read about once in a magazine: I whistled – but it didn't

92

work. Maybe because I can't whistle. I tried doing really high-pitched screams, which sounded similar, but I gave up when Chloe kicked me in the shin.

Mum just had to stop that racket. I couldn't take any more so I remembered another thing I read in a magazine: to put her finger in a glass of water. It's not really meant to stop snoring, but apparently it makes people wet the bed. If she was wet, it would wake her up and she'd stop snoring. Elementary, Whitney Houston. I got up, half filled a glass with water and took Mum's hand to single out a finger, but I didn't have time to do more than that because she woke with a start and I spilled the water over her.

After that she couldn't get back to sleep. Something was wrong. She was breathing really quickly and sweating, I asked if she was okay, and she said everything was fine, but I only half believed her because her teeth were chattering as she said it. Chloe asked if she'd like to sleep in our bed, and she came and lay down between us. Chloe put her arms around her and rubbed her shoulder, so I did the same on the other side. I don't know if they slept, but no one snored.

At breakfast this morning Chloe and me told Mum we wanted to join Julien's group from now on. It makes sense, even if it does mean putting up with a load of people. It's not that I don't like people, it's just I can cope without them, a bit like the kidney beans in chilli con carne. She asked if we were sure about this, she'd prefer to carry on just the three of us but never be too far from the others, but that's not the same. In the end, she agreed it would be better and we'd feel safer 'in the event of burglaries, breakdowns, rat attacks or glasses of water'.

So today, after visiting a place called Kalmar (which is a scam, because it's not calmer than anywhere else we've been) (and that's like not being free to roam in Rome), we joined the other campers on this sort of parking area by the sea, looking out at an island we're visiting tomorrow.

I don't remember all the names but there are four campervans:

- Julien, the organiser and his son Noah, who's thirteen
- Two parents with their two children, a boy (little) and a girl (older)
- Two old guys (Diego and I can't remember who)

Luckily, we don't have to spend the whole time together, but we had supper with them this evening to 'celebrate' us joining. They put all the folding tables outside and pushed them together into one

big table. I sat next to Noah – at least I could be
sure he wouldn't bore me to death talking. I don't
know what the grown-ups have been drinking, but
right now Diego (the oldie) is singing 'Killing Me
Softly', and I just wish someone would.

Okay, I'm off now. I'm going to look for
something to stuff in my ears so I can sleep in
peace. I think I saw some tampons in my mum's
wash bag.

Lily x

PS Sometimes I wish I was like you (not flat) (but
earless).

The Chloe Chronicles

While we were on Öland island I used one minute from my daily ration of thirty to check whether Kevin had got back to me. Still nothing. Just WhatsApps from Ines with gossip from school.

But I know he read my message four minutes after I sent it. I've read it over several times to try to see what might have annoyed him.

'Hi Kevin, I'm so glad to hear from you! I've gone away. Not sure exactly when I'll be back, but it would be really great to message each other every day, kind of like old-fashioned penpals! What did you want to talk about? Xx'

I don't understand. I don't think I came on too strong – I even deleted a heart smiley before sending it. He probably hasn't had time. Which is *not* a problem we have here.

The days drag out slowly, and it feels as if Mum, Lily and I have exhausted every topic of conversation. Silence is the fourth person in our camper. Mum makes an effort to get us talking, but it doesn't catch on. Lily's always miles away and I don't have much to say. It's weird. I've always wanted Mum to work shorter hours, like before Dad left, so we could spend more time together, and now that's happened, it's not how I thought it would be. Maybe it takes time. Maybe we need to relearn each other, like relearning a foreign language if you haven't spoken it for a long time.

'We're here!'

Mum put on the hand brake. We'd just driven down to the far south of the island on a narrow stretch of road with, on the left, cows, sheep, windmills, stones and red sheds against green grass, and on the right, the sea shimmering almost silver in the sun.

We got out, facing Långe Jan lighthouse. It stands there alone, braving the elements, impressive.

Mum started walking over to it, and we followed her. Lily, who had permission to bring her rat out, pointed to the top of the tower.

'Are we going up it?'

'We're not planning to,' Mum said, shaking her head.

'That's a shame. Mathias and me would have liked that.'

Mum looked up to the top. She didn't need to say anything for me to know she was calculating how many steps there were. She said okay.

At the door to the lighthouse a woman told us we were in a bird reserve and you could see lots of different species of bird with binoculars, and she lent us a pair.

Mum let us go ahead of her, and we started climbing.

We got there five minutes before she did! I think that, for the first time in her life, she'd have liked to swap places with a rat.

It was worth the effort. A cold, salty wind blasted my face and all around me blue dissolved into green. There was an edge-of-the-world feeling to the place and a smell of adventure. We stayed up there for a while, swaddled in our coats, and walked around the lookout point so we could see the view in all directions. We handed each other the binoculars to admire the birds. There were swans and seagulls and loads of smaller birds I can't name. We had the lighthouse to ourselves. I didn't need to wait till my eighteenth birthday to feel free up there.

We were about to go back down when Lily screamed and pointed out to sea.

'Look! That rock! It's moving!'

There was a cluster of big grey rocks in the water, just like the standing rocks all over the island. Mum instinctively put her hand on Lily's forehead to check her temperature, but Lily wouldn't calm down.

'Pass the binoculars. I saw it move, honest!'

I handed them to her and she focused them and started hopping from foot to foot.

'OMG, there's seals, *there's seals!*'

I didn't even try to take the binoculars from her to check – she would have bitten me. I took out my poor incapacitated phone – at least there are some things it can still do – and zoomed right in. Lily was right. There was a group of seals lounging on the rocks, basking in the sun. It was magical.

We ran down the stairs, hoping to get closer to them, but the caretaker lady said we shouldn't. We might frighten them. So we watched them from a distance before heading back to the camper. Slowly, as if we wanted to delay returning to the real world.

It's funny, it was like we were in a state of shock. Mum didn't start the engine straight away. Even Lily kept her mouth shut. But this was a different silence. It brought us together.

We'd just been blown away by the beauty of the world.

Anna

After spending three evenings with the campervan gang I asked Lily and Chloe if they'd like us to carry on with them or hit the road on our own again. They voted loudly and unanimously for the first option.

That wasn't my plan. I'd pictured this journey as just the three of us, a sort of close-knit experience for us to reconnect through, a restricted space so we'd have no choice but to live together. Get to know each other better, spend some time together and learn to trust in each other again. I'm convinced it's what they need. But maybe I overestimated what I'm capable of.

At home I was short of time but could always come up with solutions. Here, it's the other way round.

Being permanently busy meant I didn't have a chance to think. Every day was an endless succession of chores, housework, shopping, admin, work, changing lightbulbs, cooking meals, putting on the dishwasher, leaving a note for the girls to empty it, leaving a note for the girls to say they'd forgotten to empty it, emptying it . . . I collapsed into bed every night and fell asleep as if I'd been knocked out with a sledgehammer.

Here, I ponder. Analyse. Take stock. Sometimes I don't think about anything. A resting brain is a panic attack's chosen target.

What if I had a little panic attack now, my emotional brain suggests.

No need for that, my rational brain replies.

But that's the perfect excuse!

No, but thanks all the same.

Oh, go on! I haven't really tested you for a while – you'll end up thinking you're safe. Here, look, I'm sending an army of ants to tingle your fingers.

No, seriously, I can manage without this.

Too late. Accelerating heart rate incoming!

Stop, or I'll . . .

Or you'll what? You're no match for this, you know you're not. Come on, I'll chuck in a few hot flushes and get the shaking going. Can you take it?

No reply.

Are you still there, rational brain?

Silence.

Right, that's that. I've won again.

To be honest, I'm not afraid of being burgled or breaking down. I'm scared of having a panic attack and not being able to handle it. I dread the idea of passing out, leaving my girls on their own. I'm terrified at the thought of all those horrible symptoms. The symptoms of fear. Basically, I'm frightened of being frightened. I'm frightened of myself.

I thought we could loosely follow the same route as the group without being in each other's pockets the whole time. Never getting too far away, but not actually being with them. Occasionally spending the night in the same place, mostly not. But perhaps surrounding myself with other people is the solution to feeling safer.

After three evenings with them I'm getting to know the campervan crew. We meet up whatever time suits us after dark. Julien reserves the parking slots and all we have to do is get settled in. We bump into each other and chat as we do our little chores, then have a drink together and a meal, if we feel like it.

There's Julien, the group's founder, who's travelling with his thirteen-year-old son Noah, a sweet-faced boy who never speaks but watches his luminous spinning top for hours on end. Julien may have managed to persuade me to join in the karaoke, but I intend to come up with a rock-solid excuse to avoid the next themed evening: mime and impersonations.

There's Clara and Greg, a young couple from Biarritz, and their dog, Jojo. Every day they try to find a postcard of wherever they've visited to send to the residents of the retirement home where they both work. I think I'll get on well with them.

There's Diego and Edgar, two old boys in their eighties from the Auvergne. They were originally meant to make the trip with their wives, Madeleine and Rosa, but they died within a fortnight of each other last month.

They don't say much, and when they do it's to talk about their wives.

There's Françoise and François and their children Louise and Louis, who are seventeen and nine. She's a solicitor and he's 'in business', and they're on this road trip because their children have got too accustomed to a luxurious lifestyle. They hope that what they call the 'culture shock' will put the children's feet back on the ground. To help with that, they've gone for a smaller vehicle with rudimentary creature comforts.

The light's on in Julien's van. I knock at the door and he opens up, a chequered napkin knotted round his neck.

'Noah and I always have a hot chocolate before going to bed. Is everything okay?'

'Yes, yes, everything's fine! I came to say we'd like to travel with you from now on, if that's still okay with you.'

Without giving me time to react, he jumps down and gives me a hug, patting my shoulder.

'I'm so glad. You've made the right choice.'

On my way back to the campervan I try to convince myself I'm as sure of that as he is. The girls don't hear me come in.

'I never thought I'd say this,' Lily is saying quietly, 'but I even miss school.'

'I can't take being cooped up in this tiny space a minute longer,' Chloë agrees. 'Okay, fine, it's very nice, we've seen some lovely views, but can we go home now?'

'Do you think we should, like, tell her?'

'No, it'll upset her.'

'So what do we do?'

Chloe thinks for a few seconds.

'We just need to make sure she regrets the whole idea and wants to go home,' she suggests.

'Oh yes, yay!' Lily cries excitedly. 'We can make the whole thing a nightmare!'

I go back out very quietly, take a moment to assimilate what I've just heard, then open the door noisily to join my delightful daughters.

Lily

18 April

Hej, Marcel!
   Jag heter Lily, jag är 12 år gammal.
   (You don't look like you speak Swedish, so I'll tell you that means 'Hello, Marcel. My name's Lily and I'm twelve.')
   I hope you're okay and not too cold. There's something I've got to tell you, but I'm really worried Mum'll find you and get you to talk, so I'll do this as a riddle:
   My first is what a landlord does.
   My second is the opposite of pull.
   My third is keeping quiet.
   My fourth is finished.
   My fifth is really simple, so I'll just tell you it's 'the'.
   My sixth is to move slowly.
   My whole is what me and Chloe want to do.
   So, have you got it?
   Give me a sign if you've got an idea.

105

Pffff. You're not that bright, are you?

Fine. I'll give you the answer, but if anyone ever finds you (and it's not me), you'd better snap shut in their face and fly away, okay?

So the answer is: 'Let's push Mum over the edge.'

Me and Chloe talked it over. True, we've had some good times on this trip, but the camper's okay for about five minutes at a time. If someone had told me when I was born that this would be my life one day, I'd have gone back where I came from. I want to go home to my room, my bed, my magazines and my rocks and minerals. I want time on my own. I want to dance any way I feel like and not have Chloe taking the mickey. She wants to go home, too, so we thought we should do something about it.

We got on with it and made a first attempt this afternoon, and I can tell you we really went for it! We were visiting this medieval town, Vadstena, on the lake Vättern. Okay, so it was pretty, but all pretty things are the same: once you've seen one, you've seen them all.

Mum got us to look round the castle and when we were standing at the foot of a tower Chloe gave me a sign meaning that this was our big moment. She said she'd quite like a little rest and then I waited till Mum wasn't looking, took Mathias out from under my coat and put him at her feet (really hoping he didn't run away). She didn't notice him at first. Gotta say she wouldn't stop talking – 'Oh, the moat here and the ramparts there!' She missed her vocation – she could have been Wikipedia. My little rat must have twigged what was expected of him, coz he gripped on to Mum's jeans and started climbing up her leg. She's gradually got used to him and can cope with him being within a couple of metres of her, but she's never touched him and still screams every time she sees him. I watched as her eyes bulged with horror, and she really froze when he wrapped his tail around her calf. Chloe shot me this little look of satisfaction, and I held my breath, I was worried she'd kick off and send him flying. Well, anyway, Marcel, you may not believe this, but not only did she *not* scream, she actually smiled at me and said how affectionate Mathias is. I think she was in a state of shock.

We were seriously peed off, but we're not giving up – we'll find other opportunities. We'll just step it up a gear.

Okay, I'd better go. It's 'mime and impersonations' this evening, and Mum said we couldn't be the only ones who don't join in. Luckily, there's Noah. I showed him how to make music with a glass and I think he was really into it.

See ya.
Lily xx

PS I can't stop eating Kanelbullar, these sort of little cinnamon rolls. My stomach'll be bigger than my eyes soon.

The Chloe Chronicles

I woke up first this morning and snuck out quietly. I needed some air and a bit of time to myself. We reached Stockholm yesterday, and we're spending three days here. Mum's not giving up.

Louise, the posh people's daughter, was out doing yoga poses. She was all gushy hellos but I just gave a little grunt. I can see she's trying to be friendly with me – she comes over and talks to me whenever she can – but I don't have anything to say to her. The only thing we have in common is our age. She wears woollen dresses and matching tights, she smiles at everyone she meets (probably even if they have trunks and branches), her voice is soft as velvet and – stop press – she sneezes silently.

I walked away so I didn't have to watch her any longer and ended up bumping into the old guys having their breakfast in the sun. Edgar asked if I'd like to join them, and I said yes. Diego went to get me a chair and I sat down. Their coffee was rank, like every coffee I've ever had. I live in hope of enjoying it one day, and cigarettes, too. In the meantime, I put two sugars in one and don't inhale the other.

The olds aren't very talkative, but I knew what subject to get on to so it didn't look as if I was criticising their cafetière.

'What were your wives' names?'

Diego sighed and his eyes misted over.

'Madeleine. She always wanted to visit Stockholm . . .'

Edgar grabbed hold of the table to pull himself to his feet and walked stiffly over to their campervan. He went in and came back out moments later with a framed photo in his hand.

'That's Madeleine on the left and my Rosa on the right,' he said, handing it to me. 'They were great friends.'

The picture was of two silver-haired women roaring with laughter, standing arm in arm by the shores of what looked like a lake.

'They're here with us every minute of the way,' Edgar went on. 'We're making this trip for them. Then we can go and join them.'

'That's right,' Diego agreed. 'I've been terrified of death my whole life. The phobia hasn't gone but, now, living without my wife frightens me even more than death.'

Edgar blew his nose noisily. I downed my coffee in one and thanked them as I stood up. I've always preferred crying alone.

Most girls my age have a string of flings but don't really get serious. No commitment, and even less emotion. But

I'm looking for more than that – I'm looking for the love of my life. I want him to be in my every thought, I want to feel incomplete when we're apart and for him to understand me without words. I want to know everything about him and to be reassured by it, I want to have butterflies in my stomach when I look at him, I want his voice to make me quiver and to be happy only when I'm with him. I want to love the way Edgar and Diego love their wives. I want to be loved the way Mum is by Dad.

I met Mum and Lily on my way back to the van. They were off to find out about hiring bikes. Mum's phone was on the side, so I took it and went and sat on the bed. Kevin still hadn't replied, but he was online. I typed in the words and sent the message before I could regret it.

'Hi, Kevin, I just wanted to say I'm thinking of you. I miss you. Chloe x'

The answer came straight back. My heart bounced up and down like a yoyo.

'Hi, how much r u thinking bout me?'

'A lot'

'Prove it'

I wondered what he meant, but he sent the subtitles soon enough: 'I miss your tits send a photo'

The string on the yoyo snapped. It wasn't exactly what I was expecting but maybe, with Kevin, love doesn't manifest itself in his heart.

I glanced around. Theoretically, no one should be able to see me. I unhooked my bra, then pulled up my jumper and T-shirt with one hand. With the other I turned the phone towards my chest. I was just considering whether it was better to take the image from above or below when the door opened. It was Mum. I dropped the phone, but not the jumper.

'What are you doing?' she asked.

I didn't answer. I thought the scene was explicit enough.

'Are you taking pictures of your breasts?' she ploughed on. 'Answer me, Chloe! Why are you doing that?'

My stomach lurched. With my tits out in the open on a not very comfortable bed, prepared to exchange my naked body for a few morsels of love, I could see how pathetic I looked to my mother. I was ashamed. Angry with myself. So I turned on her.

'Leave me the fuck alone!' I roared. 'Leave me alone and get out! Can't you see you're smothering me? You're so judgemental and bossy.'

'Chloe, stop that right—'

'Stop what, exactly? Stop showing my tits, stop getting off with boys? Have you wondered why I do all this? Have you, Mum? Have you ever wondered whether you're a bit to blame? Maybe if you hadn't left Dad, we wouldn't have come to this . . .'

She didn't rise to that. I wanted to stop, but it was irresistible, overflowing. I had to hurt her. I loaded my weapon. Aimed. Fired.

'And maybe if you'd had a mother, you'd be a better one yourself.'

Anna

I have a mother. She's called Brigitte. I talk to her a lot. I ask her advice – she's the first person I tell when things happen to me. I take her flowers once a year, on her birthday.

She died on a Friday. The mimosa was in bloom, and I'd just nicked some sprays of it from Monsieur Blanchard, our neighbour. I walked all the way back home smelling those fragrant yellow pompoms; I couldn't wait for their perfume to fill the living room. They were her favourite flowers.

She was lying on the floor in the kitchen, in front of the oven. Cauliflower cheese was cooking.

I tried to get her up. I shook her, patted her cheeks, screamed, begged, cried. A mummy always wakes up when her child cries.

'Look, Mummy, I brought some mimosa. Mummy, please . . . I recited my poem and the teacher said it was good. I got a sticker. Look at my sticker, Mummy! And I saw some cranes flying over. Come on, Mummy, come out and look. I'm sure we'll see some more. Mummy . . . pleeease, Mummy . . .'

I wanted to go for help but I couldn't leave her on her own.

I put my hands on her chest and pressed. I'd seen someone do it on TV once and the man woke up. I pressed for a long time, until there was no strength left in my arms. Then I knew. I went to get the throw from the sofa and I lay down next to her with my face burrowed against her neck. I covered us with the throw and hummed the songs she used to sing to herself every evening.

I was still singing when my father came home from work. He told me all this. It was dark; the cauliflower cheese was burnt. I just remember the pompoms of mimosa scattered over the cold tiles of the kitchen floor.

I was eight years old and an only child. My father was thirty and an only parent. Nanny was fifty-four and suddenly childless. We wove our grief together into one vast, devastating, insurmountable pain. We probably hoped that, between the three of us, it wouldn't be so heavy a burden. But the opposite happened. The grief of those we love intensifies our own.

I grew up with an impatient longing to be a mother.

From their first cries, my life was reduced to a single goal: making my daughters happy.

Their father often had a go at me for giving too much of my life to them. He was right – perhaps even a little below the mark: I give my *whole* life to them. Everything I do is dictated by my need to see their faces light up with smiles. It's no sacrifice. To be honest, it's almost selfish: making them happy makes me happy.

I absolutely loved the baby years, when we were everything to each other. My gentle little Chloe who fell asleep in my arms, dedicated every picture she drew to me and swore she'd never leave me. Lily, my little clown, who stole my skirts to wear as capes, who begged me to tell scary stories: 'Pleathe, lovely Mummy, becauthe I love you tho much.' Watching them grow up was the best show on Earth.

I have a whole cupboard full of things I can't bear to get rid of. Their first babygros, their first dummies, all their drawings – even the ones that don't look like anything – the 'thoft round pebbleth' Lily brought home from school every evening, Chloe's plaster cast, their cuddly toys, their milk teeth, their first shoes, the mobile that played songs to them till they fell asleep, and so many other things that hold memories. I rarely delve into it because the nostalgia drowns me. People warned me that the time flies by. I didn't realise quite how fast, though.

It feels to me as if we're all on buses speeding inexorably towards a common destination. We come across each other, lose each other, occasionally travel together. Some people get off before the terminal. You can't put the brakes on, you can't stop for a moment; all you can do is try to feel as good as possible.

When I got on the bus, thirty-seven years ago, I shared my seat with two people: my parents. Until my mother got off. I carried on alone, with my father and grand-mother never too far away. Mathias came and sat next to me and I clung to him. Then came Chloe. Then Lily.

Since then, the journey has had a meaning. Despite the bumps and accidents, I feel good on this bus. I know why I'm here. But I can already tell there's a crossroads ahead. It's getting closer very quickly. Chloe's going to move to another seat. Lily will, too, one day. I'll be so happy for them, but I'll weep for myself. The views will lose all their glory, the seats won't be so comfortable. There'll be nothing interesting about the journey. I'll watch my life flit by through the window.

I don't claim to be a good mother. My daughters are not in a good place. I've made mistakes. With every deci-sion I make and every response I have to situations, I question whether I'm doing the right thing. Every action, however insignificant it seems, has repercussions. Par-ents are tightrope walkers, carrying a fragile parcel along a wire stretched between 'too much' and 'not enough'.

You have to be attentive but not let your children think they're the centre of the universe; you have to make them happy without letting them take things for granted; you have to balance their diet without depriving them; you have to give them confidence but ensure they stay humble; you have to teach them to be kind but not to be doormats; you have to explain things to them but not justify your own actions; they need to burn their energy but get plenty of rest; they must learn to love animals but also be wary of them; you have to play with them but also let them get bored; you have to give them autonomy but always be around; you have to be tolerant but not lax; you have to be firm but not harsh; you have to ask their advice but not let them make all the decisions; you have to tell them the truth without compromising their innocence; you have to love them without smothering them; you have to protect them without imprisoning them; and you have to hold their hand but let them walk away.

This road trip seemed like a solution to me. Over the last few years, I've had to work much longer hours to pay the bills. I thought my being out of the house so much was what was causing my girls' problems. I thought being together would be enough to plug the gaps. They're not toddlers any more. My cuddles aren't enough to heal their wounds.

Maybe Chloe's right. Maybe I shouldn't have cut their father out of their lives. Maybe if I'd had my own mother at their age, if I'd had her as a role model, I'd have made fewer mistakes.

I go into the campervan and close the door behind me. I go up to Chloe without even thinking, not sure whether I'm going to scream at her or try to talk to her. She turns to look at me and her face is distorted with anger. This is a woman I'm looking at, a woman who hates me and wants to provoke me. But, deep in her eyes, in that almost black blue that she inherited from her father, I can see my little girl asking for help.

Lily

21 April

Dear Marcel,

Things are so messed up here, you have no idea.

First there was the screaming row. I heard shouting: it was Chloe's voice. I went into the campervan and she was in Mum's arms. She couldn't stop saying, 'I'm sorry, I'm sorry,' and they were both crying. It was like a musical without the music. I asked if someone had been chopping onions, but they didn't answer. Tbh, I can't see the point of crying, especially seeing as the planet's short of water – basically, it's a waste.

Then came the disaster. I've still got goose lumps from it. We were at Skansen, which is a living museum, like a town that's stuck in a time warp. There were people in old-time clothes, we visited a haberdashery, a printing press and an old school, and we even watched a glass blower. It was like being in the olden days. I really liked it, until Mum noticed that I couldn't stop scratching

my head. She wanted to have a look, and I
wouldn't let her but she didn't take no for an
answer. It's like I'm just a tenant in my body and
she actually owns it.

When she saw the lice she jumped away and
screamed. It was an invasion and we had to find a
chemist's and destroy them. I said she'd have to
destroy me first, there was no way anyone was
killing my lice; they hadn't chosen just anyone's
head, they'd chosen mine and I needed to protect
them. I thought her eyes were going to pop out of
her face. Chloe laughed so hard she cried. She
must have thought I was playing another trick on
Mum to get us to go home, but this time I really
meant it. Mum said, 'Fine,' and we carried on with
the rest of the day as if nothing had happened.

Back in the campervan in the evening they
launched themselves at me. Chloe pinned me down
and Mum sprayed this horrible smelly stuff all over
my hair. I fought and yelled that I'd report them
for failing to help endangered lice, but they didn't
give a stuff.

My poor little headlice all died in the attack. I
made a coffin for them out of a matchbox and
buried them under a pine tree and made up a
special send-off song for them about headlouse
heaven where everyone has such long hair no one
knows whose is whose. Mum and Chloe wanted to

come to the funeral, but I refused to let those murderers anywhere near. But I did let Louise and Louis come along, even though I got the feeling Louis was laughing at me a bit.

And that's another thing that's not right. Their parents, Françoise and François, are completely bonkers. Get this: they make them wash with cold water and sleep on thin mattresses and they only have 10 krona a day to spend on food. Louise explained that they live in a really big house with a pool and electric blinds and even a fridge with an inbuilt ice machine. They have apartments in other countries and they fly more than air stewardesses. Which means living in comfort is completely normal for them, so they don't understand the value of money, and that's why their parents want to show them a different type of life. I don't really understand how you can't see the value of things. I mean, I can tell you, if I had a fridge that made ice cubes, I'd give it a massage every day as a thank you. Like that's ever going to happen – I'm never going to be rolling in it.

Then, the icing on the cake was Dad phoning. And I was made to talk to him this time. He asked me loads of questions about how things are going here, but I just answered yes and no and handed him back to my sister. It's like he thinks he can be a dad by doing it all over the phone (if you are happy, press 1; if you are sad, press 2; if you would like to speak to a real live parent . . .)

Right, that's enough, Marcel. I'm feeling pretty rubbish this evening so I'm not very good company.

I'm going to stop writing, but I'm still thinking of you. You're my BFF.

Lily

PS I hope there really is a headlouse heaven and they have parties with fleas and bedbugs.

The Chloe Chronicles

Today Mum asked if I'd like to go for a walk in Gamla Stan, Stockholm's old town. Just the two of us.

After the headlice fiasco, I really thought she'd want to go home, but her enthusiasm is still untarnished. Lily and I tried to think of new ways to get her to turn back, but I think that, in her heart of hearts, we both know this journey's going all the way, if only to honour the promise she made to Nanny. Maybe it's not such a bad thing after all. I quite like this little game against Mum. Not just because it's a laugh, but also because it's a long time since I've got on so well with my sister.

I agreed to the walk. I can't remember the last time I spent time alone with Mum. I promised myself I wouldn't be nasty, so she'd forgive me for the things I said when we argued.

We wandered through the cobbled streets and went into lots of little shops, each more adorable than the one before, we walked down the narrowest street in the city, Mårten Trotzigs Gränd, and ate sweets. I took lots of pictures: the colourful façades against the blue sky, reflections in the water, Mum posing on Riksbron bridge,

Mum outside the Royal Palace, Mum outside Stockholm Cathedral.

'Pass it here, I'll take a picture of you,' she said at one point.

She really had to insist. I always feel uncomfortable posing, particularly if the person taking the pictures takes quarter of an hour to frame it and even then it comes out blurred. That's fine by me – I don't like seeing myself. It doesn't matter that, ever since I was little, people have told me I'm pretty and photogenic. They've said I have a lovely face, gorgeous eyes, a full mouth and a perfect profile, but when I see myself on a screen or in the mirror I'm assaulted by all my flaws. So I stick to a perfectly regimented routine in the bathroom every morning. A blob of foundation to smooth out my skin, bronzer to contour my cheekbones, a cat-flick of eyeliner and three layers of mascara to bring out my eyes, lipstick to highlight my lips, a misting of perfume, a few locks of hair curled on hot tongs, and that's my mask. I'm untouchable.

We were suddenly hungry so we bought some fried strömming with mashed potato and sat on a bench by the water to eat. We'd almost finished when it became clear Mum wanted to talk.

'Are you angry, Chloe?'

'What makes you say that?' I retorted, to avoid answering.

I could feel her eyeing me but kept staring at the opposite bank.

'I just get the feeling you are. Am I right?'

I wiped my mouth with my little paper napkin.

'I dunno, it's weird. It actually changes all the time. Sometimes I'm sad, just, like, for no reason, and the next minute I'm overflowing with happiness. Then I can be seething with anger. It's horrible and that's when I say terrible things, which makes me even angrier, but I can't stop myself saying them. I think . . .'

I stopped talking. If I formulated this thought that's been haunting me for a while now, it would become too real.

'What do you think?' Mum prodded.

'No, nothing.'

'You can tell me, Chloe. I'm not your enemy, I just want to try to understand you.'

I thought it over for a long time. It's hard showing what's going on inside me. Every confession I make feels like peeling away a protective layer. And this piece of information was particularly sensitive. If I was right, it would be better to keep it secret. But if I was wrong, perhaps Mum could put my mind at rest. I turned and looked right into her eyes.

'Promise you won't judge me?'

'I promise I won't.'

'Okay. I think I'm mad.'

She tried not to show anything, but I could see the concern in her face. She took my hand.

'I don't think you're mad. You're just a teenager, sweetheart.'

'But none of the other girls in my class are like me! I'm the only one who's always confused and questioning, who keeps changing her mind and can't control her emotions. I know I'm over-sensitive, but it's ridiculous! I feel so different . . .'

She didn't say anything, just stroked my hand.

We didn't stay out very late. Lily wasn't yet back from her trip to the Vasa Museum with Clara and Greg. Mum walked away from the camper and I could see through the window that she was on the phone.

Just after supper she handed me her mobile.

'Here. I asked Pops to scan these for you.'

She left me on my own. I looked at the screen and there was a page of handwriting. Then another. Then dozens more.

It took me more than an hour to read them all. They were mostly poems, written by Mum. Judging by the dates, she must have been between fourteen and twenty. Right up until I was born.

Very poetically and melancholically, they tackled subjects like the passage of time, absence, death, childhood and abandonment. She was looking for some meaning to life, talking about world crises, about love, loneliness and fear. Several of the pieces were dedicated to her mother, her father, her grandmother, to the child she'd once been, to the children she would one day have.

Ever since I was born, people have said how like my father I am: my red curls, my dark blue eyes, my slim legs. My mother never seemed offended by this; she would smile, as if it was all the same to her. Most likely because, deep down, she knew that I was actually much more like her.

Anna

'Hey, these flowery curtains are very sophisticated!' Clara coos, stroking the fabric.

I thank her, before realising she was being sarcastic. If Jeannette hadn't married my father, it would be possible to accuse her of dubious taste.

I've invited Clara and Greg for supper to thank them for taking Lily to the Vasa Museum. She'd been on and on about going, but in the end she loathed it.

'I can't see the point of having a museum about a ship that sank, like it's an achievement,' she announces as we all huddle around the table. 'Soon they'll be making statues of planes that crash out of the sky.'

Clara throws her head back and laughs.

'Your kid's so great, I love her! She almost makes me want to have one.'

I fill the plates with meatballs, except for Lily's (she's suddenly decided to go vegetarian) and Chloe's (she had too much to eat in Gamla Stan). They're being very discreet, but I see them exchange conspiratorial smiles.

'So,' I say, turning to our guests, 'have I got this right – this is your honeymoon?'

'Well, we've extended it,' Greg replies, pronging a meatball with his fork. 'The initial plan was just to do a quick tour of Europe, but we so loved being in the camper we felt like carrying on. We did some number-crunching and took a year's sabbatical. Mmm, these are delicious!'

'Thank you. I can't really take the credit. I bought them at a deli in Stockholm, all I've done is heat them up. I'm going to open another bottle of wine. Who'd like some?'

'Always up for a glass of wine!' Clara says, holding out her glass. 'Anyway, what about you? Why are you three girls making this trip? And where's the daddy?'

I'd noticed that Clara's pretty direct, but I hadn't realised quite how much. Greg elbows her in the ribs.

'What?' she asks in surprise. 'Everyone else is talking about it. I'd rather ask her straight out.'

I'm about to reply when Lily beats me to it.

'He abandoned us.'

'What the hell!' Chloe retorts. 'He calls regularly, and he'd have us with him more often if he could.'

'Yeah, right! Do you really think he can't afford to have us to stay?'

'Girls, that's enough!' I intervene.

'That's not the point,' Chloe snaps. 'It's Mum who doesn't want us to see him, he told me so himself.'

I thump the bottle noisily on to the table to settle my daughters . . . and my heart, which has set off like a train.

'These meatballs are so tender,' Clara says, attempting to change the subject. 'You should try them, girls – you're really missing out.'

Lily glances surreptitiously at her sister, who's sulking ostentatiously. But her anger can't quite outweigh her curiosity. She slowly uncrosses her arms, takes a helping and very tentatively tries the sauce. She frowns, has another try, then passes the fork to her sister, who also has a taste. I casually carry on chatting with Clara and Greg, not revealing that I know precisely how my daughters' silent conversation is going.

Lily: It's not spicy!

Chloe: I know, I don't understand.

Lily: Are you sure you put enough in?

Chloe: I emptied the pot! Their mouths should be on fire!

Lily: And we should be in the firing line!

I contain my laughter. My darling daughters have no idea I found the empty pot of harissa in the bin, rinsed off the meatballs and improvised another sauce. They have no idea they're not the only ones playing games . . . and their mother has never liked losing.

My head's spinning by the time Clara and Greg wander back to their campervan. Swedish wine goes down very easily. Lily's writing her diary and Chloe's taking her make-up off. A green light flashes on my phone.

I didn't mean to open the message, I just wanted to check the time. The picture fills the whole screen: it's aggressive, violent. Underneath it someone called Kevin says, 'Your turn!'

I feel sick. How did I bring up my daughter to think you have to sell yourself by exchanging intimate photos? Where did I go so wrong that my baby thinks flirting has to involve these disgusting messages?

I delete the repulsive picture and write a reply: 'Hello, Kevin, I'm Chloe's mother. I'd have preferred to get to know your face before your penis, but I'm guessing you're shy. Because your relationship is so far advanced, it's time you and I met so we can discuss the wedding. Do let your parents know my daughter can't wait to introduce them to her vagina. See you soon. From your dear Mum-in-law. PS Please cover yourself up, it would be a shame to catch a cold.'

Send.

Delete all trace.

Regret.

Sleep.

Lily

24 April

Dear Marcel,

I hope you're well. I'm fine, thanks.

We've just reached Falun and my mum and sister keep oohing and ahing every time we see a red wooden house or a lake, it's like a flipping Justin Bieber concert. I can't take any more of the endless forests and endless trees – they're everywhere. I keep thinking Leonardo di Caprio's going to appear dressed in furs and covered in blood.

I've already told you about Noah, the boy who doesn't talk. I like spending time with him, maybe *because* he doesn't talk, or maybe because there's something gentle about him. When I look at him I get that feeling like when they gave me a pill to relax me before my appendix operation.

I wanted to introduce him to Mathias yesterday evening. I asked his dad if I could see him and he invited me into their campervan. Noah was lying on his bed, watching the lights moving on the ceiling. I sat down next to him and talked to him (I wasn't sure he'd noticed I was there). I took Mathias out from under my jumper and put him on the bedcover. I told him loads of times he had to take it easy, but he ran straight over to Noah's head and hid under his hair. Noah jumped up and screamed and screamed and screamed without even breathing in between. I tried to calm him down, stroking his arm, but that made things worse so I grabbed Mathias and put him back under my jumper. Noah's dad came running and bear-hugged Noah, holding his arms tightly to his body. He threw me a filthy look and told me to leave. I could still hear Noah screaming from outside. I didn't mean to frighten him, I swear it. I just wanted to make him happy.

Later, Julien came to see us in our campervan. Mum was wearing ugly pyjamas and I could see she was embarrassed, but she let him in.

He asked me what had happened so I explained, and the look Mum gave me – don't even. Julien said it was a nice idea but with Noah you have take things slowly, and you mustn't put the cart before the gift horse's mouth. Apparently, he's autistic, which is why he hardly speaks, he screams a bit, doesn't like being touched or looked at, and we can communicate with him, just not in the same way as with other people. He loves lights, anything that spins and horses. And his favourite thing is anything natural – trees, mountains, big open spaces, the stars, rain, the northern lights, the midnight sun. And that's why Julien's given up his job to take him on this trip. The rest of the time Noah goes to a special school.

When Julien left, my mother said I had to be nice to Noah and I mustn't make fun of him because he's different. And I was like, I wasn't planning on making fun of him. At school I'm the one who's different.

Lily xx

PS Have you noticed that there's only one letter different between autistic and artistic?

Lily

25 April

OMG, Marcel, me again!
   Can you see it? Tell me you can see it! Isn't it
GORGEOUS!!!
   Wooooooooooooooooooooooooooooooooooooooooo
ooooooooooooooooooooooooooooooooooooooooooooooo
oooooooooooooooooooooooooooooooooooooooow!

The Chloe Chronicles

I didn't think we'd get to see them. Everyone said it was rare at this time of year because there's no proper darkness, just hours of twilight.

I was fast asleep when someone came and banged loudly on the van door. It was Julien, yelling at us to come out quickly. It was after midnight and I nearly buried my head back under the duvet. That would have been a big mistake. Huge.

The cold hit me. Swedish nights are no joke. Julien, Noah and all the others were outside, staring up at the sky. Lily squealed. I opened my mouth wide.

Overhead, the northern lights were playing out a hypnotic ballet. It was like a vast silk scarf hovering languidly against a dark sky. A diaphanous veil dancing in a halo of green and pink light. Waves unfurling across the stars.

I remembered Lily's presentation and how fascinated I'd been by the videos she watched when she was doing her research. But that wasn't a patch on what I felt now. It was indescribable. Powerful.

We watched the show till the curtain fell. We hoped there'd be an encore, but there wasn't. We all went back to our campervans saying the same things: fantastic, unbelievable, magical, spectacular. I slipped under the duvet, moved my legs around to warm the bed up, put my hand under my pillow on to the picture of Dad and went to sleep with a smile on my face.

The Chloe Chronicles

We took a boat to the small island of Trysunda in the Gulf of Bothnia. Mum had seen on the internet that there was a perfectly preserved fishing village there, frozen in time. I wasn't expecting it to be so beautiful. If Lily hadn't been in such a state of excitement about our latest ploy to get Mum to give up, I probably wouldn't have gone through with it.

Picture this. A cove edged with little red houses on stilts reflected in dark water, small, neat gardens surrounded by white fences, green roofs, fishing boats tied to pontoons, the whole place surrounded by the protective arms of a pine forest, by lapping water, birdsong, the wind in the treetops, the smell of resin. This is serenity on Earth.

We'd put together a picnic so we could spend the day there. We took lots of pictures of the fishing village and then headed into the woods to walk to the other side of the island.

Lily was complaining about a dream she'd had: 'I was turned into a tree and woodcutters sawed off my arms for firewood. It's messing with my head!'

I felt great. Walking through the conifers, listening to the wind, walking on soft earth and smooth pebbles – it was soothing. The forest eased the constant racket inside my head.

Lily stopped whingeing when we got to the other side of the island and were confronted by a wild sea. Waves crashed down on to the white rocks before drawing back to gather themselves up again. The stormy wind buffeted my hair and the sea mist whipped my face.

We found a place on the edge of the forest, sheltered from the gusting wind, and Mum took out the sand-wiches she'd made. I ignored Lily's silent pleas to set in motion our latest scheme, but she didn't leave me any choice.

'Chloe, wasn't there something you wanted to tell Mum?'

I shot her a stony look.

'Oh, really?' Mum asked, raising her eyebrows. 'I'm all ears.'

I knew what I had to say and, even though it wasn't true, it still wasn't easy. I was worried about how she'd react, worried I'd hurt her. We'd look really clever if she had a panic attack on a near-deserted island.

I cleared my throat and recited my lines, my sister nodding excitedly.

'So here's the thing, I, um . . . basically, I was a bit late so I bought a test at a chemist's in Stockholm, you know, when you gave me an hour of free time.'

I hoped I wouldn't have to finish the sentence, but she just stared at me silently, encouraging me to keep going.

'I don't really know how to say this . . .'

Lily did, though.

'Right, come on, spill the baked beans – Chloe's pregnant!'

I ducked away as a precaution in case Mum's hand flew at my cheek, but it didn't move. For several long seconds I tried to read some sort of sign on her face, but it was expressionless. A wax statue. Lily prodded her with the tip of her finger, probably to check she was still alive. When Mum finally looked into my eyes, hers were full of tears.

'Oh, my darling! I'm so happy, if you only knew! I've waited such a long time for this . . .'

I tried not to show how weirded out I was. She, meanwhile, wouldn't stop talking.

'It would be great if it's a little boy – we could call him Tom, I've always loved the name Tom. Oh my goodness, I'm going to be a granny. Thank you, sweetheart, that's the most precious gift you could ever give me.'

She threw herself at me and hugged me so hard that, if I really had been pregnant, I'd have given birth to a flat baby. I let her get on with it, my own arms hanging limply at my sides. My sister sat facing me, watching us, staring in fact, her mouth gaping open – gobsmacked personified.

Anna

The nights are getting shorter, and the temperatures lower: we're getting close to the Arctic Circle. Chloe really wanted to visit Umeå because Julien had talked so much about this charming town nestled in the countryside. I struggled to stifle my laughter at her astonished expression when I told her I'd rather she stayed at the campervan. Better to be safe than sorry, in her condition.

Lily, wearing her snuggly hat with the rabbit ears, comments on everything we see. Françoise and François keep casting knowing glances in her direction, but I suspect my daughter has a good reason for all this.

'I bet you don't get bored!' Diego whispers as we head into the art museum. I just smile. Julien has a soft spot for this town, and yesterday evening he suggested we had a group outing here. As soon as we were settled at the campsite he set off to hire a minibus, and he's been introducing us to incredible sights all day: Umedalen sculpture park, Lake Nydalasjön, the nature reserve . . . only Chloe and a tired Edgar are not with us.

On the third floor we go into a perfectly dark room.

Luminous shapes form and dissolve on the walls and ceilings – Noah is captivated.

'He's adorable,' Greg says quietly to Julien. 'Are you his full-time carer?'

'I am now, yes. I used to be a chef, but I stopped that three years ago so I could come travelling with him. He loves the natural world, especially Sweden and Norway. If we could, we'd move here, but he loves his school and needs to attend it regularly. So we alternate. We do two road trips a year, always the same itinerary. He likes it – he's starting to get his bearings.'

'Always travelling in a group?'

'At first it was just the two of us, which was good, but I like the idea of meeting other people and I'm convinced it's good for Noah. I'm signed up to a campervan forum and last year there was a couple looking for a guide for a trip to Scandinavia. I said I could do it, and two other families joined us. Now that's what we do every time.'

'Did his mother die a long time ago?' Clara asks, diplomacy to the fore, as usual.

Julien strokes his beginnings of a beard with an awkward smile.

'It's funny. Everyone's convinced my wife's dead, as if it's impossible for a man to look after his own child! She left five years ago. When Noah was eight.'

The obvious amazement on the young couple's faces encourages him to expand: 'I don't hold it against her she was so sure she could cure him of autism. She tried everything: ABA, TEACCH, PECS, psychoanalysis, healers, a gluten- and casein-free diet . . . she refused to accept that he might never be able to hug her, tell her about his day, play with other children or call her Mummy. When she finally took that on board, she couldn't handle it. I got home from work one day and she handed Noah to me and nipped out to the shops. She never came back. She'd emptied out all her stuff during the day.'

He tells the story as if it's someone else's, his eyes distant.

'She calls me from time to time to check everything's okay. She's always very apologetic and cries a lot. It was very hard for her. She persuades herself that Noah doesn't notice she's not around, and maybe she's right.'

'Aren't you angry with her?' Greg asks.

'I dunno. Sometimes I get angry and I wonder how she can cope without him so easily after living with him for all those years. I couldn't do it.'

Françoise, François and their children – who had gone straight on to the next room – come and join us.

'We're moving on. Are you coming?' Françoise asks.

'I'm going to stay here for a while,' Julien says. 'Noah seems to like it. But you go on without us. Shall we meet back outside in an hour?'

The whole group does just that, except for Lily and me. I don't have the heart to leave Julien on his own after he's confided in us. Lily takes up her position next to

Noah and looks back and forth between the teenager's face and the lights he's gazing at.

'I think she's trying to understand how he works,' I murmur to Julien.

'Your girl's wonderful. It's the first time someone her age has taken an interest in him.'

'Yes, she's a star. She's not usually very outgoing with other people, she prefers animals, but there's definitely something there with your boy.'

We lean against the wall and watch our children, silently harbouring a shared emotion.

It's almost time to go and join the others when Françoise runs in, looking frantic.

'Come quickly, come quickly! Something terrible's happened.'

Lily

2 May

Dear Marcel,

How are you doing? I'm okay, in case you're interested. Didn't your parents teach you any manners? Fine, I'm not the sort to bear a grudge, I'll talk to you anyway, specially coz something really crazy happened.

We were visiting this lame museum (except for the room with lights, which was very cool – it even made Noah smile) when Françoise came in screaming like she'd seen her own reflection in a mirror. Clara had fainted. She was there one minute, then bang! she was down. Everyone was worried because she took a while to come round and because she'd knocked her head on the wall. It was bleeding a lot. I almost looked away.

The paramedics took her to hospital for some tests. Greg was in a total panic – you could tell from his forehead, which was all crumpled, like an accordion. They spent a whole night there, so

144

we got to look after Jojo, which made me happy, but not too happy obvs, coz I really like Clara.

I introduced Mathias to Jojo and he was a bit snooty. He didn't want to kiss him hello and I don't know if that's what upset Jojo, but he bared his teeth and they kind of agreed to differ.

We waited for Clara to come back before setting off again. She had a dressing on her head and, apparently, she'd had stitches. She looked tired. But Greg seemed all happy to see her again. He did the driving and Julien and Mum went in convoy with them in case she fainted again.

This evening we had a Swedish theme because we'll soon be moving on to Finland so we had to say a proper goodbye. We ate bakpotatis, mashed potato, herring, and those monsters ate reindeer. I was almost sick, but Clara got there first. It went everywhere and Greg just stroked her back – OMG, love is so gross!! After that she cried and told us all that the hospital had said she was pregnant. Everyone congratulated her, so she cried even more. She said she was going to officially complain to Durex (I dunno who he is) and it wasn't planned and she wasn't ready. Diego said no one could refuse a gift like that and she said she knew and, really, she was happy, but now that the gift was in there she'd have to get it out and she was scared. Françoise said she nearly died it hurt so much. François told her to be quiet, but she kept going and said a colleague of hers died – she actually died for real. Clara was sick again.

When we went off to bed my mum's eyes were shining. She couldn't stop saying how wonderful it was, all these pregnancies – it reminded her of her own.

Right then, I'd better go. She's just got into our bed with us.

See ya

Lily x

PS You could say goodbye, too. Just saying.

Anna

The three of us are lying on our backs on this cramped bed, staring into the shadows.

'With you, Chloe, I realised I was pregnant on a Saturday evening. It was what I longed for from the depths of my heart. For several months I'd been heartbroken every time I got my period. But this time I was a day late, too early to know, too late not to hope. It was all I could think about. We'd had our dog Brownie for a few months by then. She wasn't very cuddly, more the timid sort, but she couldn't leave me alone that evening. When I sat down on the sofa she jumped up and nosed my tummy for a long time, then rested her head on it. The pregnancy test was positive a few days later.

'I became a mother before I even met you. I could feel you growing inside me, I talked to you and stroked my tummy the whole time, I ate lots of fruit and vegetables and avoided certain movements. I took exercise and looked after my body in a way I never had before. I loved it for the first time. It had a use for the first time. I tried to imagine you and wondered if you'd look like me or more like your father, if you'd sleep a lot, if you'd be constantly hungry, if you'd be born with hair, blue eyes, all your fingers and toes . . .

'I had morning sickness, I couldn't bear any sort of smell, I went ballistic if anything annoyed me, I was even rude to an old lady at the supermarket once because she pushed in front of me at the check-out, but oh, I so loved being pregnant! As it got nearer to your due date I was torn between dying to hold you in my arms and nostalgia for these times when you were mine alone.

'And then you were born. My little sweetheart, my little cuddly bear. You came out quietly, without a sound. The midwife slapped your bottom to get you to cry and you cried. It broke my heart. I took you in my arms and stroked you, I smelt you and counted your fingers and toes. I felt strange. I wanted to cry and dance at the same time. It was like part of me was missing, but I'd never felt so complete.

'You slept for six hours. I watched you, and I just couldn't get over you. I thought about my own mother a lot. Then I fell asleep, too, with you gripping my index finger, and I knew that from then on my happiness would be completely bound up in yours. When you were sad, I'd be even sadder. When you were happy, I'd be even happier.'

Silence.

The girls are lying motionless under the duvet. I hope they haven't gone to sleep.

'And I longed for you for ages, too, my Lily. I'd almost

given up hope when you planted yourself inside me. It wasn't Brownie who noticed this time but me. When I cried over an advert for sliced ham I got the message my hormones were sending me. I couldn't have been happier. My dream of having two children was coming true and I couldn't think about anything else.

'I didn't have morning sickness but I spent the whole time eating, and I craved gherkins. I got fatter by the minute but I couldn't care less. When I had a scan they told me you were a boy. I had this little snag of disappointment, but it soon passed. I would have loved to have a sister for Chloe, but everyone seems to think it's great to have one of each. I got everything ready for you – blue pyjamas, dinky little trousers and bibs embroidered with your name, Tom.

'I wasn't as frightened as the first time. There wasn't the element of the unknown, I knew what was in store. I knew it would hurt but that I'd forget the pain the minute I saw your face. I knew that a wave of infinite, explosive, intense happiness would flood through me when I felt your tiny body next to mine. I knew it, but when it happened it was even stronger. The reality was more powerful than the memories.

'It was like a volcanic eruption – I overflowed with happiness. You cried so loudly, my little tornado, screwing up your eyes and your little fists, and you weren't a boy. You didn't quieten down when they put you on my chest or when I talked to you softly. You howled, you were *not* happy. I watched you take your first lungfuls of

life and I knew that from now everything you felt I would
feel too. When you were angry, I'd be even angrier. When
you were euphoric, I'd be even more euphoric.'

Silence.

Silence.

'Are you asleep?'

'No,' Chloe mumbles.

'No,' Lily whispers.

Still lost in magical memories, I can feel my eyes filling
with tears. I wasn't expecting an effusive reaction – I
know my girls too well. But an answer, a word, a gesture . . .
If only I could feel them one more time, tiny and snuggled up against me. If only my words could still reassure
them, my kisses still make everything better, my arms
still comfort them. If only the things they worried about
were just how happy their teddies were and how many
more sleeps it was till Christmas.

I'm just about to go back to my own bed when I feel
Chloe's hand move. She wraps her fingers around my
index finger. I stay there for several long minutes, savouring that feeling, then slip out of the bed.

'Goodnight, my darlings.'

'Goodnight, Mum,' Chloe murmurs.

'Mum, Mathias wants me to tell you something,' Lily
says.

'What is it?'

She pretends to listen to what the rat's saying.

'He says he's glad he landed up in this family.'

The Chloe Chronicles

It was our last day in Sweden.

We were still feeling the side effects of what Mum had told us about when we came into the world. We smiled about nothing in particular, talked to each other gently. I didn't even make a fuss when Lily finished the cereal at breakfast or when Mum kept saying she was happy she'll soon be a granny.

It was weird, actually. At one point I found myself really believing it, and it was nice, because for the first time in a very long while, I didn't feel alone.

We listened to music on the way from Skellefteå to Luleå and even sang along when we found songs that the three of us knew, Ed Sheeran, Beyoncé, stuff from *A Star is Born* . . . We sat in the front, in a row, the whole way. Then Lily suddenly shrieked and Mum slammed on the brakes. I went to take a picture. A herd of elks was strolling casually across the road just metres in front of us. They were magnificent. Till then, we'd only ever seen them on our little TV. We talked about it the whole rest of the way.

We visited Gammelstad, a church town. Julien explained that church towns only exist in Scandinavia. They have a cluster of wooden houses built around a church, and the houses are used by churchgoers from the surrounding area when there are services. The rest of the time the village is empty. We explored its narrow streets, took pictures of each other in front of windows with white curtains and then made our way towards the church . . . only to realise there was a service going on.

We tiptoed inside and sat at the back. A woman was taking the service and we didn't understand a word, but the worshippers' faith didn't need any translation.

It was only about ten minutes till it was over. We wanted to get out quickly so we weren't in anyone's way, but an old man came after us and asked if we'd like to have a cup of tea with them.

It was pretty special. We experienced a bit of their culture and they took an interest in ours. We were sad to say goodbye, knowing we'd never see them again . . . but then we'll never forget them either.

That's what I like about travel. Meeting people like that is why I wish I could go to Australia. Gaining something from other people, enriching myself, broadening my mind. I feel like I'm shrivelling on our estate.

The three of us ate in the van. We sat on the bed with the duvet over our legs, eating pasta with cheese. Mum gave me a double helping because of the baby. We'd almost finished when the phone rang. It was Dad. He listened to what we'd been up to then asked to speak to Mum. Which surprised her as much as it did me. He never wants to talk to her. She asked if everything was okay and, after a while, she went outside. When she came back in she acted like everything was fine, but her hands were shaking so badly it took her two attempts to lock the door.

'What's the matter?' I asked.

'Nothing, nothing.'

'What did he want?'

No answer.

'Mum, are you okay? Are you having a panic attack?'

She looked at me, and I could see the terror in her eyes. She lay down on the bed and we put the duvet over her, but it wasn't happening. She kept saying she was fine, but her voice was like a little bleat.

I didn't know what to do, so I went to get Julien. He asked Lily to keep an eye on Noah, or maybe it was the other way round, and came over. He said we had to get Mum to think about something else, so he started telling her jokes.

'What do you call a blind deer?'

Mum didn't answer, so he asked her again.

'I don't know,' she said, shivering.

'Do you mean you've no eyed deer?!'

She didn't react to that. He soldiered on.

'What's black and white and red all over?'

No response.

'Anna, what's black and white and red all over?'

'Haven't a clue . . .'

'A newspaper! Geddit? Read?'

The worst of it was he looked proud of himself.

'What do you call evangelical Swedes?'

Mum groaned. She was about ready to bite.

'Do you know?' he kept going bravely.

'I couldn't give a stuff what you call them!'

'Björn again Christians! Okay, here's another. What would you call a Russian inventor?'

'Julien, I'm tired . . .'

'Ivan Idea!' he roared.

I couldn't help chuckling, but Mum still wasn't really on board. So then I tried my luck.

'Did you hear about the man with five penises?'

That was met with total silence. Braving the lack of enthusiasm, I gave them the punchline:

'His underpants fit like a glove.'

Julien looked at me, his eyes popping out of his head. Mum slowly turned towards me. I saw all sorts of expressions flit across her face – it was like watching a slot machine when you don't know which image it's going to stop on. It finally stopped on a laugh. It was just a shaky little snigger but enough to elbow the stress out of the way.

An hour later Mum was sleeping, Julien had gone back to his campervan and Lily was back in ours. On the other hand, I was having trouble getting to sleep. My thoughts made it difficult. For Mum to be in that state, Dad must have said something really major.

Lily

5 May

Dear Marcel,

Mum's been seriously weird since her little turn
the other evening. She's almost stopped eating
and just drives along without talking, not even
trying to strike up a conversation. I think there's
something brewing, and it's not a cup of tea.

She didn't even want to go and visit Rovaniemi,
when she was the one who'd been banging on
about how she couldn't wait to explore Finland.
She said she was tired and stayed in the
campervan, so we had to put up with Françoise
and François – just don't even.

They took us to visit Father Christmas's village.
No, honestly, the Finns have built a Father
Christmas village. Can't wait till they build a tooth-
fairy village and one for the Easter bunny. If only
we'd gone with Clara and Greg, but no, we had to
get the Pollyanna family. Little Louis running all
over the place shouting (I wonder if he's actually

human), Louise raving about how wonderful it all was (she needs to get out more) and the parents taking so many selfies the phone decided to commit suicide. I can tell you, François was properly hacked off – that actually shut him up. When Louis said it was just as well coz now they could really live with no modern comforts, I thought he was going to feed his own son to the reindeer.

Chloe seemed to enjoy herself, except when Louise came to talk to her – then she snarled a bit. I know where she's coming from. That Louise girl is stuck on smile mode. She freaks me out – she's like Barbie on drugs.

The only cool thing was this big white line painted on the ground to show us we were going into the Arctic Circle. We're a really long way from home now.

When we got back, Françoise wanted to have a chat with Mum. We didn't hear anything coz we waited outside but when she came back out she said we were having supper with them and Mum needed a bit more rest. We ate boiled potatoes – *AND NOTHING ELSE*!! Françoise and François want their children to lose their spoilt-brat habits. Chloe thinks they're a bit extreme; I think they're a bit extremely messed up in the head. At the end of the day, Mum's not all that bad, even when she snores.

They asked if we'd like to sleep in their van, and I don't know what got into me but I said I sleepwalk and hit people in my sleep. They said, 'Maybe another time.'

Mum was waiting for us when we got back. We told her all about our day as we ate our way through the sweets left from Stockholm, and when we went to bed she promised she'll be feeling better tomorrow. I hope she is, otherwise this campervan won't exactly be a barrel of laughs.

Goodnight, Marcel

Lily xx

PS I found a cool thing: if you don't blink when it's very cold, your eyes cry, I love it.

Anna

The words keep going round and round inside my head. In order, out of order, bumping into each other, leapfrogging each other, knocking each other over. I'm obsessed with them, consumed by them.

'I could have let my lawyer tell you. I'm calling out of genuine friendship.'

'Sole custody. They'll see you every other weekend and half of the holidays.'

'I've been very tolerant, till now. It broke my heart knowing my girls were on their own, left to their own devices.'

'You're not in your right mind. A road trip to Finland . . .'

'Who do you think the judge will choose, between a father who works nine to five and has a salary and a mother who's unemployed, in debt and takes her daughters out of school to take them on the road?'

'I agreed to lie to them, but I'm taking things in hand.'

'Chloe's told me about your panic attacks. You're putting the girls in danger.'

'You've never made this easy for me. If you hadn't been so selfish, they could have seen me much more often.'

'I'm not doing this to hurt you but to protect my girls.'

'*If you let me come home, you can see them every day.*'
'*I want custody of the girls.*'
'*I want custody of the girls.*'
'*I want custody of the girls.*'
I don't know what's going to happen.
I don't know if I'll have to pay for my mistakes.
All I know is that if he takes them from me, I'll die.

Lily

9 May

Dear Marcel,
    I can't write, my fingers are too cold.
    Love you anyway.
    Lily x

The Chloe Chronicles

I called Dad. I wanted to know what he said to Mum, and he didn't try to hide anything.

'I want you to come and live with me,' he said. 'You're a big girl now, you can do what you like, but Lily's still young, and your mother can't cope with the two of you any more.'

I didn't understand. He'd always said how wonderful Mum is and how sad he is that she didn't want to live with him. He's never had another girlfriend and claims no one could replace her. This was the first time he'd badmouthed her.

'What do you mean, she can't cope with us any more?'

'You know what I'm saying. She was already having trouble making ends meet, and now she's out of work it'll be impossible. You can't live with that sort of insecurity.'

'But she'll get another job. And, anyway, you're not working either. You can't even have us to stay at your place because it's too small.'

He gave a huge sigh.

'I've actually been in work for a while now. I have a four-bedroom house.'

'What? Since when?'

'I don't know . . . quite a while . . . maybe two years.'

That was like an electric shock to my heart.

'Two years? But, Dad, I don't understand, why didn't you say? Why didn't you have us to stay, at least in the holidays?'

'That's not what this is about,' he said, a bit more firmly. 'We're talking about your mother at the moment. It's not just the money. She's taken you out of school to go off camping in countries she doesn't even know. She's out of her mind! You told me yourself she'd lost the plot.'

I couldn't begin to think what to say. I didn't even know what to feel. How could I explain that when I criticised Mum to him it was mostly to give him comfort? I listened as he got increasingly angry, listing his arguments and convictions, and then I said I hoped he had a nice day and hung up.

While I had the phone, I used it to do a bit of research.

Mum looked amazed when I said we should make a little detour.

'It's a surprise,' I told her. 'Trust me. Oh, and by the way, on the subject of trust, I'm not pregnant.'

She did a cartoonish sad face and Lily shook her head.

'That's awful, my darling. Have you lost the baby?'

'No, I was never pregnant, it was just because I wanted to go home. Lily and I were trying to make you give up.'

My dear sister said I was a snitch, but Mum seemed genuinely upset.

'Oh, and I was so happy that I was going to be a granny. I'm so, so disappointed . . . and you must be very sad. Are you sure there isn't just a tiny chance?'

I nearly answered, but I saw the glint in her eye. She kept her smile in check: she knew that I knew. Neither of us said anything.

The detour cost us a couple of hours. On the way there Mum asked several times whether I was sure of what I was doing. The address on the satnav gave her no clues. The thaw hadn't reached this latitude and the landscape was still cloaked in white.

When we arrived it was five in the afternoon. And the temperature was –1°C. The owners were very friendly, and not just because they understood my Franglais. They took us over to the log cabin, gave us everything we needed and explained the instructions. It took Mum and Lily a long time to get it. A really, really long time. They must have been subconsciously blotting out the situation with a huge dollop of denial.

And then Mum's eyes nearly popped out of her head.

Anna

'Do you honestly believe I'm going to have a dip in a semi-frozen lake?' I squeak.

Chloe bursts out laughing. This is more serious than I thought.

Lily tries to sneak away while Chloe's talking to the owners, but her big sister grabs her by the scarf.

Vesa, one of the owners, asks us to follow her into the log cabin. The room is heated by a wood burner and has just a table, two benches and some coat hooks.

'The sauna's over there,' she says, pointing to a glazed door at the end. 'You can get undressed now.'

Vesa sets the example: she takes off her coat, boots, jumper . . . she's in her underwear and fur boots before we've had time to react.

'Well?' she asks with a smile. 'Don't be frightened, it's an incredible experience. Once you've done it, you'll just want to do it all over again!'

'Looks like the cold fries your brain cells,' Lily groans. 'I'm not going.'

'Come on, let's do it!' Chloe says, stripping rapidly. 'Mum, Lily, come on, I've read it's really good for your health.'

'I'd rather live a shorter life and be warm,' Lily announces.

'The thaw's started,' Vesa interjects. 'The water temperature's now 4 degrees, which is perfectly manageable.'

She must think we're muppets.

Chloe's hopping from foot to foot. She really wants to do this. I can't let her down; she organised this for me.

I slowly take off my clothes, privately thinking that people seriously need to consider all the consequences when they have children.

'Lily?' Chloe asks.

'No. I'll wait for you here,' Lily replies, burrowing her chin further under her scarf. 'I'm too cold just from looking at you.'

Petri, the other owner, is waiting for us outside the cabin – in yellow underpants. If my jaws weren't paralysed by the cold, I'd laugh.

We run the short distance to the lake. Chloe's teeth are chattering and I suspect she regrets this surprise. We come to a small pontoon and at the end of it a ladder drops down into the dark water. Petri explains the procedure: we climb down, stay in the water at least a minute, come out, run back to the cabin and shut ourselves in the sauna. If we're brave enough, we do it again.

'Alternating cold and heat is beneficial for the body,' he explains, casually climbing down the ladder. 'Come on in!'

He's now swimming. Unbelievable. He's going to turn into a stalagmite, then he won't look so clever.

Vesa joins him, positively purring with pleasure. These people must just like the cold. I can't think of another explanation. I bet they make love in the freezer.

Chloe takes off her boots and steps over to the ladder.

I do realise that I'm going to have to move. I must make up my mind to do this. I try to convince myself the water's not as cold as the air but, honestly, I'm one of those people who struggle to wash their hands if the water's not piping hot, so this . . .

'HAAAAAAAAAAAAAAAAAAA! HAAAAA AAAAAAAAAAAAAAAAAAAAAAAAAAAAAA! FUCK ME SIDEWAYS!'

That was Chloe. She's in the lake.

I've stopped thinking. I go for it and put one foot in the water.

Oh shit.

Then the second.

Fuck me sideways indeed.

Chloe pushes me aside to climb back up the ladder and I find myself completely submerged. It's as if I'm being attacked by thousands of blades. I can't feel my legs. and my arms are going, too. I'm just saying a final farewell to every part of my body when I hear a great screech coming towards us.

'BANZAAAAAAAAAIIII!'

In her knickers and bra (and with her scarf still around her neck), Lily runs along the pontoon, pinches her nose and jumps into the water, holding her knees up to her chest.

Her horrified face emerges a few seconds later. Her lips are blue.

'I'm dying! Help me!' she begs, her frozen features pleading.

No one responds.

'Well, come on!' she howls, *'Do something! Pee on me or something!'*

Petri – whose conviviality does have its limitations – unceremoniously hauls us on to the pontoon and we all head for the log cabin, Petri and Vesa walking while my girls and I trot along with rigid arms and legs. We look like table-football players. The sauna greets us with its enveloping warmth. Our hosts go back to their house, leaving the three of us alone.

We drop down on to the wooden bench. I lean my head against the wall and close my eyes. My body gradually comes back to life and my skin warms through.

I try to visualise what we must look like, all three of us almost naked in a sauna somewhere in the depths of Lapland. I picture our apartment, the home where we really only pass like ships in the night. I think back over my misgivings, about this improvised trip and the consequences it may have. And if only for this experience now, for this moment, for Chloe's excitement when I grasped what the surprise was, for Lily's face when she jumped in the water, for this easy shared silence, for this memory that will bring a smile to my face in the bleakest time . . . if only for this, I'll never regret it.

The Chloe Chronicles

For our last evening in Finland we had to respect tradition and get together for a typical Finnish meal. We crammed into the biggest campervan – Diego and Edgar's – with our plates on our knees, to sample food bought in the market at Inari: grilled sausages, elk soup, weird cheese and other specialities whose names I can't hope to remember.

The atmosphere was cheerful until Clara picked up the framed photograph.

'Are these your wives?' she asked.

Edgar told us about when he first met Rosa, and then Diego described his and Madeleine's wedding. Clara cried and blamed her hormones, Françoise wiped her eyes, Mum sniffed, Greg had to leave the room, Julien told a joke and Louise turned into a waterspout.

When we got back I checked whether Kevin had been in touch – something I do three times a day. Still nothing since he requested a photo. Maybe he thought my lack of response meant I'm not interested. So I showed him I still am: 'Hi Kevin, I hope you don't mind about the photo. I'd rather we talked a bit first, if that's ok? Chloe xx'

The reply came the next morning when Mum and Lily were having breakfast and I was in the shower. My heart skipped for joy when I saw there was a message.

'Hi, u betta just ask yr mum'

My heart did a nosedive.

'Mum, have you spoken to Kevin?' I asked as I came out of the bathroom.

Lily asked who Kevin was. Mum went red. She sent Lily off to see Noah and told me everything. I was so shocked I couldn't react, not even cry. I got to my feet and I couldn't bring myself to look at Mum. She was still talking to me, but I'd stopped listening. All my senses were clouded by anger. I opened the door and, as I walked out, I turned round to give her my parting shot:

'I hope Dad does get custody.'

The cold outside was like a smack in the face. I went to sit on a bench by the lake where we'd parked up. My fury at Mum had to fight it out with my fury at myself for being so spiteful to her. Just as my tears started to flow Louise came and sat next to me.

'What do you want?' I asked, wiping my cheeks with the back of my hand.

'I saw you here on your own and felt sorry for you.'

'I don't need your pity. Leave me alone.'

She didn't move.

'Piss off!' I yelled, turning to look at her. 'Can't you see I don't like you?'

It was the first time I'd seen her close up like this. Her eyes were as grey as the sky; as mournful, too.

'Yes, of course I can,' she said quietly. 'What have I done to you?'

'Not now, please. Leave me alone. I don't want to be a bitch.'

She got up, started walking away, then turned and stood squarely in front of me.

'Basically, you're jealous.'

'What?'

'You're jealous, that's why you don't like me.'

Now, I got to my feet and our faces were just inches apart. Louise drew all my anger towards her like a lightning rod. I roared with laughter, to avert any other sort of roaring.

'What exactly am I jealous of, then? Of your perfect little spoilt-brat life, where you're so lost for things to do with your money you have to pretend to be poor? Oh please, don't be ridiculous.'

'Not as ridiculous as wearing designer fakes.'

I wanted to wipe that superior sneer off her face, get rid of her snooty eyes and her pretentious manner. I wanted to satisfy the violence seething in my veins. A violence that's been overwhelming me recently.

'Piss off,' I growled between my teeth.

'Or you'll do what, bitch?'

I took a slow, deep breath, walked round Louise and stalked off, trying to ignore her chuckling. I walked for a while, and the sound of my footsteps on the snow dispelled my anger to reveal something else, like chipping away a layer to see what it's protecting underneath. And I was flooded with boundless sadness. It tied my stomach in knots, scratched my throat and darkened the sky.

It's a painful transition from childhood to adulthood, when all your illusions are blown apart and your dreams come crashing down in the face of reality. I miss that easy openness, that cocooned world where every little ouch evaporates when you go beddy-bies. I miss the life before, I miss the bubble of happiness kept in the air by Mum and Dad. I'm heading towards adulthood, leaving pebbles of innocence along the way. I don't want to lose them all. I don't want to grow up any more.

Lily

15 May

Dear Marcel,

I hope you're okay, but personally, I'm not okay
at all, and not just coz I've got a cold. We're now in
Norway, which should be called Noway: there's no
way you can ever get warm here. I have to watch
out when I sneeze – I'm worried an iceberg will
shoot out of my nose.

But that's nothing compared to the hideous
hideousness that's happened. I'm not even sure I
can cope with telling you about it.

Before we set off this morning I was with Noah in
his campervan, playing with his spinning top (he
doesn't mind lending it to me now, but I can never
get it to spin for as long as he does so I have to
pretend I'm letting him win on purpose).

Someone knocked on the door. Julien opened up
and there were men in uniform. He told us they
were customs officers and wanted to search the
van. I asked if that was normal. I couldn't see why

they'd come just like that, with no warning, just drop in out of the blue sky thinking, but apparently it happens a lot. It's to check we're not trafficking drugs or cheese.

I instantly thought about Mathias (Mum had said we'd better not be checked) and I ran to get him, but it was too late; they were already in our van. I rock-bottomed out. Mum came out of the van with a weird look on her face, and she squirmed as she walked. I mean, it looked like she wanted to do a wee, but in fact she'd hidden Mathias under her jumper. I took him back before she started shaking all over. He was very happy and snuggled round my neck.

The customs men climbed down from the van and said it was clear. They must have missed the cage, or they thought it was for decoration.

While they were with the two oldies (who were seriously freaked out), checking their campervan, Clara came to see us all wild-eyed. Her stomach was huge – I thought her baby had skipped a few months of pregnancy and was coming early, but it was coz she'd hidden Jojo under her poncho. She asked if we could keep him with us while her place was searched because they hadn't had time to give him one of his jabs, or something like that. We agreed to (obvs), because no way was that poor dog going to prison.

The problem was, he sniffed out Mathias and started barking. I tried to introduce them again to calm him down, but this time Jojo didn't even bare his teeth, he just launched his attack.

My little Mathias died instantly.

I gave him heart massage and mouth-to-mouth, but he didn't come round. My stomach and throat both hurt at the same time. I wanted to tell him how much I loved him (so much), but I couldn't seem to speak. I hope he knew.

I didn't bury him. I've put him in a Tupperware tub and I'm going to let him out tomorrow at North Cape when we do my great-grandpa's ashes.

Chloe and Mum were nice to me all day, even though they're both very careful not to speak to each other. I don't really know what they're angry about, but apparently it's about someone called Kevin.

That's all for now, Marcel. I haven't got the heart to write any more. That's the second time someone called Mathias has abandoned me, you know.

Lily x

Anna

North Cape.

Two months ago, my world comprised my apartment, a restaurant that was eating away at my morale and the commute between the two. North Cape was just an obscure place my grandmother mentioned when she talked about past travels.

Now, I'm at the northernmost point of Europe, having crossed the continent in a campervan with my daughters. Our day-to-day lives are over two and a half thousand miles away.

I turn off the ignition. It's ten o'clock at night and we're in broad daylight. We've been in immaculate silence the whole way: Lily's in mourning, Chloe's sulking.

'Come on, girls. Can't you make an effort for this important moment?'

I'm met with unenthusiastic groans. Nanny must have pictured a rather different atmosphere for my grandpa's last journey. I pick up the urn and stow it under my jacket.

'I'm not sure you're allowed to scatter ashes here. We'd better try to be discreet!'

My words bounce off their total lack of interest. Chloe's fiddling with her gloves and Lily's stroking her little plastic box. We come out of the campervan and head towards our first midnight sun.

The view from the top of the cliff is stunning. More than 300 metres below us, the Arctic Ocean stretches away as far as the eye can see. The dark rock with a smattering of snow is a stark contrast with the washed-out blue of the sky. The sun has started its downward journey. We take up positions behind the safety barrier to wait for midnight.

Lily doesn't seem to notice the wonder of it. Chloe is visibly making an effort not to go into raptures.

I make several attempts to start a conversation, with no success. Tense atmospheres are easier to deal with in a grey apartment.

At five to midnight the dozens of people waiting fall silent.

At midnight, as we stand facing the sun, which is still reflected in the sea rather than having vanished below the horizon, everyone claps and champagne corks pop. Strong emotions have a way of bringing together anyone who shares them. I feel close to the people around me – we're all a little alike tonight. I glance at my two girls, their dumbstruck smiles and shining eyes – they're three years old again.

We wait for the crowd to disperse.

'Do you want to start with Mathias, Lily?'

She shakes her head. Her chin's wobbling.

'It's okay. I've already done it.'

'Really? When?'

'When everyone clapped. It seemed like the right time. He flew off like a film star.'

Chloe strokes her cheek and then tucks her hand quickly back into her pocket, as if she'd never made the gesture.

'Okay, then, let's do what Great-grandma asked us to do,' I say. 'Will you film it, Chloe?'

I take off my gloves and take the urn from inside my jacket. I look around, but no one seems to be paying us any attention. In the distance, I can see Françoise, François, Louise and Louis heading back to the car park.

I remove the cover. I'm overcome with emotion – I know how much this means to Nanny. I don't remember much about my grandfather; I was very young when he died. A walk through the woods, him teaching me to lift dead leaves with a stick to find the most delicious mushrooms. His deep voice coughing. Him rubbing a clove of garlic on a slice of bread. That's all.

I reach my arm as far out as I can and tip the urn so the ashes can fly north.

Goodbye, Grandpa.

'What the hell's that?' Chloe cries.

It's not ashes flying north. It's sand.

I look into the urn, and there's an envelope taped to the inside. In the envelope is a sheet of paper folded in four and smothered in writing. I immediately recognise my grandmother's handwriting. Chloe and Lily press up against me and we read the letter together.

My dear Annie,

I'm picturing your face and laughing here on my own. You know how much I love you, so you'll know there was only one reason for this ploy: to help you.

I've watched you struggling with life for years. You fight like a lioness, but life always hits back. Every strike is allowed. I'm here to support you, to fill you with new strength and motivation, but I feel so helpless.

Losing your job is a stroke of luck. An opportunity to start afresh. When you told me you wanted to go on this trip but had your doubts about it, I was worried you wouldn't see it through and would turn back for home. I had to give you a good motive. I knew you'd do it for me.

Life has become your adversary. Make it your ally.

You've often told me that your girls are all that matter to you, that it pains you to see so little of them and if you could start all over again you'd do everything differently. You can't start all over again, but you can choose another way.

You know I'm closer to the end than the beginning, I can almost see the finish line. My legs have stopped working and the rest of me isn't in very good shape. All I have left are my memories. I sometimes think about places I've visited, books I've read, films I've enjoyed, but the things I never forget are your mother, your grandfather, you, Chloe, Lily, my parents, my grandmother . . . Everything comes to an end eventually, Annie. Anger, disappointments, obstacles, joys, exhaustion. What keeps us going to the very end, whether they're still alive or not, are the people we love.

I didn't completely lie to you. North Cape is a significant place. In the summer of 1957 your grandfather – whose ashes are still in my bedroom – and I visited Norway. The midnight sun was our most wonderful experience and we stayed there admiring it till the early hours. Your mother was conceived the next day, and I've always thought that's what made her such a luminous character. As you read these words, four generations of our family are together at North Cape. She'd be so proud of you.

I don't want to lecture you, I can't stand people who moralise. I just want to light the way for you, to show you the way before I go.

I hope this trip will help you love each other even more. I know how everlasting the bond is between a mother and daughter.

I love you, my Annie. Don't be angry with me.
Nanny.

I fold the piece of paper and put it back in the envelope before my tears dilute the words. The sun is still hovering over the horizon and we watch it in silence for a few more minutes.

I imagine my mother beside me, her hand on my shoulder. It doesn't hurt any more. I couldn't say when it

179

was that memories of her became soothing. The pain tiptoed away. You get so used to having it there you stop noticing it; it becomes an integral part of you. And then one day you realise it's gone, giving way to a few scars and all the good memories. The times when I think of my mother have almost become bearable because they bring her back to life a little.

'Shall we go?' I eventually ask the girls.

They nod and we walk reluctantly back to the van. The silence isn't as dense as on the way over, but I daren't break it. I don't know whether they're ready.

Nanny's right: if it weren't for her, I would never have left. If it weren't for her, I would probably have found a new job and paid my debts. I'd even have a bit of money left over and we'd be eating something better than tinned food warmed up on the hob, we'd be sleeping on comfortable mattresses, the girls would have proper teachers, it would be twenty degrees warmer, I wouldn't be risking losing custody of them and we would have avoided a fair few arguments. But. We'd see each other for a few minutes a day, I wouldn't know how sensitive Chloe is and how like me she is, I wouldn't know how funny and generous Lily is, I wouldn't have shared all the hysterical laughter, the in-depth conversations, the long nights, the new discoveries and the fears with them. I wouldn't have forged all these unforgettable memories with my daughters.

Nanny didn't give me advice, she gave me a gift.

I close the door to the van to keep the warmth in. The girls undress quickly and slip into bed. I settle down on my bench and pull the duvet over my face to block out the sunlight and stifle my sobs.

Only a few minutes pass before I feel a small body slide in beside me. Then another. I lift up the duvet and Chloe and Lily come and join me in my refuge and snuggle up against me. Well, I say against me, but given the size of my bed, they're more or less on top of me. Lily starts to giggle first, then I succumb and soon the three of us are laughing so much we almost fall on to the floor. We make the wise decision to decamp together to the double bed.

Thank you, Nanny.

The Chloe Chronicles

Mountains reared up between the lakes, green and white vied for prime position, the sea was never far away – it was like being in one of those amazing screensavers. We'd been on the road for more than an hour when Mum wanted to talk. Lily had fallen asleep.

'You don't have to do everything boys ask you to, you know.'

I'd have been happier talking about the scenery, but she kept going.

'Are you in love with Kevin?'

'I think so.'

'What makes you think you are?'

I thought for a few seconds.

'Because I'm sad when he doesn't answer my messages.'

'And that's all?'

Her voice was as honeyed as the snake in *The Jungle Book*. I thought she was trying to soften me up. But I played along.

'No, he's kind to me, he tells me I'm beautiful and attractive, he's affectionate . . .'

'Fine, but do you think it's okay for him to send you

pictures of his penis and to ask you to show him your breasts?'

'I don't know,' I said with a shrug. 'I haven't really thought about it.'

'Did you want to do it?'

'No, not really. But I'm worried that . . .'

I ground to a stop, but she wouldn't drop it.

'You're worried what?'

'I'm worried he won't be so nice if I refuse to. I'm worried he won't like me any more.'

Then she gave me a long speech about what I should and shouldn't find acceptable, about how all boys are different, about love definitely not depending on explicit photos, and about affectionate behaviour not being proof of love. I nodded, but thought to myself that she just didn't understand.

I don't like showing my breasts. I don't like giving my body. What I like is being given compliments and cuddles and promises. What I like is being loved. Knowing someone's thinking about me. And that I matter.

When I show my breasts and when I give my body, they give me love. When I don't give them anything, they don't give me anything. It's as simple as that.

I'd like to believe my mother when she says that's not how you get love, that charming someone doesn't necessarily involve sex and that boys might want something else from me. I really would like to, but how can I believe someone who's been with only one man?

'Do you promise you'll be careful next time?' she asked.

I didn't promise, I just nodded my head and secretly crossed my fingers. I'd like to try, but I already know what will happen next time. He'll try it on, I'll put up some resistance, he'll be disappointed, I'll be frightened of losing him, I'll give in.

We reached the car park at Stabbursdalen National Park early in the afternoon. It was cold and grey, but Julien had convinced some of the group that the best way to get a feel for Norway was to go for an invigorating walk through the pine forests. Apparently, a breath-taking sight awaited us at the far end.

After walking for two hours through the trees, the patchy snow, Louise's exclamations, François's photo-taking and Mum's whingeing, we came to the promised surprise. A lake fed by a waterfall that was no rival for the ones we passed every day on our travels. You could hear the disappointment in our silence.

We had a picnic by the water's edge and then set off unenthusiastically to walk back. Mum, who didn't seem to have realised that the return trip would be as long as the way out, came close to asking us to come back for her with a helicopter. Françoise floored her when she said she needed a little moment to go and 'powder her nose'. We waited on the track and Françoise walked off into the trees, whistling. She reappeared three minutes later shrieking, running as fast as she could, waving her arms in the air, her face distorted in terror. She tripped, jumped back to her feet, clawed at the trees to help her on her way and vaulted over tree roots. When she reached us, we saw it. It was not far behind her, huge, majestic and followed by two babies. An angry elk.

'Help me!' she squawked.

Julien grabbed her hand and pulled her towards the group. Louise and Louis put their arms around her, sobbing. François focused his zoom on the animal.

'Strange,' Julien whispered. 'Elks aren't normally aggressive, she must have thought her fawns were in danger. We'll back off, that should reassure them.'

We took a few steps back, very slowly, but that wasn't enough to calm the protective mother. She came closer to us, head lowered, ready to charge. Mum hugged us to her. Then Julien's dignity left the building.

He took a step towards the animal with his arms *en garde* in front of his face.

'Hey! Back up!' he cried. 'I'm a ju-jitsu blue belt.'

The elk peered up at him. It came closer still. Julien gave a guttural cry, clearly intended to frighten it. I think he only frightened his own vocal cords. I heard a stifled laugh behind me and had to bite my cheeks to stop joining in.

Realising intimidation was having no effect, our hero tried to communicate with the animal.

'Don't worry,' he said. 'We don't mean you any harm.'

The elk, which didn't seem to understand the spoken

word, stepped even closer. It was now only three or four metres from Julien, who decided the time had come to launch his secret weapon.

As if in slow motion, he pivoted on his left leg and jabbed his right leg in the air – I discovered later this is called a circular kick. A cry rang out, and it didn't come from the elk. Julien put his foot back down very casually, as if we hadn't all realised that he'd torn a muscle.

The elk – probably feeling sorry for him – paced restlessly for a few more seconds then went back to where her fawns were, by the side of the track. Julien tilted his chin towards it.

'That's right,' he said, but not too loudly. 'Be very afraid.'

Then he turned round with a half-heroic, half-pained smile on his lips, limped back to us and encouraged us to keep walking. Which we did. No one disobeys Chuck Norris.

Lily

19 May

Dear Marcel,

It's me (Lily). I hope you're well, even with this
horrible weather. We've reached Alta, which is
very pretty, but I'm sure it would be better without
the fog. It's like someone's having a hot shower in a
cold room. We parked all the vans next to
Altafjord, which is a fjord (the clue's in the name),
and a fjord is a flooded valley (no clue in the name
there – I thought it was a kind of car).

Seeing as there was water around and that's all it
takes to get them going, Françoise and François got
out their fishing rods. They were well up for killing
some fish, I can't tell you, specially their daughter,
she couldn't stop chuckling – anyone would think
she was the cat's cradle who'd got the cream. She
really is stupid, you know, Marcel. If you stuck
your ear to her head, I bet you'd hear the sea.

So anyway, they set themselves up, and I wasn't
too fussed – they look more the sort to hook

themselves a bit of smoked salmon from a fancy deli. But ten minutes later Louis gave a squeal of excitement. His mum had caught a fish. The poor thing was thrashing about in every direction and the Pollyanna family thought it was funny. When they turned back to do some more fishing I decided deep down inside myself that I was not okay with that.

I picked up some pebbles, sat down next to them and threw a pebble into the water, right where the float was. François laughed, he thought I was doing it for fun, so I threw another one. He asked me to stop and I said I was trying to practise skimming. His duh-brain daughter said I'd need flat pebbles, and that made me throw another one. After a while they got fed up with this (François frowned so hard I thought he'd get cramp in his forehead), and they moved away. I waited till they'd got themselves all settled, then went and sat next to them and started again. They were seriously hacked off, but I don't care. I'd rather the fish liked me than that family.

After five minutes of this Louise started screaming at me. Her sugary smile had completely disappeared. I knew she was two-faced and, well, they say you must let sleeping dogs lie in the manger.

I heard my sister's voice behind me, and it didn't sound like she was coming to make friends. She 'advised' Louise to stop talking to me like that, and Louise asked, 'What if I don't?' to which Chloe said, 'If you don't, you'll get a faceful of my fist.' Louise was about to reply but her mother told her to calm down and not get roped into arguments with badly brought-up girls.

I swear I didn't do it on purpose, Marcel. I swear my arms disobeyed me and there was nothing I could have done to stop them pushing Miss Ditz into the water. She screamed (apparently it was cold) and while her parents heaved her back out Chloe and I locked ourselves in our van.

My mum was really angry, specially as Françoise dressed the whole story up loads. So, to apologise, she went and bought some fish and made us cook it for them for supper, sort of to make up for the ones they didn't catch. Chloe started gutting them and scraping off the scales, but I told her to do the rice instead and I gutted the poor little fish, apologising to them as I did. I hope Chloe got the fact that I did that as a thank you to her, because it was hard.

Okay then, I'll leave you now, or you'll start smelling of fish.

Lily x

PS Do you know how you say McDonald's in Norwegian? McDonald's! Bonkers, isn't it?

Anna

Chloe sits down next to me with the phone in her hand.

'It was Dad,' she says. 'He wanted to talk to you, but I said you were busy.'

I nod. I know she knows, but we've never talked about it. I can see from the look in her eyes that now's the time.

'What do you think about the whole thing?' I ask.

'What does she think about what whole thing?' asks Lily, coming into the van.

I give Chloe a questioning look, and she nods her consent. I gesture to Lily to sit down with us and I tell her what their father is asking.

'I don't want to live with him!' she wails. 'I don't know him! I don't have anything to say to him!'

'I don't know why you're so hard on him,' Chloe says.

'I don't need a reason,' Lily retorts.

'But he *is* your father. He hasn't done anything to you! He's sad – he thinks you don't love him.'

'Well, he's right, I don't love him.'

'You really are—'

'Shush.' I interrupt Chloe before she goes too far. 'Let's all calm down. Your sister's right, Lily: he's your father, you must be kinder to him. It's no good pulling faces. I won't let you talk about him like that.'

'Well, why don't you go back to him if he's so nice!' she snaps.

Lily was only five when we separated. She's lived longer without her father than with him. She must have only vague memories of him, and the few times the girls have stayed with their paternal grandmother won't have helped her change her mind. But I just won't let her personality be shaped by these misunderstandings that don't relate to her. She can think of him as geographically distant, busy, not very committed, even not nice if she wants. But he is not devoid of feeling for his girls. No one grows up well with a lack of love.

'Listen to me, Lily. Your father loves you both, and I'm sure if you knew him better, you'd love him too.'

'So you're going to let him get his way?' she blurts.

'Of course not. Don't you worry. I have every intention of keeping you. Don't . . .'

'Well, *I'd* like to see him more often,' Chloe mumbles, with tears in her eyes.

'I know, sweetheart. We're going to see how we can sort that out.'

The tears tumble down her cheeks.

'But he's had a house for two years now!' she sobs. 'I don't understand why he kept that from us. It means he could have had us to stay, we didn't have to go to Gran's, but he didn't have us!'

'You see, I'm right,' Lily announces sharply.

'I'm sure it's more complicated than that,' Chloe says, sniffing. 'I remember when we were little he took care of us loads, and even now on the phone he always asks me how I am. I know he loves us. He must have good reasons.'

Lily shrugs. Chloe blows her nose.

'I miss him,' she sighs.

I sigh, too, torn between my elder daughter, who wants to see more of her father, my little one who wants to see even less of him . . . and myself.

'Your father and I are going to find a solution,' I say, to conclude the conversation. 'Don't worry, we're responsible adults, we'll handle this.'

I wait till the girls have drifted away before looking at the messages on the phone and, like the responsible adult that I am, typing a reply to their father:

'You'll never get custody of the girls. I won't let you.'

Anna

The girls have gone straight to sleep. The visit to Tromsø got the better of their stamina. Mine is on a roll, though. I'm squirming and fidgeting on the banquette, trying to empty my mind and concentrate on my breathing, but these thoughts have wedged themselves in and are clearly planning to spend the night in my head.

I get up quietly, put on my coat and boots over my pyjamas and go out to get some air. It's nearly midnight and the landscape is bathed in golden light. There are lots of campervans overnighting here, but I walk away from them and gaze admiringly at the snow-covered mountains in the distance. People told me Scandinavia was different, but I never imagined to what extent. The architecture, vegetation, topography, alphabet, climate, roads, food, culture – everything's different, and the most astonishing thing is the sun, which shines twenty-four hours a day in summer and then disappears completely in winter, giving way to a gloaming half-light. This place is stark and unadulterated, there are no half-measures.

We've done more than half our trip now. In a month, we'll be back in France. Each new leg of the journey brings us closer to our everyday life, and all I want to do is turn back towards the far north, get as far as possible from my letterbox, which must be overflowing, my bank manager, the bailiffs, the paperwork and hassle. As far as possible from Mathias. I want to stay in this digression from the real world.

The sound of a dog barking drags me away from my thoughts. Jojo is running towards me with his hackles up. I crouch down to reassure him and he bounces up happily to say hello.

'Not sleeping, then?' Greg asks, coming over to me.

'No, I couldn't. How about you?'

'Jojo needed to come out. Come and join us. We're playing French Tarot with Julien.'

I don't hesitate for long. I just can't resist an evening surrounded by adults with no teenagers on the horizon.

Clara is delighted, explaining – as she makes me a cup of herbal tea – that Tarot's better with four people.

'I'd have liked to give you a glass of wine, but I'd be too tempted. I've already had to stop smoking overnight, I mustn't mess with my head . . . I hope the baby remembers this and comes out without causing too much damage. Did it hurt a lot when your girls were born?'

I picture the scene, my screams of pain, how I wanted to tell the midwives to leave me there to die because I was slowing them down. I'm about to reply with a softened version of the truth but not an actual lie when I catch Greg's imploring eye.

'I didn't feel a thing,' I say. 'Not a thing, both times. When I heard my girls' first cries, I was amazed they were already out.'

I gather from Clara's expression that she's relieved . . . and from Greg's that I went a bit too far. Julien is falling about laughing.

'What's so funny?' Clara asks. 'Was Noah's birth complete carnage, then?'

He pulls himself together and tries to look extremely serious.

'Absolutely not, it was very quick.'

'Oh, that's good to know!' Clara almost whispers.

'He was ejected like a cannonball,' Julien adds. 'He almost smacked into the obstetrician and landed in one of the midwives' handbags.'

Clara stares at him, baffled. Greg has gone bright red and is trying not to laugh.

'Are you taking the piss?' she eventually asks.

We all chorus our denials and she consents to believe us. Anything rather than the truth.

Between two hands of Tarot Julien checks that Noah is still fast asleep and I nip out to cast an eye over my girls. Lily is snoring – I really should record her!

'It's good to have an evening without children,' Julien whispers behind me.

I'm startled, I didn't hear him come over. I close the door to the van carefully and turn round.

'Yes, it's been a long time.'

'Are you going to play another round or go to bed?'

'Do you honestly believe I'd give up after a defeat?'

He smiles.

We go back to join Clara and Greg, and when Julien helps me up into their van, that's all the encouragement Clara needs.

'You two would be good together, you know,' she says.

A moment of acute embarrassment. I roll my eyes. Julien clears his throat.

'Stop it, Clara, you've embarrassed them,' Greg scolds, shuffling the cards. 'Right, are we playing this hand, then?'

'But what's the problem?' Clara asks, amazed. 'I think they're a good match, there's no harm in that. When I find a belt that matches a pair of shoes, I say so, and no one gets upset about it, or not that I know of.'

'There's no problem at all,' Julien admits with a broad smile. 'By the way, has anyone warned you an episiotomy's bloody agony?'

I giggle, hoping Clara's attention will now turn to much more important subjects.

'Do you have anyone in your life?' she asks me with affected innocence.

That didn't work, then.

'I have two daughters, and that's plenty.'

'Come on, Clara, we're playing!' Greg cuts in.

She spreads her hands in capitulation.

'Okay, okay! I'm sorry. My hormones are making me all sentimental, I see couples everywhere.'

I organise my hand, relieved we've moved on to something else. I have good cards, lots of trumps, including the 21 and some court cards. I'm not sure whether to pick up, and glance around at the others. Clara is busy arranging her hand, Greg seems to be thinking, and Julien, all shining eyes, is staring right at me. And unsettling me.

The Chloe Chronicles

I've had an anonymous letter. It's written in capital letters, probably to disguise the writing, on a folded sheet of paper slipped into the door handle of the campervan. Mum found it, but it was addressed to me.

CHLOE,
YOUR SMILE IS IMPISH
YOUR VOICE IS BELL-LIKE
YOUR EYES ARE CAT-LIKE
YOUR MOUTH IS DIVINE
ALL OF YOU MOVES ME
ALL OF YOU APPEALS
YOU MAKE ME HAPPY
I LOVE YOU FOR REAL.

I chuckled and asked Lily why she would play such a stupid joke, but she swore on her life it wasn't her. She shouldn't have done that – I mean, I don't want her to *die*.

I asked everyone in the group, and they all denied any knowledge or just looked completely confused. The only person I didn't ask was Louise, because I refuse to talk to her. But she's the one I suspect. As far as I know, she's the only person who would have it in them to do this, just to piss me off. Not to mention the simplicity of the poem, which is about on a level with her mental abilities. That girl's so empty just looking at her makes me feel dizzy.

I tidied the piece of paper away . . . in the bin.

I have to confess that, just for a moment, I wondered if it could be a real declaration of love. The thought that someone secretly loves me gave me butterflies, but common sense soon won me over. I'm surrounded by men who are either married or decrepit. It must be a joke.

Shame.

Since I've given up all hope on Kevin, there's been something missing in my life. I've missed having someone to think about. I put my lipstick on in the morning and don't wonder whether he'd like it, I choose what to wear without hoping it'll appeal to him, and I fall asleep without a headful of dreams. I feel lonely. And pointless.

I think that's another reason I've started this blog. I could have written my thoughts down in a book, but sharing them with you, knowing that they make you laugh, they move you and give you food for thought, knowing I'm not the only person to feel what I'm feeling and think what I'm thinking, is precious to me. I know it's only virtual, but I don't feel so alone.

Even negative comments do me good. At first, they hurt me, made me question everything I said, I couldn't take a step back and get some perspective, but as I've got used to them they've taught me that I can't please everyone and it doesn't matter that much. There will always be someone to criticise, but that doesn't mean what I'm doing is wrong.

I'm nowhere near being the person I'd like to be. I envy people who don't worry about their image and about what others think of them. People who have so much self-confidence nothing throws them. I do so much soul-searching that I can end up feeling guilty, even if I'm the one who's been wronged. There are some people who are so afraid of not being liked they daren't speak up when they disagree with someone. Well, I daren't even *think* the opposite of someone else. I envy anyone who doesn't need other people's approval to love themselves.

I wish the only approval I needed was my own.

Lily

23 May

Dear Marcel,

It's a good thing you can't overdose on emotions because otherwise I'd be dead by now. I hope you'd be sad without me.

First of all, there was no cereal left for breakfast. The stock we brought with us has run out, which meant I had to eat these really thin brown cracker things with jam – it was a bad start. Mum says everything's more expensive here, so we have to make sure we don't eat too quickly, but I'm having a growth spurt, I'm not going to hold back. You shouldn't count your chickens until they've done a hatchet job.

After that we had to go to the launderette to do a wash. It took forever, and I really can't see why you have to wash clothes when you're going to put them on again afterwards and get them dirty again. Logic is in danger of extinction, I'm telling you.

Then we did a little detour to see the
Målselvfossen falls. Noah (and his dad) came with
us, so that was great. The waterfall isn't high, but
it's very wide, makes loads of noise and the water
goes really quickly, throwing itself off like
someone's chasing it. If you ask me, it thinks it's in
trouble. I think if you swim in that water it tumbles
you around so much you'd come out looking like a
Picasso portrait. Julien showed us a ladder to help
the salmon get upriver. We tried to spot one, but
it's not the right time of year.

At one point Mum was chatting to Julien and
Chloe and I turned round to see Noah heading off
towards the trees, peering at the ground. I realised
straight away he was looking for his top. I went and
joined him and helped him look, but there were
rocks and plants, and it wasn't easy. And anyway,
they do say you find things when you're not looking
for them. I once tried to explain that to my maths
teacher, because he couldn't understand why I
didn't do any calculations to find an answer. All I
got in return was two hours' detention 'for
insolence'.

Anyway, I was concentrating so hard I didn't
notice how far we'd gone, but eventually Noah
realised and he was frightened. I tried to find the
way back but, what with all the trees, I think I got
even more lost. Noah kept looking around and I

could see he was scared; he started rocking backwards and forwards really hard, and that made me flip out, too. Specially as I'd heard there are bears round here. Noah started screaming and hitting his head with his fist, and I didn't know what to do. I tried to talk to him really softly, but that didn't change anything. He was wailing, and it made me feel terrible seeing him in such a mess.

Then I suddenly remembered what his dad does to calm him down. He's much bigger than me, so it's not exactly the same but, well, nothing ventured nothing ever again. I put my arms around him and squeezed him really hard. He tried to struggle free, but I held on. It was hard work, but I didn't let go and I gradually felt Noah's body relax, and his cries got quieter and eventually stopped. That was when his father came running. He must have heard us. We weren't actually far away at all, but my sense of direction is like a GPS with Alzheimer's.

Mum gave me a bit of a field dressing down, but Julien said it was fine. Of course I was sorry I hadn't been more careful, but I was also quite pleased I'd managed to calm Noah – that means he accepts me. I really hope I can see him again after we get home, I wasn't sure it would be possible, but I still asked his dad where they live. You'll never guess where, Marcel! I'm so happy I feel like doing cartwheels in the air I breathe! They live in Muret, near Toulouse, which is basically twenty minutes from us! I can see him again, and that deserves a shedload of exclamation marks!!!!!!!!!!!!!!!!!!!!!!!

In other words, that was quite a lot of emotions already but, can you believe, we came across some reindeer on the way back. I'd already seen some in the Father Christmas village, but they're even more beautiful roaming free. To top it all, we found Noah's top (see what I did there?). It was stuck behind the passenger seat in their campervan.

So you see, Marcel, my heart must be made of pretty strong stuff to put up with all that. I think I'm now ready to be told I've won the lottery.

Lily xx

PS I've thought this over and I think my future husband's surname needs to be White.
PPS If he's clever his first name could be Brilliant.
PPPS And we could call our children Pure and Snow.

Anna

The schoolwork is the most restrictive aspect of this trip. Every morning Lily baulks at doing the exercises I set her, and Chloe argues with me, telling me to give up trying to push her into sitting her exams. The sessions quite often end in a row. That's what's happening this morning, and it's more heated than ever.

'You're taking up too much space,' Chloe snaps at her sister, who's almost lying over the table.

Lily doesn't react.

'Hey, can you hear me in there?' Chloe rages, prodding Lily's head. 'You're not the only one here, you know.'

'Shush, I'm trying to learn,' Lily grumbles.

'Say something, Mum!'

'Lily, make a bit of room for your sister.'

No response. Lily is apparently immersed in her book. I try to think of a solution.

'Why don't you sit on the bed, Chloe? You're not actually writing today, are you?'

'Oh yeah, that's right,' she snarls. 'Always me who has to go out of my way. Tbh, I've had enough of coming second to your little favourite.'

'What the hell!' Lily cries, sitting up. 'I'm not the favourite!'

'Calm down, girls.'

'Of course you are, you know you are, and oh how you milk it!' Chloe retorts, red with rage. 'It's been like this ever since you were born – I come second after Princess Lily.'

'Right, that's enough, Chloe. I don't have a favourite, and stop arguing the whole time, the pair of you. It's exhausting.'

'I'd be very happy to stop arguing,' Lily says, 'but she needs to stop being so stupid.'

Chloe stands up and leans over her sister.

'Like I'm the one who's stupid! Oh, very funny. You've got the IQ of pond life, sweetheart. You can't even put two words together without getting something wrong. I've heard it all now!' Chloe roars, gesticulating wildly to give her words more impact. Lily peers at her in silence.

'Chloe, that's—' I try to intervene, but she keeps going.

'No, seriously, I've had enough of you! I mean, what the hell's the point of you? All you do is criticise Dad and get all the attention: "Oh, Lily's so sweet, Lily's so funny!" Well, do you know what?' she asks, glowering at her sister with hate in her eyes.

'Chloe,' I say, coming over to her and taking her arm. 'Calm down now, you're saying terrible things that you'll regret later. Stop right now.'

She's stopped listening to me. She opens her mouth to speak and I can feel her hesitate, but her anger is stronger.

'I wish I was an only child,' she says. 'I wish you'd never existed.'

'Chloe, I forbid you to . . .'

She couldn't care less what I forbid her, she's already walked out, leaving us like two trees still standing after a storm.

'I wish I was an only child, too,' Lily announces before going back to her exercise book.

I drop down on to the bench seat, dazed.

I would have so loved not to be an only child.

How many times since my mother died have I wished I had a brother or sister to share the memories? It would have been so wonderful not being the only person who remembered her loud kisses in the crook of my neck when she came to say goodnight, the funny voices she put on when she told stories, her high heels clacking on the school playground, the little notes she slipped into my schoolbag, her soft hand on my cheek . . . My father wept for a wife, Nanny wept for a daughter. I would so love to have had someone else there to weep for a Mummy with me.

Later, much later, I learned that she was expecting another baby, a little boy. It was the pregnancy that caused the blood clot.

I definitely didn't want to have an only child. Girl, boy, dark, redhead, blue eyes, brown eyes – I couldn't care less. There were just two things I wanted: to have at least two children so they'd never have to keep their memories alive alone, and not to die before they were old enough to heal their wounds without their mum.

They fight and tear each other apart and reject each other, but they love each other and they're not alone.

I pick up the phone and leave the campervan. The sun is gently caressing the mountains. This evening we'll be at the Lofoten Islands, an archipelago famous for its magical scenery, and it looks as if the fine weather is planning on coming with us.

I make the call and Nanny's voice instantly soothes me. She seems happy to hear from me.

'How are you, my little Annie?'

'I'm fine, Nanny. I'm really sorry I haven't called you all week. The days are pretty full-on here.'

I've been calling her regularly to tell her about each leg of the journey and describe the landscapes she once saw. I fill her in on the latest stages and she listens attentively. I can just picture the smile on her lips.

'How are the girls?' she asks.

'I think they're okay. Chloe's talking to me a lot more. She's terribly sensitive, but I think that's just who she is – she experiences everything very intensely.'

'Now, I wonder where she gets that from!' my grandmother teases.

'Yes, she's definitely very like me, more than I thought. But, unlike her, my teenage years were easy.'

'They certainly were.'

I'd have liked a few explosive teenage outbursts, a bit

of rebelling, arguing and drawing attention to myself, pushing myself, kidding myself . . . but I didn't let any of that happen. Make no noise, make no waves, keep small and quiet so nobody notices you. Don't make things worse than they are. Tiptoe through the world. They've suffered enough. We've all suffered enough.

'And little Lily?' she asks.

'She's made friends with Noah, who I've told you all about. She seems very fond of him and I think she's enjoying the trip. Well, here I am telling you the girls are fine, but they've just had a massive row and said the cruellest things to each other. I know it'll pass and it's normal for sisters to fight, but it always breaks my heart.'

'Oh, Annie, they're having to live together twenty-four hours a day. It would be worrying if they *didn't* rub each other up the wrong way!'

'You're right. At least they're communicating, which they weren't doing at home. And how are you, Nanny?'

'Oh, well, you know me.' She chuckles. 'Every day's a bonus, I won't complain. But let's talk about you. Have you found what you set out to find?'

I pause for a moment. I hadn't really thought of it like that. Have I found what I set out to find?

'I'm getting warmer, Nanny. I'm getting warmer.'

The Chloe Chronicles

Mum asked me if that's really what I think, and I said no so she doesn't have a horrible guilt trip, but the truth is I really do think she loves my sister more than me. She hides it well – I can't find a single clue even if I go looking. But I know it, deep down, because it can't possibly not be true. Lily's more likeable than me. She's sweet-natured, always even-tempered and funny she's everything I'm not. She's the child all mothers dream of having.

Let's be honest: you have two pairs of shoes, and one of them's comfortable, pretty and cool; the other's uncomfortable, ugly and naff. Which would you prefer?

'You know I don't have a favourite,' she insisted.

'I know, Mum, I know.'

When I walked past Lily I said sorry, but she acted as if she hadn't even heard.

I can't help loving her either. I don't know if it's because she's my sister – maybe we're programmed to like the people we're related to. Mind you, I can think of several examples to prove the opposite. So maybe it's because she's her.

We'd driven along tiny roads snaking between mountains and waterfalls and we'd just reached Lødingen on Hinnøya Island. The old saying is right: in Scandinavia, the journey is as beautiful as the destination. The wind had swept away the clouds and the landscape was made up of three colours: blue, green and white. Mum was tired from driving and was having a rest before going to explore the area, and Lily was writing in her red notebook, so I went out for a little walk. Julien and Noah had gone off to watch the ferries manoeuvring in the harbour, and some of the others – Françoise and François, and Clara and Greg – hadn't yet arrived. Diego was sitting on a folding chair, enjoying the sun.

'Edgar's having a siesta,' Diego said, offering me Edgar's chair.

I declined and sat cross-legged on the ground.

It's weird how you can sometimes feel close to someone when you've exchanged only a few words with them. It's like that with Diego. There's something in his expression, a gentle sort of sadness, that makes you want to love him. He filled his pipe, lit it, drew in a few breaths then blew out some thick white smoke.

'You know these anonymous poems I've been getting?' I found myself saying, to start up a conversation.

He studied me, his eyelids quivering.

'I've had three. Someone's writing them and slipping them under the door handle of our van, but I don't

211

know who it is. At first I thought it was a joke, but now I'm not sure.'

'What are the poems about?'

'They're very short, quite simplistic, they're from someone who wants to tell me they love me. It must be someone from the group. Do you have any idea who it could be?'

He frowned and his wrinkles grew a little deeper.

'I do have an idea, yes, but I'll keep it to myself. I've never been the type to snitch! But I don't think they're a joke, it's someone who's taking the risk of realising a dream.'

I nodded slowly.

'Do you have dreams, my dear?' he asked.

'How do you mean?'

'Do you have dreams for your future?'

'A few, yes,' I replied before I had time to think.

'What are they?'

'I'd like to find my soulmate, have children one day. And be happy.'

He smiled, drew on his pipe for a long time and blew out his smoke. There was something comforting about the slightly caramelised smell.

'Don't you have any more personal dreams? Something just for you?'

I didn't have to think long for the answer to come to me.

'I'd like to live in Australia.'

'Well then, you must go there.'

'I can't. My mother needs me here. I've got to start earning money to help her. If things ever work out better for her, then I'll see.'

He sighed.

'I don't know your mother very well, dear, but I've known enough mothers to be sure of one thing: a mother can't be happy if her children aren't happy.'

He was gazing off into the distance with a dreamy smile.

'Madeleine and I wanted three children, you know, but we only had one, which is very lucky in itself. We cherished him, our whole world revolved around him. For twenty years we were parents and nothing else. It didn't make us unhappy, quite the opposite – our son repaid us for our love a hundred times over, he was happy, kind, funny, generous ... When he was twenty he suddenly announced he was going off to live in Canada, and our world fell apart. Madeleine got depression and I tried looking into ways to follow him out there: we needed to find work and an apartment, it couldn't be that difficult. But the psychologist Madeleine was seeing helped us change our minds. Our children don't belong to us – we're like stakes supporting saplings, we help them grow. A child taking flight like that is a reward. Of course, we didn't accept it overnight – it was hard not seeing him every day, we had to find new goals and new occupations – but it was wonderful seeing him grow into a fulfilled young man.'

He fell silent and drifted off into his thoughts.

'Does he still live in Canada?' I asked.

'Yes. He'd like me to go and live with him now, but I can't.'

'Why not?'

He straightened his sunglasses over the top of his reading glasses.

'Because we don't have children in order to become their children.'

Anna

I've just bought five little trolls in a shop in Svolvær.
They're the classic souvenir you can buy all over Norway. The first will go next to the TV in the living
room, two are for my father and Jeannette, and the
other two are for the girls. The funny one with his hair
in a mess is for Lily and the warrior is for Chloe. My
first instinct was to get an identical pair so they couldn't
read any preference into the distinction. I thought better of that.

I've always made a point of being fair with them. I'm
careful to give them presents of the same value for their
birthdays and not to spend more time with one than the
other. I've shared out my considerations as if weighing
out bird seed at a packaging factory. I had such a terrible
feeling of abandonment as a child myself I've done everything in my power to spare my girls the same thing. I've
failed. I once read that a first child always feels rivalry
from subsequent children – it's inevitable, whatever the
parents do. But I think I must take my share of responsi-
bility here: perhaps it was precisely in my efforts to be
fair that I lost sight of their individuality.

Chloe and Lily are different. They shall have different trolls.

My phone rings as I close the door to the shop. I take off my gloves and delve my hand inside my jacket. I hesitate before answering when I see the number on the screen but, as Lily would say, I'm only taking a step back in time to get a better run-up.

'Hello, Mathias.'

'Well, hi there, Anna,' he croons. 'How are you?'

'What do you want?'

'I want us to find a solution, I don't want a war. I just want what's best for my daughters.'

I pause for a moment to calm myself.

'I don't even want to talk to you, Mathias. This is getting out of hand.'

'Nothing's out of hand, I'm just a father with natural concerns.'

I have a sudden urge to scream. I take a slow, deep breath.

'You know,' he says, 'if you'd let me come back, we wouldn't have come to this.'

'You disgust me. You don't give a stuff about the girls, you're only thinking of yourself. It's seven years, for fuck's sake! Can't you move on to something else?'

There's silence on his end for a long time. I stop walking and swap the phone into my other hand. It's shaking.

'As you wish,' he says eventually, his voice harder. 'I'll call my lawyer and ask her to start proceedings. You'll lose, you can be sure of that. I have the funds and the evidence to prove that, of the two of us, I'm the better parent. Afterwards, I'll call the girls and tell them you've been forcing me to lie for seven years. How do you think they'll take that, then, my darling? How do you think they'll react when they realise that if it wasn't for you, they could have seen their father much more frequently?'

I gulp hard and it burns my throat. I feel sick at the thought of his tense, thin lips as he says these words. I can hear the halting way he's breathing as he waits for my reaction. Waits for evidence of my fear.

'If that's what you want, Mathias,' I manage to say, trying to control the quiver in my voice. 'But if you tell them the truth, I'll have to do the same.'

Lily

27 May

OMG, Marcel, you have no idea! You'll never
guess what I saw today. I pinched my hand so hard
to check I wasn't dreaming I popped a blood
vessel. But that doesn't matter, I can die happy
because I SAW SOME WHALES!!!!!
     What the hell! I thought you'd be jumping for joy.
     Okay, I'll tell you all about it. Yesterday evening
I was reading a story to Noah (it was in
Norwegian, so I didn't understand much) and I
heard his dad telling Françoise and François how
you can get to see whales. My heart skipped a beat
around the bush, I listened carefully and then
afterwards I told Mum word for word . . . except
then she went and ruined it. I'll cut to the chase:
apparently, it's really expensive and we're really
poor and the two just don't go together. But there
was no way we weren't going to do it – this could
be the only time in my life I come close to whales.
It's not like I'm going to bump into them on every

street corner in Toulouse. Or if I do, they wouldn't be feeling that great.

I begged and pleaded and wheedled. I even offered to sell my little fingers to make some money – I've never really seen the point of them myself. In the end, she got the fact that this was something I seriously wanted to do and she said yes. Later, she asked if I'd rather be anaesthetised before they were cut off. I thought she meant it. Not even funny.

We went across the Lofoten Islands to Andenes in a minibus. The views along the way were pretty, but all I could think about was the whales. They gave us these ugly overalls to protect us from the cold, the water and the wind. I have to say if Jack in *Titanic* had had them he wouldn't have died, but I'm not sure he'd have pulled Rose either. We got into a little boat, which Mum said was called a Zodiac. I remember that because I wondered why it was called that – maybe the inventor liked reading his horoscope. There were eight of us and the other people were an English couple with three teenagers (I think that's why Chloe whinged about wearing the overalls).

I was worried I'd be seasick after Mum's driving made me nearly sick, and I can tell you this wasn't just a 'nearly'. There were loads of little waves and it's like with bad marks at school – it's better to have one big one than lots of little ones. The wind was very cold and there was snow on the mountaintops in the distance (someone needs to tell the Norwegians it's nearly summer). Eventually, Magnus stopped the boat. There were several black fins moving through the water together. Apparently, they were half dolphin, half whale – it was weird, like being in a nature programme. We watched them for a long time but all we could see was their backs; they didn't want to show us anything else. A bit later Magnus got a message and we sped off further out to sea. I was sick again and Mum rubbed my back and insisted I chewed some gum.

Are you ready for this, Marcel? I'm going to describe THE BIG MOMENT. I saw it before the boat stopped. It blew some spray from its blowhole. Lots of people think they blow out water, but I've watched so many documentaries about them I know that's wrong, it's actually air and water vapour. It was magical, wonderful, fabulous. Actually, there aren't words to describe it. It just was.

We could only see its back. It was almost motionless, and we were just a few metres away. I wanted to dive in and swim alongside it, but I think Mum guessed because she warned me that the water was even colder than the air. The whale slid past slowly and then suddenly dived down and its tail stood up out of the water for a few seconds. Those were the most beautiful seconds of my life, Marcel. I mean, I almost cried!

We saw another one after that and then another on our way back. I swear to you, my head's still full of them, and I hope it always will be. They're too big to come out through my ears, anyway.

I told Mum that when I'm older I want to work with whales. She laughed. I don't know how old people are when they give up on their dreams, but I hope I never get to that age.

Okay, that's enough for today, I need to go and tell Noah all about it.

Best wishes

Lily

PS It turns out English people and Norwegians make the same face as us when they're surprised.

Anna

Clara and Greg have invited me over to play Tarot again this evening, and my girls had trouble disguising how glad they were to get rid of me. I pretended to take it well.

They're in the middle of a Skype call when I reach their campervan: on the screen is a young woman with a child in Buzz Lightyear pyjamas on her knee.

'It's her cousin, Pauline,' Greg whispers to me, gesturing for me to sit down.

The conversation doesn't go on for long, but I hear how thrilled Pauline is about Clara's pregnancy.

'I'm so happy for you both! You'll see, it's the best thing ever, and you'll be amazing parents.'

'Am I going to have a cousin?' the little boy asks in a squeaky voice.

'Yes, Jules, a little baby cousin!' Clara says.

'I hope it's a boy.'

Everyone laughs and then Pauline gives them her news: the African dance classes she's loving, the way young Jules finds a good excuse to sneak into her bed every night and her parents' trip to the Bahamas. The conversation winds up with the two cousins promising to speak again soon and a resounding kiss from the little boy.

'Would you like a tea?' Clara offers, stroking her stomach.

I smile, and Clara realises what she was doing then gets up to boil the water.

'She doesn't want to admit it,' Greg says, winking at me, 'but she loves it already.'

Clara shrugs and tries to stop the corners of her mouth curving upwards.

'What are you talking about? I've looked on Google, it isn't even five millimetres long at the moment. How could I love something the size of an ant?'

'All I'm hearing is that you've looked on Google,' Greg replies. 'Have you been researching ideas for names, too?'

She blushes, and Greg laughs out loud.

'Okay, fine,' she concedes. 'Maybe I've slightly got used to the idea of being a mother. Don't make such a thing about it. One sugar for you, Anna?'

'Yes, please. Your cousin's right, you know, nothing's ever made me happier than my two girls. Sometimes I just have to look at them and I feel my heart swell with happiness. I can't explain it.'

'Yeah, yeah,' Clara says, putting a steaming mug down in front of me. 'Don't try getting me on to another subject to avoid the one about you. So, how are things going with Julien?'

Greg gives me an apologetic smile.

'What do you mean, "things" with Julien?' I asked innocently.

'Don't go all innocent on me! I don't have many talents, but I can spot when there's something going on between two people. And in this case, I can smell the attraction from ten kilometres away!'

I gulp down a scalding mouthful. Three little knocks on the door interrupt my embarrassment. Greg opens the door to Julien, who comes in, followed by a blast of cold air.

'I waited till Noah was fast asleep,' he says, putting his baby alarm on the table. 'So, are you ready to lose?'

We work our way through several games, a lot of laughter and a few confidences until tiredness creeps up on us. When Clara falls asleep sitting up with her cards in her hand, it's time to take our leave. I'm just pulling my hat on to my head when she resurfaces without even realising she's been gone.

'Did I win?' she asks.

'Of course,' Julien lies, buttoning up his coat.

Pleased with this result, she gets up and puts her arms around my neck to kiss me goodnight.

'You'd be so adorable together,' she whispers.

I give her a peck on the cheek and hop out into the cold fog.

'Wait, I'll walk you back,' Julien offers, slipping his arm around mine.

My van is parked on the far side of the plot, and we walk over to it slowly.

'So, do you regret agreeing to travel with the group?' he asks.

'Yes, it's a real pain being with such horrible people.'

'You're right. Clara and Greg are particularly unpleasant.'

'I can't stand them. But the worst one is still the organiser. What's his name again?'

He nods in agreement.

'Oh yes, the bloke with the son, erm, Julien. Completely agree with you, I'm not keen on him either . . .'

'He's ghastly, always trying to make himself helpful. Who are these people who constantly want to help everyone out? It's repulsive.'

'Yup, they should bring back the death penalty.'

I can't help laughing. We've reached my door and the fog wraps itself around us like a cocoon. Julien turns to face me, still holding my arm.

'I heard what Clara said to you,' he says quietly.

'She's got this idea into her head,' I stammer, caught off guard. 'I don't know . . .'

'Maybe she can see things other people don't see,' he whispers, looking at me intently.

My heart goes off at a gallop and I gently extricate my arm.

225

'Goodnight, Julien.'

'Goodnight, Anna. Sweet dreams.'

As I reach for the door handle I feel Julien's hand gently stroke my cheek. I open the door and shut myself inside, shivering from head to foot.

The Chloe Chronicles

François asked me to help Louis with some creative-writing exercises. His sister's no good at that sort of thing and Mum had been boasting about my grades. I had absolutely no desire to spend half a day with a nine-year-old boy, until his father offered me a decent fee. My willingness comes pretty cheap.

We got settled in their van, and Louis took out his exercise book and opened it on the last page. There was a poem by Prévert and his job was to imagine how it might go on.

'What do you want to write about?' I asked.

He stared at me with his big, dark eyes as if he didn't understand the question. I had ideas jostling for attention inside my head and I was tempted to pick up the pen and do the work for him, to carry on with this poem and write some more, too.

'I dunno,' he said.

'Do you understand the poem?'

He shook his head and blushed. At his age, I used to cram notebooks full of my thoughts. When teachers asked me what I wanted to do in life, I would say 'write stories'.

I explained to Louis what he was being asked to do and he started to write, hiding his work with his other arm.

I looked around the campervan. Louise was lying on her stomach on the bed, watching a TV series on her father's phone, Françoise was peeling carrots and François was chopping them into rounds.

My parents used to cook together. When Dad came home from work he'd join Mum in the kitchen, take off his jacket and tie and make supper with her. I would sit down nearby and listen as they told each other about their day. They laughed a lot. Dad often put his arms around her, and they kissed and fed each other spoonfuls to taste whatever they were cooking. I've often thought back to those times as I've closed my eyes at night before going to sleep. Trying to find an explanation. A ten-year-old girl can't understand why her parents would separate when they were kissing only yesterday.

I asked a lot of questions, but the answers were always vague. For months, every time I heard a key in the lock I hoped it was Dad coming home. I wanted to hear his voice in the living room, to see his jacket on the back of the chair, I wanted to smell his deodorant in the bathroom. I wanted our family to be whole again.

Lily was five; she didn't really notice. I never heard her ask for Dad. I never saw her cry. I remember a few temper tantrums, she'd wake in the night screaming, she hit her friends at school and argued with Mum, but it didn't go on for long.

I still don't understand why they separated, but I've given up on the idea of watching Mum and Dad laughing as they feed each other spoonfuls of whatever they're cooking.

'Finished!'

Louis turned his book towards me with a satisfied expression on his face. He seemed to have understood the task, the end of the poem was coherent, the rhymes worked, the writing was . . .

The writing.

Blue felt-tip.

The blood rushed to my cheeks. There was no room for doubt. Sitting there facing me with a big smile on his face, my little anonymous poet was waiting to hear what I thought of his work.

Anna

When we set out on this trip nearly two months ago, one of the things on my mental list of fun activities was kayaking in the fjords. It was one of those dreams you think will never be realised – it would be too good to be true.

It *is* too good to be true.

We're doing it.

Before getting into the kayaks I asked the girls which of them wanted to come with me. They both pointed to each other. So we took to the water individually and I've been trying to get the hang of the paddle on my own for the last ten minutes.

Lily is leading the three of us, ploughing on at a good rate so as not to lose sight of the instructor and the rest of the group. There's a rippling wake behind her kayak as she carves through the clear waters of the Norwegian Sea.

Chloe is alongside me. She must have felt sorry for me when she saw me going backwards instead of forwards. The sun is gleaming on her red curls and she's going into ecstasies about everything.

'Wait, I want to take a picture,' she announces, setting down her paddle across the front of the kayak.

She takes her phone from her waterproof bag.

'Careful you don't fall.'

'Chill, I've got this.'

Our kayaks have come to a stop, and the sound of paddles plying the water has been replaced with silence. Total silence. Disturbing silence. My heart thuds in my ears and I have a pins-and-needles feeling in my cheeks. We're surrounded by dark mountains topped with their caps of snow. The scenery is reflected in the perfectly smooth water. We're tiny. My breathing accelerates.

'What if I had a little panic attack right now?' suggests my emotional brain.

'No, thanks – no offence,' replies my rational brain.

'But look, she's on the water, surrounded by threatening mountains, miles from anywhere. It's the perfect opportunity!'

'Sweet of you to offer, but she's trying to give up.'

'Too late! I've already sent out the rampaging heart rate and the pins and needles in her fingers,' my emotional brain says smugly.

'Well, you can call them back because she won't let them in.'

'We'll see about that! You know perfectly well I always win. Here, look, I'll throw in a couple of hot flushes.'

Chloe peers at me.

'You okay, Mum?'

'Fine, sweetheart. It's magnificent here.'

I watch as she captures the panorama, and my heart gradually returns to its usual rate.

'Give us a smile!'

I have no trouble complying. If it wouldn't mean risking capsizing, I'd dance for joy because I just overcame a panic attack! Even though I know the next one's never far away, and they're always there, crouched in a corner, waiting for the right moment to have another go at me.

'You look gorgeous in this picture!' Chloe cries. 'Will you take one of me?'

I paddle closer to her, take the phone from her and immortalise my daughter and her smile, which I've missed so much.

'Right, we'd better get going, they'll be waiting for us.'

Chloe puts the phone away and we set off to join the group . . . as quickly as my paddling abilities will allow. The figures in the distance are motionless, except for Lily, who's waving to us frantically. I try to speed up, but that just makes me spin round to the left. I correct myself and I decide I'll have to be patient. I can feel Chloe beside me, watching me.

'What?' I ask, turning to look at her.

'Can I ask you something, Mum?'

'Of course you can.'

She pauses for a moment, which I don't find reassuring, and hits me with, 'Now that I'm older, will you tell me why you left Dad?'

Anna

The first time he hit me he broke my nose.

That was two months before our wedding. He came home from work grumpy, going on and on about how his boss had criticised him for something that wasn't his fault. I tried to comfort him, but he brushed me aside harshly. We'd been living together for six months and – having come to know him as tender and good-natured – I was now seeing a new facet of his personality. In the first few weeks, I'd even wondered if he was too kind, if I wouldn't be better suited to a man with a bit more character to him.

He didn't like it when I tried to find excuses for his boss. His fist flew out of nowhere – I didn't have time to duck. I didn't have time to understand what was happening.

You get a lot of blood, with a broken nose. He begged me to open the bathroom door. I ran the water in the basin and my blood mingled with it. I just stared at that watery choreography, completely paralysed.

He apologised. It was his fault, he shouldn't have done it, he'd never done it before. He loved me. He loved me so much he wanted to die.

We told people I'd run into a closed door. Everyone laughed – what are you like, Anna, can't see doors now?

He did everything to secure my forgiveness, telling me he loved me the whole time, being thoughtful and cuddly, fulfilling my need for love better than I could ever have hoped. The punch became just a memory. A little accident along the way, not important enough to stop us travelling further together.

The second time, he avoided my face.

Chloe was three months old. She needed to have me near her every minute of the day and I was happy to be there for her. He asked me whether I still loved him. This was the attentive father, the kind and considerate husband, the man I felt lucky to have met. It seemed so obvious to me that I loved him I gave him a big grin and said, 'Of course I don't!' I didn't have time to say the next bit – I felt his fist barrel into my still-tender stomach.

He spent a month at his mother's house. I made it absolutely clear: I would never live with him again. He called me several times a day, but I didn't answer so he left messages. He didn't understand what was happening to him, he was frightened, frightened of himself, he didn't want to be violent, it was stronger than him, he was consumed with guilt. He started some therapy, took up sport. He loved me too much, he was scared I'd think he wasn't such a good person, that I'd stop loving him. It was all too much for him, it was breaking his heart.

I forgave him, and for a long time I congratulated myself on this decision. He'd succeeded in overcoming the monster that was trying to take his place. He had his faults, but then, who doesn't? I wasn't easy to live with every day either. Now that I was working part-time in a restaurant I was often tired in the evenings. I sometimes rejected him and forgot to show him I loved him.

I was back with my soulmate, the man who knew everything about me, the man who made me laugh, come alive, dream . . .

It was a Sunday morning. Chloe had spent the night with her little friend Ayna next door and Lily was still asleep. She was five. I got up to get ready for work; I had a shift at midday. He was still in bed. He pulled me back by my arm.

'Is his bigger than mine?'

I didn't understand what he was talking about. I thought it was a joke, so I laughed. He yanked me brutally down on to the bed then straddled me and put his hands round my throat. His eyes looked right into mine and I didn't even recognise them. I tried to fight, but he was stronger than me. He squeezed. And squeezed. I couldn't breathe. I was watching the man I loved kill me. He let go before I lost consciousness.

'Little tart, you'll pay for this.'

I hit out at his arms and chest and scratched his cheeks and legs. He let me pull myself free and I rolled on to the floor and crawled to the door. A savage kick in the ribs knocked the breath out of me. I could hear our little dog Brownie scratching at the other side of the door.

He pulled me up by my hair and smacked my head against the wardrobe. I was reeling but still lucid enough to think he was going to kill me. I was petrified. I thought about Lily and Chloe being left alone with him. Who would find my body? Lily? Chloe? Like me with my mother?

He hit my head again, harder this time. I was bent double when the door opened. Brownie raced in, wagging her tail, and Lily stood in the doorway with her hair all mussed up. Terrified.

I tried to stand up to take her in my arms, but he was faster than me. He gave me one final kick in the shin and pinched our daughter's face between his fingers.

'If you talk about this, your mother'll pay for it.'

We went to live with my father for a week. I told him everything. He and Jeannette were horrified. Who would have thought that this charming man, who couldn't bear injustice of any sort, was violent?

Mathias begged me to give him one last chance. He was going to have treatment, would go to hospital, would find a solution so it never happened again.

I was the one who found a solution so it never happened again. He had to leave.

It wasn't easy to achieve – he tried emotional blackmail, appealed to me for pity, threatened to hurt himself or me or the girls. He went to live with his mother in Marseille.

When I got back to the apartment Brownie was dead. The vet told me her liver and spleen were both ruptured.

I smile at Chloe, who's watching me as she paddles. She's waiting for my answer.

'We separated because we just didn't get on any more, sweetheart.'

The Chloe Chronicles

I've been sent another poem. It was in the usual place when we got back to the campervan after spending the afternoon at Nusfjord. A new addition: there are now hearts dotting each 'i'. Any hint of a doubt has now disappeared . . .

> I'D FIND JEWELS TO GIVE TO YOU
> AND FLOWERS FOR YOUR HOME
> FINE PERFUMES TO MATCH THE VIEW.
> AND, ON THE OUTSKIRTS OF ROME,
> I'D BUILD A VILLA IN THE HILLS OF GREEN
> WHERE LOVE WOULD BE THE ONLY THING
> WHERE LOVE WOULD RULE LIKE A KING
> AND YOU WOULD BE THE QUEEN.

It seems little Louis has run out of inspiration.

I was first into the campervan, really pleased with the photos I'd taken in the fishing village: quaint red and yellow houses reflected in the still waters of the fjord – the place was a picture postcard.

The first thing I did was check whether Kevin had

replied to the message I'd sent him in the morning: 'I'll be home soon, hope we can see each other. I think about you a lot Xxx'

He had replied, and his feelings were pretty clear.

'Piss off.'

I threw the phone on to the banquette and went out without a word to Mum and Lily. I needed to be on my own to think. I walked across the site and off along the road, not knowing where I was going. The view down into the fjord and over the village below was mind-blowing.

Luck was so much on my side (not) that I ran into Louise, sitting on the grass with her arms around her head. I passed her, trying to make as little noise as possible so she wouldn't hear me, but she's not only a pain, she's got sharp hearing, too. She seemed startled and peered up at me.

'What are you doing?' I asked.

'Nothing.'

'Why've you got your hand over your mouth?'

'Like I said, it's nothing.'

She was very red, and frowning.

'Well, show me, then,' I persisted. 'You can't spend the rest of your life with your hand over your mouth.'

She shrugged, and her eyes filled with tears. She slowly lowered her hand and the carnage appeared: Louise's face bore a magnificent brown moustache.

'What *is* that?'

'Well, I was trying to wax but the stuff was too hot . . . so I've got a scab.'

I tried not to laugh. I promise, I tried. But you really had to see her looking like a muppet with her scab moustache. You wouldn't have managed it either.

It was a silent, contained chuckle which could have stopped at that if Louise herself hadn't burst out laughing. The problem was this stretched the scab, which hurt her, so she was laughing and wincing in pain at the same time and pressing her fingers into the sides of her mouth. I couldn't keep up the fight. It came up from the pit of my stomach, it broke through the barrier of my compassion and exploded – long, loud, hysterical laughter, the sort that hurts your stomach and makes you cry. Louise was screaming with laughter, too.

When we eventually calmed down, several minutes later, we were lying on the grass with tears streaming over our cheeks.

I sat up and wiped my face.

'You're lucky, it's very fashionable.'

'So are small boobs.'

Maybe there's more to her than meets the eye.

When we came back to the site we behaved as if we hadn't just spent an hour chatting. Diego was outside smoking his pipe and I went over to see him. The things he'd said about parents and children were still buzzing round inside my head.

'A bit low?'

'I'll be okay. How about you?'

'I'm fine. Better than Edgar, who spends the whole time sleeping. I hope he doesn't leave us before we get back.'

He must have taken pity on me as my eyes popped out of my head, because he smiled and asked, 'So, what's bothering you? An affair of the heart?'

'You could say that . . .'

He drew on his pipe slowly and blew out the smoke, gazing at the fjord.

'Do you know something, my dear? If I could relive my whole life knowing the things I've learned along the way, I'd be a lot happier. We often get in such a state over nothing much. The things we think are negative may actually be positive, and vice versa.'

I asked him what he meant and he explained.

'When I was twenty-two,' he said, 'I had a serious cycling accident. I had several fractures, but what upset me most was that I couldn't go to the party I was meant to be going to that evening. I'd been thinking about it for days because I would be seeing Lucie, a young lady I liked very much. I spent the whole day trying to persuade the doctors to let me out, but it was no good. I cursed them! Lucie got close to a young man from the neighbouring village and stopped answering my letters. I was in despair, I thought my life was ruined. And a month later I met my Madeleine. That same year, my brother, who I was very close to, was appointed head of the glassworks where he worked. It was a big event – no one in our family had ever risen to that sort of level. His days started earlier and he came home later, but there was no dampening his enthusiasm. On his way home one evening he lost control of the car on a corner. He died on the spot. I could give you dozens of examples like that. If I hadn't been injured, I would never have met my wife. If my brother hadn't been promoted, he might have lived longer. All through our lives, we assess the things that happen to us and we either celebrate or grieve, but we won't actually know whether it was right to celebrate or grieve till the last minute. Nothing is fixed, everything keeps changing. Don't be sad today, because whatever's happening now might bring real happiness.'

I listened attentively to what he said. He communicated his wisdom well. Then I went back to the campervan wondering whether what he'd told me was a good thing or a bad thing.

Anna

It's midnight, and this will be the last time we see the sun at this hour. We'll be leaving Bodø tomorrow and dropping back below the Arctic Circle.

The campervans are parked on a site at the top of a hill overlooking the town and the sea. The girls and I wanted to make the most of this, so we're sitting on a rock, sheltered from the cold by a snuggly duvet and watching the magical show of the sun refusing to set. We don't say a thing. Experiences like this don't need words.

'Can I join you?' We hear Julien's voice from behind us

'Take my place. I'm falling asleep!' says Lily, getting up. 'Goodnight.'

'Me, too, and I still need to write my blog,' Chloe says, giving me a kiss on the cheek and following her sister.

I almost go in with them, but I wouldn't want to upset Julien. He stands there awkwardly in front of me, apparently unsure, so I lift up the duvet and he sits down next to me.

'That's Landegode Island over there,' he says, pointing to the mountains that are partially masking the sun.

'Well, could you tell it it's in the way?'

'I'll see what I can do,' he says earnestly.

He puts his mouth to his baby alarm.

'Hello, Landegode, this is the director of the Centre for the Preservation of World Beauty. We've received some complaints because you're parked right in front of the sun. We'd be grateful if you could find somewhere else. Otherwise, I'll have no choice but to send you my top agent, Anna, to deal with you. And I can tell you, she doesn't mess about. Have you heard of Atlantis? Well, that was one of her jobs. All the best!'

He puts the handset into his jacket pocket and turns to face me.

'There, that's sorted. The island's just getting its things together and it'll move along.'

'Excellent, Mr Director. Of course, if it doesn't move, you could always get it in a ju-jitsu hold.'

He smiles, and the golden light makes his eyes twinkle. He looks right into my eyes and I can't seem to look away. His smile gradually fades, his eyes peruse my cheeks, drop to my mouth and linger on my lips. For a long time. A long, long time. A wave of warmth spreads through my body and Julien slowly brings his face closer to mine. I want to move closer to him, too, but it suddenly occurs to me that we can be seen. I pull away and we both go back to gazing at the midnight sun.

Lily

30 May

Dear Marcel,

I hope you'rc well!

Btw, I think Mum's been telling Françoise stuff about me. It was so random – she came to find me to tell me I mustn't let people push me around and bullying is very serious and she was an escaped goat at school, too. She told me her life story, and at first I just listened to be polite, but then I listened because it was interesting. I told her I wasn't being bullied and I couldn't care less that the twins were horrible to me, and she was, like, that's exactly what she used to say but, actually, it <u>did</u> hurt her. Like me. I really didn't expect that from her. Well, then I asked her how she dealt with it and she gave me some tips. I'll write them out for you. You never know, you could find they come in handy some time.

1. If another diary is horrible to you and you're frightened, picture it with terrible diarrhoea.

2. Instead of being nasty back (or not replying at all), you have to give them a big smile and a compliment. I can't see how that helps, but Françoise swore it works.

After she'd gone, Chloe came to see me. I think she'd heard the whole conversation, but she didn't say anything. She couldn't stop going on about the weather and the gorgeous scenery we were driving through. I could tell she wanted to talk to me about something but just couldn't get it out, and then in the end she did. She admitted that she didn't really mean what she said the other day and she's glad she's got a sister, and she's even more glad that it's me (who's her sister). I tried not to smile too much – I can't have her thinking I'm a pushover – but still, I did say that I was glad it was me, too (who's her sister).

Oh yes, on the way home, you need to remind me to find a shop where I can buy some brunøst. It's this brown cheese that has a slightly caramelly taste. It's so good I could eat it all day. Here, I'll put a lump on the page. Have a taste and let me know what you think.

Okay, I'm off. We've just stopped to look at a waterfall. I hope there'll be salmon jumping this time (and maybe some bears).

Lily xx

PS I don't know who invented all the weird
words in Norwegian with ø and å and æ, but
if you ask me, he was drinking more than
water.

The Chloe Chronicles

'Do you like Julien?'

Mum wasn't expecting that. She asked me to repeat it.

We were sitting outside on the ferry to Vevelstad with bowls of soup warming our hands. The ferry was slaloming between small islands surrounded by magnificent scenery with big white clouds drifting across the sky.

Mum swallowed hard.

'Why do you ask?'

'I dunno. I get the feeling you like him. Do you?'

She gave a shrug, but her embarrassment sent out a clear message.

In all the time since she left Dad, I've never asked Mum this sort of question. I never did it because I didn't want to hear the answer.

Of course I wanted to see her happy, but Dad just wouldn't cope with it. He's told me so several times.

Even after seven years, his only aim is to rekindle Mum's feelings for him. Every time I speak to him on the phone he tells me about the letters he writes her and the prayers he offers to someone he's not sure is even listening. He describes his memories and his voice gets choked.

I can tell how upset he is, it's so obvious. He's lonely where he lives, so far from the love of his life and his daughters. It's killing me.

I know she'll find someone one day, and I know it won't be Dad. It's horrendous knowing that one parent's happiness will destroy the other's.

Men like Mum. I see the way they look at her. I've seen the phone numbers slipped under the windscreen wipers. I've heard the security guy in the supermarket telling her how charming she is. I imagine she's had relationships in these seven years. Flings, flirtations. She's always covered her tracks. This is the first time I've suspected anything.

I've noticed the way she looks at Julien. She can say whatever she likes, there's definitely something missing in comparison when she looks at Edgar or Diego.

She thought for a moment before saying, 'I do like him. He makes me laugh. How about you?'

'Stop answering my questions with questions, Mum. It's a pain.'

'That's a shame, because I've got one for you. Would it bother you if I was with someone?'

'With Julien?'

'With anyone. Enough already about Julien!'

I thought it over.

Everything I thought I knew has been turned on its head in the last two months. I've spent more time with Mum than I have in the whole of the last two years. Dad deserves to be happy, and so does she. Whether that's on her own or with someone else.

'It might be a bit hard at first,' I admitted. 'But I'd get used to it.'

She smiled, and then I added one clarification, 'But please not the campervan-whisperer in his lumberjack shirts!'

Anna

I was eleven when my father introduced me to Jeannette. My mother had been dead three years.

He came to pick me up from school and told me we were going for a meal in a restaurant. We never ate in restaurants.

He worked long hours at the time and I often spent the night at Nanny's. She and I had woven a little cocoon of habits and when I was at her house I felt nothing could harm me. Every evening was the same. I'd come in and put on my slippers. I liked it when they were a bit old; they glided over the tiled floors more easily. Nanny would make a snack for me, a glass of hot milk, a pancake or a waffle with icing sugar that she ground up herself from ordinary sugar. If I spilled any on the oilcloth I would dab it with my fingers and suck them greedily. Then we'd do my home-work and some crosswords if there was time before making supper. She sometimes let me fill the words in but, more often that not, it was my job to look up definitions in the dictionary. Next we'd go to the kitchen. I had my own apron, a red one with purple flowers on it. She read out the ingredients and I fetched them; she let me beat the eggs, roll our pastry and grease dishes. I was always frightened when it came to lighting the oven. I struck the match then reached it over to the little hole while Nanny pressed the button to release the gas. While we waited for supper to cook I would put on my pyjamas and she would close the shutters, then we'd sit on the sofa and watch game shows on TV. The house would gradually fill with wonderful smells and my tummy would rumble. We'd talk a lot over supper. I liked it when Nanny told me about her memories: I liked hearing about the little girl she once was, I liked her telling me about her parents and about my grandfather, who'd died when I was little. What I liked best of all was when she told me about my mother: her childhood, her laugh, and that December evening when she announced that she was expecting me. I was allowed to read before going to sleep. Nanny had completely redecorated my mother's bedroom specially for me. We'd chosen the wallpaper and the furniture together. She'd kiss me three times on the cheeks, then say, 'Goodnight, my Annie,' and it was a good night, because Nanny was there.

The plan had been for me to sleep at her house that night, but my father was waiting for me outside school. We stopped off at home for a while and he put on lots of aftershave, then we went to the restaurant. It was a table for three, but I didn't suspect a thing until she arrived.

She was wearing a red blouse and an uncomfortable smile. She handed me a parcel and my father encouraged me to open it straight away. It was a notebook.

'Your father tells me you write poems.'

I had burger and chips, then chocolate ice-cream. It wasn't very good. Jeannette was nice. She talked a lot, as if she didn't want to leave any room for awkwardness. She was divorced and had no children – her smile faded when she mentioned that. She worked at a day nursery and she and my father had met in a doctor's waiting room. She'd sprained her right ankle and he his left wrist and they saw that as a sign.

While we were eating dessert she put her hand on my father's. He withdrew his gently.

We said our goodbyes on the pavement. She whispered that she was happy to have met me, and I said I was happy to have met her, too. In the car my father asked me what I thought of her and I told the truth: I said she seemed nice and had pretty eyes.

It was a long time since I'd heard him whistling in the shower: I was happy for him. He hugged me tightly before going off to bed.

'Goodnight, my darling,' he said.

'Goodnight, Daddy,' I replied, smiling.

He closed the door to my room and I slipped under the covers and cried all night.

Anna

'Hello, Jeannette?'

'How are you, my darling? Come here, Pops. It's Anna on the phone!'

I can hear my father's voice as he comes over to the telephone.

'Ask her if she got my message,' he tells Jeannette.

'Wait, I'll put her on loudspeaker,' she replies.

'Did you get my message, Anna?' he says, and his voice is clearly right up next to the handset.

'Yes, I did. I'm really sorry I haven't made the time to call back . . .'

'That's a good thing – it means everything's going well,' Jeannette says cheerily. 'Last time we spoke you were in Lofoten. Are you still there?'

I tell them about the latest legs of the journey, the midnight sun, the kayaks . . . they ask for all sorts of details.

'We were planning to go to Italy for our first campervan trip, but you're making us question that,' my father says.

'There's nothing to stop us doing both . . .'

'Oh, there goes my darling Poppet!' He chuckles.

'Coo-ee, I'm here!' I interrupt, before it descends into canoodling. 'I highly recommend Scandinavia. The countryside changes the whole time – you really get an eyeful. I even know someone who could give you a guided trip.'

We spend several minutes planning their next holiday, and they're buzzing with excitement. My father eventually goes back to whatever he was doing, but not before reiterating snippets of advice about the campervan.

'And the girls?' Jeannette asks.

'They're on good form. I feel like I'm rediscovering them. It's wonderful actually living with them.'

'You were so right to listen to your instincts, my darling. Have you talked to them?'

'No. Not yet. I'd better go, I need to do some washing. We haven't got anything clean left to wear.'

'Okay, give the girls a big hug from me. And there's one for you, too. I can't wait to see you back, you know.'

'I can't wait either. Love you.'

Lily

1 June

Dear Marcel,

How's tricks? Actually, don't answer that, there isn't time. I have to tell you about something so crazy even I think it's crazy.

There we were, happily walking through the Old Town in Trondheim, and Chloe was taking photos of all the historical buildings and Gamle Bybro bridge, when she suddenly had an idea she shouldn't have had. She wanted to go to Ikea, because it was a shame to come to Scandinavia without going to one of their stores. I almost chucked her in the water. It's boring enough shopping in France. I was on the brink of despair.

Mum agreed with her, and whatever I tried to get them to change their minds, telling them it was a Swedish shop and we really should have gone while we were in Sweden, I could see I wasn't tipping the scales (and I say that because Mum says she's put on ten kilograms).

Ikea in Norway is the same as Ikea in France, except that the names really mean something to the people here.

We did our little trot round. I tried to lie down on a bed to wait till they'd finished, but I could tell from the look on the salesman's face that I'd do better to move along. His expression didn't need any translating.

I think they looked at EVERY item in EVERY department. I was just about to throw myself from the top of the Sniglar wardrobe when I spotted something that gave me back the will to live. I couldn't believe my eyes, even though they're not liars, so I asked Chloe to come and have a look, and her eyes said the same as mine.

Okay, I'll stop keeping you guessing. I can see you can't take the suspense a moment longer – it's like the end of an episode of *Game of Thrones*. So this was in the department with all the frames and posters. There were loads of them in every shape and size; there was even a big one you could slot twenty different photos in, and it made me laugh because they'd put twenty copies of the same one. And that photo was the crazy thing. I clocked the fact that I'd already seen it somewhere, but it took me a few minutes to work out where.

Are you ready for this, Marcel? Watch out, this is heavy stuff. Don't go having a car-jack arrest.

Okay, I'm going to tell you.

It was the photo of Edgar and Diego's wives. Two older-looking ladies laughing in front of a lake. It was them, definitely.

I swear, this whole thing is too weird, I just don't get it, but Chloe and me decided we'd do some investigating. We're good detectives – we've played a lot of Cluedo.

And anyway, we started thinking it over, and there are zillions of explanations.

Theory one: Ikea stole the photo of Madeleine and Rosa and that's really really really really serious, specially because the ad is, like, lying, because in real life they're dead.

Theory two: Edgar and Diego don't know the women in the photo and that's really really really really serious, because I don't understand that at all.

But don't you worry, Marcel, we'll find the answer. All good things come to those who pull their wait.

Lily xx

PS I took Noah's hand this morning when we were watching his top and he didn't mind at all.

The Chloe Chronicles

I wanted to play it really discreetly, sniffing out the secret of this photo. Sadly, it turns out we're not especially private detectives. The two old men knew something was up as soon as we asked to see the picture of their wives again.

'Why do you want to?' Edgar asked.

'Just so we don't forget them,' I said.

He eyed me warily.

'We saw the same photo in Ikea,' Lily piped up.

'What does that mean?' Edgar asked, frowning.

'It means we're toast,' Diego said.

'Oh.'

They invited us in, and we sat down on the banquette. Lily had her sunglasses on. She thought they gave her more gravitas.

'What do you know?' Diego asked.

I explained that we'd found the exact same photo in a frame. The two men listened, their heads lowered. Diego suddenly jumped to his feet, picked up the framed photo and put it on the table. It was true, they weren't Madeleine and Rosa, he admitted in a shaky voice. But Edgar shouted over him to stop, not to say another word.

Diego reassured him with a hand on his shoulder.

'It was too painful seeing their faces the whole time,' he explained. 'We opted for a neutral image in case someone asked to see them.'

Lily lowered her sunglasses and knitted her brows.

'Hold your horses! We weren't born yes today – no, tomorrow.'

'She's right.' Edgar nodded. 'Your story doesn't stack up. Tell them. I think we can trust them.'

'You can!' I promised.

Diego poured us a glass of orange juice each as he revealed their story.

Ever since his wife had died, his son had been concerned about him living alone and kept insisting he should move to Canada to live with him. The old man refused: he didn't want to be a burden to his son. But he didn't want to give him cause for concern either, which is why he moved into a retirement home three months ago.

'Giving up my home filled with all my memories was heartbreaking,' he sighed. 'But it was the price I paid for my boy's peace of mind.'

It was at this home that he met Edgar, who had been in the room next door since his own wife had died, nearly a year earlier. *He* hadn't had any choice: his daughter and son-in-law had decreed that he couldn't stay at home after he'd set fire to the microwave when he was warming up some pasta.

Their shared loneliness brought them together. Sand

trickled through the hourglass so slowly, the days dragged by and conversations burbled on. All they could look forward to was deliverance.

It didn't come in the way they'd expected . . . but in the form of a campervan.

'The director of the retirement home came and showed off his new acquisition to the staff and residents,' Edgar explained. 'We watched the show from the courtyard. It was the highlight of the day. At one point, they all disappeared inside the building and we took the opportunity to admire the beast at closer quarters. And that's when everything got out of hand.'

The key was in the ignition and the papers were on the dashboard. Diego sat in the driver's seat, Edgar in the passenger seat. They watched the director running after them in the rear-view mirror for a long time – it still made them laugh now.

They hadn't planned any of it. They had nowhere to go. Just a spanking new campervan and galloping heart rates.

'We drove for hours, completely aimlessly,' Diego went on. 'We were beside ourselves with excitement, like little boys. Luckily, I had my bag with me, with my glasses, my pills and my bank card. We stopped when the fuel light came on, but we couldn't open the blithering tank. Fortunately, a man came and helped us. A man in a checked shirt.'

Julien had just hit the road at the start of his next expedition. He could immediately tell something was wrong with the picture, and the two old boys confided in him. Touched by their story, he told them he'd be meeting up with other campervans the next day for a road trip in Scandinavia. He asked if they'd like to join the group, on condition that they let their families know.

'We thought about it all night.' Edgar picked up the story. 'At dawn we bought a few clothes then called our children from Julien's phone. The director had already contacted their families. Diego's son was worried to death about us, and my daughter was absolutely livid about the campervan. They begged us to go back and we said we would. We just didn't say when.'

Lily had taken off her glasses and was hanging on their every word.

'But wasn't this a trip you were meant to be doing with your wives?' she asked.

'Not exactly,' Edgar replied. 'My Rosa couldn't bear the cold and Madeleine didn't like travelling. When Julien told us about it, it just seemed like the best way to end our journey here on Earth. Deep down, we didn't really lie: when we go to join them I'm sure they'll congratulate us for this.'

We sat in silence for a long while. The two of them lost in their memories, the two of us floundering in surprise.

'That still doesn't explain the picture!' I eventually exclaimed.

'No,' said Edgar, shaking his head. 'I'd just bought the frame at Ikea in Stockholm the morning you came here for a coffee. It was the perfect alibi to get people to believe our story. We were worried about rousing suspicions.'

'You see,' Diego intervened, 'I've never stolen anything in my life, not so much as a stamp! I feel like a runaway. I keep thinking the police will turn up any minute. I almost had a heart attack when the border patrol searched the vehicles. We needed a rock-solid backstory. We couldn't mention the retirement home, so we just tweaked the facts a little. Two widowers making a trip they had planned with their wives – that would stop people asking too many questions. I mean, we haven't heard a word, after all. We've no idea whether our children have managed to calm things down or if Interpol are on our heels. I have to admit, it's not that unpleasant – we often comment on how long it is since we've felt so alive. But we're still frightened of being found.'

He took a big deep breath then peered at us anxiously.

'Are you going to report us?'

Lily frowned.

'I'm not a snitch.'

Diego started to laugh, soon joined by Edgar. Lily succumbed, too, till she had to hold her sides. I wasn't expecting to, but found I was laughing along with them, and the four of us roared with laughter together for a long time.

Later, when we left, it occurred to me that we humans would be in a pretty rubbish place if we didn't have the gift of laughter. It would mean we always had to express our true feelings.

Anna

The children are in bed, even the older ones. This evening's theme is 'Truth or dare'. Most of us tried to wriggle out of it by coming up with massively urgent occupations, but Julien's enthusiasm relegated them to secondary activities.

The temperatures are milder now, so we've found a spot outside, a little way away from the vehicles. It won't get dark till very late. Knees more prone to the cold are protected with blankets, candles are burning and all our glasses – except Clara's – are filled with aquavit, the local spirit. My head swims just from smelling the stuff.

Julien spins his home-made wheel to determine Françoise's fate, and it stops on dare. He takes out one of the pieces of paper on which we've written our dares and questions.

'You have to tell a joke in a Canadian accent.'

Françoise takes some time to think, claiming she doesn't know any jokes, but eventually she launches in.

'A stag with magnificent antlers goes into a bank looking unhappy. "Can I help you, sir?" one of the tellers asks. "Well," he says, 'I'm just looking for my doe."'

She tilts her chin upwards, clearly proud of herself. I wait for the punchline, only to realise she's delivered it. It takes me a while to get it. I glance around: everyone looks incredulous.

'You do realise that wasn't a Canadian accent, don't you?' François asks his wife.

'I know, I can only do a Texan accent, but wasn't my joke funny?'

'Yes, yes, it was!' we all chorus reassuringly.

Satisfied, she downs a gulp of alcohol and spins the wheel for Greg.

'Truth!'

She pulls out a piece of paper and Greg waits apprehensively for the question.

'Describe the last dream you had.'

'Ah!' he says, clearly relieved. 'It was last night. I dreamed I was walking down a dark street alone, all the shops were closed, there were no cars, no planes overhead, no birds. I didn't know where to go and this beautiful blonde girl suddenly appeared with a sort of halo of light around her. She took me gently by the hand and I followed her and no longer felt lost. It was you, Clara, my darling.'

Clara throws her head back and laughs.

'It's okay, my love, you can tell the truth. I won't mind.'

'Oh, right, okay. I dreamed I was on a slide eating a hamburger and a rabbit told me it was going to rain.'

He pulls out a piece of paper before we've had time to react.

'Edgar, truth! Tell us about your most wonderful memory.'

The old man takes a deep breath, apparently pained by delving into the past.

'The most wonderful moment in my life was when I met Rosa. I was twenty-five. On my way to work every morning I used to pass the school where she taught. She always smiled at me, one of those smiles that warms you on a freezing-cold day. It took me three months to pluck up the courage to wave hello, another three to be brave enough to make conversation. I waited for her to come out one evening, with a bunch of roses, and offered to see her home. She didn't live far away, so we walked. When we reached her house she knew everything about me and I knew nothing about her, so I suggested doing the same the next day. I'll never forget the look in her eye when I stepped over to her with those flowers in my hand. Never.'

Sadness descends over the table. Diego puts a hand on his friend's shoulder. I drive away the lump forming in my throat with a mouthful of aquavit.

'Your turn to spin the wheel, Edgar,' Julien whispers.

He goes ahead and Clara has to do a dare.

'Give us ten song titles with one word substituted for another.'

She doesn't stop to think, and I suspect this is the dare she wrote. She comes out with the titles one by one, counting them off on her fingers:

' "Cocking on Heaven's Door"

266

' "Cock on Wood"
' "Rock around the Cock"
' "Jingle Bell Cock"
' "Jailhouse Cock"
' "Beat the Cock"
' "I am a Cock"
' "Cock with You"
' "We Will Cock You"
' "I Love Cock 'n' Roll." '

She comes to a stop with a smug smile on her lips. Diego draws on his pipe in silence, Edgar looks away, Françoise's eyebrows are up on her hairline and her husband has gone bright red. Greg is falling about laughing and I can't help doing the same.

Then it's my turn.

'Truth!' Clara squeals, unfolding the piece of paper. 'Who around this table do you find most attractive?'

I giggle, convinced she's teasing me. But she isn't.

'Julien,' I say before my courage escapes me.

'There, I knew it!' Clara cries.

'Well, there's not a huge amount of choice. Edgar and Diego are very sweet, but the question relates to attraction. François and Greg are married, so that leaves only Julien.'

Julien himself gives a little pout and I realise how untactful I've been.

'No, but that doesn't mean I don't find you attractive, Julien! I was just explaining why I chose you, I didn't mean . . .'

I grind to a halt – my justifications are only digging me in deeper. A gulp of aquavit shuts me up. Clara is weeping with laughter. I spin the wheel.

An hour later, Edgar has done an impression of Angela Merkel, Greg has put his boxers on over his trousers, Diego has described his 'first time', François has cut his chin open trying to do a somersault, Clara has peeled an apple with her teeth, I've confessed to my biggest lie, Julien has run round the caravan park imitating a starving bear and we've been entertained by plenty of other truths and dares.

The bottle is empty, and we are full. It's now Clara's turn to describe her greatest shame.

'Okay, I'll make this short. I was walking along a street and everyone was watching me, and I thought I'd definitely made the right decision putting on my little flowery skirt. I strutted my stuff a bit, walking like a top model, except that after a while the top model realised her skirt was tucked into her knickers and everyone could see her bum.'

Everyone laughed as they pictured the scene, and I tried to offer some comfort.

'It does happen quite a lot, getting skirts caught in knickers . . .'

'Yeeees,' she replies, 'but is there often toilet paper caught in there, too, trailing behind like a train?'

The laughing gets louder and I can't help bursting out laughing, too, so much so my stomach hurts, and Clara's pretence that she's offended as she tries not to join us isn't helping.

'Right, your turn!' she challenges me before we've had a chance to calm down. 'Dare!'

She delves for one of the pieces of paper and reads, 'You have to kiss the person to your right on the mouth.'

I turn to check that the person on my right is still who it was a moment ago – obviously, it's Julien. We're all instantly serious again.

I lean towards him without thinking and give him a peck on the cheek.

'On the mouth!' Françoise slurs.

I chuckle. I feel as if I'm in a trap, but there's still a little play in its jaws.

'Show me the piece of paper, Clara.'

She pretends not to hear me.

'Clara!'

'What?'

'Please can I see the piece of paper.'

'What piece of paper?'

'Stop it,' I say. 'You invented the dare.'

'Nonsense.'

'You do know that, if you lie when you're pregnant, you'll have a fifteen-pound baby, don't you?'

'Nonsense.'

'It's true,' Julien says very earnestly. 'And it'll have a wooden nose.'

I can't help laughing now, and neither can he. Edgar gets to his feet even more slowly than usual.

'I'm going to withdraw to my quarters,' he announces between two hiccups.

'But Anna hasn't done her dare!' Clara protests.

I also stand up and give her a big smile.

'I'm off to bed, too. Goodnight, everyone!'

Julien does the same, then Françoise and François. Clara stays in her chair with her arms crossed. I lean towards her and put my arms around her neck.

'It was a good try.'

'I'll get there before the end of the trip,' she mumbles.

'You really are adorable.'

'Hmm, thanks. You're lucky I like you.'

I whisper a few words in her ear, her face lights up and she gives a little squeak of excitement. I give her a kiss goodnight and head over to my van. The ground is lurching. An arm slips into mine. Julien.

'I'll walk you back. I've heard there are starving bears round here,' he whispers.

'You're right, and Canadians with Texan accents.'

We try to walk straight as we make our way across the site, arm in arm, then he takes his arm away as we approach my door.

'Well, goodnight, then,' he says softly.

'Goodnight, Julien.'

I rummage for the key in my coat pocket and he doesn't move. I turn to look at him and he's staring at me seriously. His hand comes up to my cheek gently and he strokes my face with his thumb. I close my eyes. When I open them again he's smiling at me. He turns and walks off towards his van. Leaving us there – me, my drunkenness and my longing.

The Chloe Chronicles

When Mum said we were going to take the Atlantic Road I couldn't understand why she seemed so excited. Now, I know.

It's a road about eight kilometres long that cuts across a corner of the ocean, occasionally alighting on small islands. So we went over a succession of bridges and reefs with views over the waves, fjords and mountains. We were driving over the sea with the water dancing all around us and spray spattering the windscreen. Mum drove slowly so we could make the most of it, but the most wasn't enough. When we got to the other end we turned round and went back for a second helping.

We were on our third crossing when the phone rang. It was Dad. I answered.

'Hi, Dad! You'll never guess where we are!'

'Hello, sweetheart, tell me all about it. Judging by your voice, it's pretty good!'

I described the scenery as we passed it, giving him every detail. I wanted him to be here with us, in a way. He sighed enviously and I promised to send him loads of photos.

'Thanks, sweetheart. Well, this may not be the right time, but I was calling to tell you something.'

I blocked my other ear with a finger so I could hear him better.

'Is it something bad?'

'No, no, don't worry. It's just . . .'

He took a deep breath. I was terrified.

'It's just, I'm not going to fight for custody after all.'

'Okay,' I replied. 'I think that'll be better, specially as we can come and see you more often now you've got a house.'

'It's a bit complicated . . .'

'How do you mean? What's complicated? You couldn't have us at your place because it was too small, but now you can, so what's the problem?'

I heard him sniff.

'I'm so sorry, sweetheart. I'd really love to have you here several times a month. To be honest, that's what I've always wanted . . .'

'Well, then, why don't you?'

My voice had become squeaky.

'Because your mother won't let me.'

He whispered that last bit. It was almost inaudible and it lacerated my heart. I looked at Mum. Her hands were clamped tensely on the steering wheel.

'Why?' I asked.

'I have no idea. I've been fighting to see you for years, but she doesn't want me to. Promise me you won't talk to her about this, it'll only make things worse. I'm scared she'll stop me even calling you.'

'I'd better go, Dad. Love you.'

'Promise!'

I didn't promise. I hung up, grinding my teeth. I stared at the waves and wanted them to go wild, to hurl themselves on to the rocks, to match the way I felt. Mum didn't say a thing. I tried not to either, to not betray Dad, but I couldn't manage it.

'Why the hell did you do that?' I tore into her.

'Why did I do what?'

'Why've you stopped Dad seeing us? Why don't you want us to go to his house?'

She put a hand on my thigh.

'My darling, I—'

'Oh, for fuck's sake! So it's true? Was he telling the truth?'

I was screaming now. My eyesight was clouding. I wanted her to say it was a misunderstanding, that he was wrong, that she hadn't deliberately kept me from my father for all these years, but that's not what she said.

'We're going to stop a little way ahead and talk about all this. I never wanted to hurt you in any way . . .'

'I couldn't give a stuff about your explanations! I'll never forgive you for what you've done.'

Tears sprang up in my eyes, spilling over my cheeks and down my neck, but they did nothing to ease my pain. Lily turned to face me and looked right into my eyes.

'Have you forgotten, Chloe?' she said. 'Have you really forgotten that Dad used to hit Mum?'

Anna

The music is on full blast in the campervan. The girls and I are singing Francis Cabrel songs at the top of our lungs. I listened to his music so much when they were little they know all the lyrics by heart.

We're just about to set off down the legendary Trolls Road. It's meant making a brief detour, but it would have been unthinkable to miss it. At the first turn in the road we cut the music and our singing, even our breathing.

The road is extremely narrow and clings to the mountainside, enough to make your head spin. We're escorted on the right by a raging torrent.

'Oh, look!' Chloe cries.

There goes one of my eardrums, but never mind. Up ahead, apparently spouting from a dark rock, a huge waterfall launches into the air. It's spectacular.

Chloe rests her head on my shoulder. She's been more affectionate than ever since our conversation the day before yesterday. I didn't go into detail but I did answer her questions. She'd never suspected a thing – she's devastated. The image she had of our family has been atomised. I was wrong to keep it a secret. Lily has also made a point of showing she's on my side – she's given me a handful of 'the softest' pebbles, like when she was little. It never occurred to me that she might remember that day. But she hasn't forgotten a thing.

We go round one hairpin bend after another, not sure where to look because it's all so magnificent. To our right, the rockface in all its steely pride; to our left, thin air and the green valley far below.

We drive past two impressive waterfalls tumbling down the mountainside just metres from us . . . then the third leaves us gaping in amazement. The water lunges down, bouncing from rock to rock, hurling itself, launching itself into the air, spewing clouds of spray amid a deafening roar. It's so beautiful I want to cry.

'I love you two,' Chloe says out of the blue.

'Me, too. I love *you* two,' I reply.

'Same,' says Lily.

And right there, at that exact moment, a wave of happiness washes over me. We're gazing at an exceptional spectacle in a magical setting, we're fit and well, and we're together. How right I was to burst my bubble.

Lily

5 June

Dear Marcel,

How are you? I'm okay, except Mum asked me if I wanted some of the 'lovely local salami' in my sandwich and it turned out it was reindeer meat – when I got the picture postcard I was nearly sick. Sneaky Mum!

We visited the stave church in Urnes. Stave church means it's made of standing wood. I can see you don't really get what that means either, which is reassuring. I'm telling you, they all laughed when I asked if the wood sat down when it got tired. So, as your chief educator, I should tell you that it's called standing wood because the builders used pillars of wood to build the walls, nave and roof. You see, you learn a load of stuff with me, don't you! So anyway, we had a look round it. It's the oldest one in Norway – even older than Nanny – so I showed it a lot of respect. It was really beautiful, considering how old it was, although it was quite cramped inside, but I didn't stay inside long because Noah was happier outside.

We sat down on the grass, looking across the fjord and not saying anything. We didn't need to. I really like Noah, you know. Apart from my family, it's the first time I've loved someone so much – someone who isn't an animal, I mean. He doesn't lie, he's kind and he makes me laugh. He was making these weird noises the other day and, when I giggled, he kept going. I swear he only did it to hear me giggling.

Mum didn't talk to Julien much; she stayed with Chloe because Chloe's sad. She didn't want to tell us why but, in the end, she couldn't help herself, because pain hurts more when it's inside than when it's out. Basically, she found out on Facebook that her boyfriend Kevin's got a new girlfriend so – well, you can imagine. She's been trying not to think about it, but I can see that's not working. Otherwise, she wouldn't keep saying no one's ever going to love her, that she's rubbish and ugly and thick and she'll end up on her own.

And plus, finding out what my dad used to do to my mum hasn't exactly helped – she's convinced the only thing men are any good at is hurting her. Maybe I shouldn't have told her, but I've had to listen to her going on about it for years, saying everything's Mum's fault and poor Dad, and blah

blah blah, so I thought it was my duty free to tell the truth.

It seems Mum thought I'd forgotten coz I was so little, but when you see your mum with blood all over her face, you don't forget – I can tell you. I haven't seen Dad much since then, but he always tries to find out if I remember. He must have thought it was odd that I'm not nice to him, like Chloe. Don't read a book by its cover story – I may not look it but I'm no pushover.

When we left the church and got back on the ferry Chloe started crying. I don't really know what to do when she does that, so I didn't do anything, but when we got back to the campervan I took you out from under my pillow, opened you on the page for 1 May and told her to read it.

So there, you see. I may not have got very far with maths on this trip, but I've come a long way with sisterliness.

With my most sincere good wishes
Lily

PS I've got a hair in my left armpit.

The Chloe Chronicles

Lily told me to read an entry in her diary, but I'm not sure I completely understand: it's addressed to someone called Marcel.

This is what she wrote on 1 May.

Dear Marcel,

I need to talk to you about my sister Chloe. Well, I've already told you stuff about her, but there's even more now.

My sister's the person I've known for the longest, second only to my mother and father, so basically, we've been putting up with each other for donkey work years. That's why we argue a lot (and also coz she's a pain). She whinges and cries, she screams and hogs the bathroom for an hour every morning, she treats me like I'm an idiot and she never wants to play the game where we pretend we can speak English fluently. But still, I could have had a sister who was a serial killer or a maths teacher, so I don't complain too much.

There are loads of good things about her, and not just her figure.

She's a good actress: you should have seen her yesterday when she told my mum she was pregnant — I came a very close shave to giving her a Caesar salad.

She's kind: she pretends not to see the bills that Mum hides in the cupboard (like me) and she always comes and checks how I'm feeling before she goes to bed.

She's intelligent: she won a writing competition last year and she always gets good marks at school. Plus, she can say the whole alphabet in burps.

She's generous: she gave me a chip once.

I don't know how she can't see all this for herself, coz I see this stuff far more than her hair and her eyes. Do you know something? When I've had enough of being weird (which is what people at school say I am), I'd like to be like her. But if you ever tell anyone, I'll have to burn you.

Lily x

PS Mathias says hi.

I took pictures of the pages, afraid I wouldn't believe it if I tried to remember what she'd written. Lily came and joined me on the bed.

'I didn't know you saw me like that,' I said.

'I asked Marcel not to tell you, the little sneak.'

I smiled. She didn't say anything else, but the message got across. Those words were the 'I love you' she couldn't actually say.

I remembered Louis's poems: naïve, simple and plagiarised, but so sincere they were disarming. Anonymous letters that never expected a reply.

A nine-year-old boy and a twelve-year-old girl have just taught me something: you can love without reciprocation.

Anna

I just can't get to sleep tonight because there's been quite an upheaval today.

When Clara knocked on the door of the van this morning I immediately understood. Her eyes were red and she had her hands over her stomach.

'Are you leaving?'

She couldn't get a word out in reply. She nodded her head and dissolved into tears. I invited her in.

'Okay, but just for a minute,' she sniffled. 'I need to help Greg tidy everything. We don't want to set off too late. Will we see each other again?'

The girls emerged from their bed, Lily with an I'm-not-happy forehead.

'Of course we'll see each other again! Toulouse isn't far from Biarritz!'

'Why aren't you finishing the trip?' Chloe wanted to know.

'It took me a while to get used to the idea of having a baby, but I'm ready now. I want to go home so I can give everyone the news and get everything organised.'

Clara hugged my two girls.

'I'm going to miss you so much!'

I joined in, struggling not to cry.

'It was really great meeting you,' I murmured, and I felt Clara squeeze my arm.

Just before they left we went over to say one last goodbye. The whole group had gathered outside their van. The sky was in a dismal mood – very apt.

They took their time getting going. There were endless hugs, countless promises, a lot of reminiscing. There was a feeling of something coming to an end.

It felt like saying goodbye to old friends. It won't be the same without them. Lily said the best people were going first, Françoise pretended to take offence and everyone laughed. Laughter's the best stand-in for tears.

They eventually drove away. Leaving a gaping void. I went back to the campervan to keep my low mood to myself. I'd hardly got inside before my phone buzzed with a new message. From Clara.

'I forgot: best of luck with Julien!'

I missed her already.

After that we visited Bergen. Lily loved the Bryggen district with its strings of colourful houses and its streets paved with wood. She even announced that all streets should be covered in wood because it wouldn't hurt so much when you fell off your bike. Chloe couldn't get enough of the trip in the funicular to the top of a hill with fabulous views over the city – that girl was born to travel.

We stopped off at the fish market and bought our sandwiches for lunch. I honestly thought Lily was going to cry when she saw that you could have whale meat in them.

The girls went to sleep early, but I can't get to sleep. I keep thinking about Clara and Greg, about people we chance across who have more of an impact on our lives than those who are part of them. I think about how paths cross and then go their separate ways. And about my girls, who'll leave some day. Soon. I need some fresh air.

I pick up my phone and type out the message. The answer comes immediately. He can't sleep either.

I put on my coat and boots and slip out quietly. Julien's outside already, his pyjamas poking out from under his jeans.

'What's the emergency?' he asks.

'I'm down in the dumps.'

He smiles.

'Shall we walk?' he suggests.

'Okay.'

The road isn't lit, but the day is still eking out its light.

'What's on your mind?'

'Watching my daughters grow up. I know it's stupid, there's nothing anyone can do about it, but whenever I think of them as babies I feel like crying. It all went so quickly . . .'

'I understand. Time really does fly. It feels like Noah was born yesterday.'

'That's it. I feel I haven't made the most of them and

here we are already, they'll be leaving home tomorrow. I can't get used to the idea.'

As these words come out of my mouth I appreciate the situation.

'Oh, Julien, I'm so sorry! How tactless of me to complain about my daughters becoming independent . . .'

'You're right. I do sort of have the opposite problem – my boy may never be independent, he won't be leaving home and that's what keeps me awake at night. But I still understand how you feel. I get all nostalgic about the past, too, the days when I could hold him in my arms without him treading on my feet!'

This makes me smile.

'When Lily was five her teacher told us she was autistic. She didn't interact with the other children, hardly talked, played with pebbles and couldn't bear to be touched. I was really worried, but after a few months the specialists reassured me. Looking back, I think I was mostly frightened she'd be rejected but also – and I'm ashamed of this – that she wasn't a normal little girl.'

'It's not as bad as all that, you know,' Julien says. 'Quite the opposite. When we were given the diagnosis with Noah my world fell apart. It took me a long time to accept that my child wasn't like other children. We're afraid of difference, so we reject it. In the end, he was the one who showed me the way. He couldn't care less about the teasing – he's impervious to nastiness. He's not unhappy – I'd even say he's happy. So no, I may never be able to show him how to build spaceships with Lego, I may never meet his girlfriends, but he's crazy about his top, he adores watching the moon travel across the sky, he's passionate about lightning. He's taught me a lot.'

We keep walking in silence. I chew over my ignorance, digest my prejudices; you could say Noah's taught me a lot, too. My daughters' happiness must be the only thing that matters.

'Shall we head back?' I suggest. 'We've come quite a long way, haven't we?'

Julien doesn't reply. He stands squarely in front of me and looks at me seriously. His face is a few centimetres from mine. He puts his hand on my cheek, his thumb strokes my lips. His eyes are ablaze with desire. He moves closer, I can feel his warm breath on my skin. His hand eases round to the back of my neck and threads through my hair. I shudder. He pulls me close and I close my eyes as his mouth finds mine.

The Chloe Chronicles

Dad wouldn't stop calling, but I didn't pick up. He sent a text to say he was worried and we needed to send some sign of life. I called back, and he definitely got proof that I was alive.

'I don't want to talk to you right now. I need time – it's a lot to digest.'

At first he denied everything. It wasn't true, he would never raise a hand against anyone, he couldn't even squash a spider, so he'd never . . . Mum was lying, she'd found a new way to come between us. He started crying, but he stopped when I told him Lily clearly remembered his threats.

'It didn't happen a lot,' he said, in a stifled whisper.

'That's still too much. And you killed Brownie! You disgust me.'

He promised he'd changed, he was a completely different person, he'd acknowledged how wrong he was. His voice was very shaky. Mine wasn't, but my heart was. I wanted to both hug him and spit at him. I was angry with him, and I felt sorry for him. I ended the call asking him not to call me again and saying I'd be in touch when

I'm ready. He said he loved me. I said, 'Me, too,' but not out loud.

Mum was happy for me to walk around Bergen on my own. I decided to take the bus because the site is about half an hour's walk away and I didn't feel like walking. Then I saw Louise was waiting at the bus stop and decided half an hour wasn't all that long a walk after all. Since our bout of hysterics over her moustache we've been getting on better, but not enough to spend a day together. The problem was, she'd seen me and she suggested coming with me. So we did the walk together, and the rest of the day, too.

We stopped for a rest at Byparken, a big flower-filled park with lots of benches, and we cadged cigarettes off a group of teenage boys. One of them couldn't stop looking at me, and I liked it.

'Do you have a boyfriend?' Louise asked when we sat down.

'I did, but it's over.'

'Shit. Over as in over over?'

'Yup. He posted on Facebook that he's got a new girlfriend.'

'Ouch.'

'Yup. How about you? Got someone?'

'Yes. We've been together three years now. We're going to get married next year.'

'Congratulations! But that doesn't surprise me.'

She raised her eyebrows.

'Really? Why?' she asked, blowing out smoke.

'I dunno, you're obviously quite focused, good at everything.'

She gave a little laugh then pushed up the sleeve of her coat.

'So good that I got this wrong.'

There was a raw new scar right across her wrist. I threw my cigarette away.

'Why did you do that?'

'Because I felt terrible, it was like I was at the bottom of a pit and I'd never be able to get out. The worst thing was how guilty I felt because everything around me seemed so right: I had a wonderful boyfriend, fantastic parents, good marks at school, but I dunno, I felt so empty. Like I couldn't be bothered with anything. It was like I was shut away from everyone else, so alone. I don't think I really wanted to die – well, if that *was* what I wanted, I didn't realise it. I just wanted the feeling sad to end.'

'I suppose your parents didn't notice anything. I get the feeling they work long hours . . .'

'Are you joking? Yes, they work a lot, but they're there for us big time. When I did this bollocks,' she said, gesturing to her wrist, 'they dropped everything to have this road trip with us – they knew I had this real thing about seeing the northern lights. They're convinced nature can help me and that, for me, all our money has got in the way of what life really means.'

'Well, you can tell them that, for me, it's lack of money that's got in the way.'

She laughed, and so did I. Our lives are poles apart – money isn't a problem for her, she feels she matters to both her parents and she has someone who loves her – but it could be me saying the things she's saying. Shut away. Empty. Alone.

We caught the bus back just before supper. I thought about things all the way back. When I opened the door to the campervan Mum smiled at me and Lily pounced on me, saying there was something she just had to tell me.

Maybe I'm not really alone.

Maybe it's just an impression.

Maybe it's time I got that impression in a fierce ju-jitsu hold.

Lily

8 June

Morn, Marcel,

   Hvordan har du det? (That's 'Hi, Marcel, How are you?' in Norwegian) (I now know a few words in German, Danish, Swedish and Norwegian) (I'm polygamous).

   I'm fine, but I am a bit sad. This trip's nearly over – we only have three more days before we leave Norway. Do you remember I thought my mum had lost the plot when we set out? Now I wish it could go on longer – it's all gone too quickly. We should be able to relive our favourite bits. But hey, there's no point whining. I'm not in charge of time.

   We spent the night near the Langfossen falls, which Mum really wanted to see because it's one of the most beautiful waterfalls in the world. And it was seriously beautiful. It's very very very very very high and it drops down into a fjord. All that water gushing down, almost like when my sister cries.

Seeing as it was a nice day and we'd soon have to say goodbye, Julien suggested we all slept together, in sleeping bags outside. He had some foam mat things. Everyone except for the two oldies said yes (they said their bones wouldn't win the fight with the hard ground), so we all set up near their van so they could still sort of be part of it. It was the first time I'd slept outside.

I was between Noah and my mum, who was next to Louise, who was next to her brother. Noah and me looked up at the sky. It was night-time but not completely dark and the stars weren't out because the sun wasn't properly down. Julien, who was on Noah's other side, kept telling jokes, and all the grown-ups laughed. Then they started telling scary stories. I pretended I was fine with it, but I wasn't really. Françoise said that once this old lady in the street followed her all the way home and kept calling her Michelle, and when she went inside and drew the curtains the lady was standing out in the garden looking up at her. Exactly as she said this we heard a cracking sound nearby and my heart hopscotched a beat, I tell you. I stopped listening to them after that. I took Noah's hand and hummed songs to him, I think he liked it.

We didn't get much sleep and, in the morning, no one had moved, except Mum, who'd gone over next to Julien because he had a pillow.

You know, Marcel, I'm not exactly going to say I like people now, but these particular people . . . well, I'd be very happy to sleep with them every night.

Lily xx

PS Edgar and I did a competition to see who could touch their nose with their tongue, and I nearly won but he took his dentures out.

Anna

On paper, this seemed like a good idea. A short walk to get to an incomparable view was acceptable – tempting, even. Everyone had told me the same thing: if I didn't see Preikestolen – a cliff nearly 600 metres high that towers over Lysefjord – the whole trip would have been wasted.

Everyone had also told me this: the climb was easy, accessible to anyone.

Well, I'm clearly not anyone. After ten minutes I already want a new pair of lungs.

The girls, meanwhile, are storming ahead as if we're on flat ground – they're practically whistling. Noah's almost running. And don't even mention Louis, who thinks he's a greyhound.

So yes, fine, the lakes, waterfalls and forests we pass are probably very pretty, but Julien said we should do the climb at night to avoid the crowds and so we could watch the sunrise from the top, which means I can only imagine these views. It's not totally dark and we have headlamps, but all I can see are the rocks underfoot.

After half an hour Françoise asks for a break. I feel like kissing her. François says, 'Maybe a bit later.'

I've never been very sporty. My work was physical, and I quite often came home stiff and cramped after a shift. At twenty-five, it wasn't a problem, but I'm no longer twenty-five. In the last few months at the restaurant I could feel my stamina flagging. I'd get out of breath and I regularly had sprains. We must all have a bank balance of fitness, and I'm now overdrawn.

'You okay?' Julien asks.

'Fine,' I say, out of breath. 'Preikestolen had better live up to its reputation, or I'll smash its face in.'

He laughs as he hands me a water bottle.

'You'll see – it really is worth it. We're nearly there.'

Nearly.

Julien's a liar. I've had more than enough opportunity to twist my ankle eighteen times, fall twice, think I was breathing my last a million times and have an urge to push Louis over the edge too many times. It's an endless succession of steep paths and piles of stones. Up and up it climbs; it just keeps on climbing. I can't feel my thighs, my calves or my buttocks. All I can feel is regret for getting up at one o'clock in the morning to do this.

'Do you need some help, Mum?' Chloe offers.

'No, why?'

'I dunno, you look tired.'

'No, I'm fine. I feel great.'

I feel great for someone who's about to die.

Ten minutes later it's Lily's turn to slow down till she's

level with me. I expect her to ask whether I need a heart massage, but no.

'Could you carry my bag, Mum? It's hurting my shoulders.'

My maternal instincts are faster than I am, so I agree and take the bag.

'Wow, it's heavy! What have you got in here?'

'I've picked up loads of pretty pebbles,' she says, haring on ahead of me.

Three hours.

After three hours of toil that should have earned me an Olympic title (or an amputation), we catch sight of the famous cliff. Preikestolen means 'Pulpit Rock' because the top of it is flat, forming a sort of terrace. Just a few more steps and we'll be there.

The sky is lighter than when we set off, a deep blue, not unlike Chloe's eyes. Two men have spent the night up here in tents. I drop my two bags to the ground, then collapse on the ground myself, my arms flung out to form a cross. A few clouds drift slowly overhead. Chloe sits down next to me.

'Get up, Mum. Look how beautiful it is!'

I sit up just as the first sunbeams break over the horizon.

'Are you going to join us, Lily?'

She whispers something in Noah's ear and comes over to us.

The sun emerges slowly from its hiding place behind

the mountains in the distance. The sky blazes and the whole scene is tinged with gold.

We're on top of this incredible rock and, far below, the fjord comes awake. Boats look tiny, trees microscopic. The wind slaps at our cheeks. It's quite magnificent. They say climbing Preikestolen changes your life. And it's a mind-blowing experience – unforgettable.

I stay there for a while with Chloe's head on my shoulder and Lily's hand in mine . . . and I'm overcome with emotion.

My girls.

My babies.

My rocks.

Anna

'So, you see, girls, this road trip was a metaphor for life.'

'What's a metaphor?' Lily asks.

'It's like a comparison, an image,' Chloe explains. 'Why's it like a metaphor, Mum?'

'Because we've had the break-in, the breakdown, panic attacks, arguments, revelations about your father, the cold, fear and exhaustion but, at the end of the day, what we'll remember are the northern lights, swimming in ice-cold lakes, the midnight sun, the fake pregnancy, the waterfalls, the colourful houses, the laughter, the karaoke evening, Noah's spinning top, the nights we've spent together and singing at the top of our lungs on the road.'

The girls don't say anything for a moment. Chloe puts her arms around my neck and plants a kiss on my cheek.

'You're right, Mum,' Lily says with a smile. 'It's a very good metafive.'

Anna

It's our last night before the ferry crossing back to Denmark, from where we'll drive home to France. We went to bed late after an evening spent with the whole group reminiscing over the trip. Lily and Chloe have been chatting in their bed. I thought they'd never fall asleep. The thing is, I've got a date.

Very softly, and listening to their breathing the whole time, I slip out of my bed, pull on a coat and leave the campervan. Julien isn't here yet. I wait for him with an idiotic smile on my face – I feel about the same age as my girls.

When he arrives – on tiptoe and carrying a big bag – I feel like a girl sneaking out of my parents' house to meet a boy.

We decide not to go too far so we would hear the children should anything happen. We find a clearing reasonably close to our campervans, and a few minutes later our tent is ready, equipped with a huge sleeping bag, a bottle of wine and some chocolates. He even thought to bring pillows for the sake of our necks – which aren't as young as they used to be.

I don't know what's giving me more of a buzz: the way we're hiding, the fact this is a million miles from my everyday life, or Julien himself. After just one chocolate we throw ourselves at each other eagerly, our clothes fly off, his hands are all over me, his tongue devours me and our skin comes blissfully into contact. I feel beautiful, and I press myself up against him and moan with pleasure when he eases inside me.

'That was magical,' Julien whispers, stroking my back.

'Oh yes,' I say, breathless and ecstatic, my face pressed up against the fabric of the tent and a stone digging into my ribs.

We spend the night talking, laughing and making love. I snuggle in his arms, revelling in his tenderness and his gentle voice, trying to have my fill of him before leaving.

'We need to go,' he says, giving me one last hug, 'Noah will be awake soon.'

I bury my head against his neck and steal a few more seconds, then I slowly uncurl my aching limbs.

'I'm glad we did this trip with you,' he whispers, sitting up.

I stroke his cheek without a word. A stroke to say, 'Me, too,' but there's too big a lump in my throat for me to talk. A stroke to say, 'It was wonderful.' A stroke to mean, 'See you soon.'

The Chloe Chronicles

It was hard leaving them at Kristiansand. We were all meant to get the ferry to Denmark together, but at the last minute Mum said she wanted to take Lily and me to Oslo, which was more than four hours away. So our paths diverged there, and I wasn't ready for it.

I like the beginnings of relationships. Meeting people, getting to know them, showing them something of myself.

I don't like the end of relationships. Saying goodbye, stopping seeing people when you've come so far with them.

I gave Diego a big kiss and thanked him for his advice. He doesn't know how much he and Edgar shook me up. If I had a great-grandfather, I'd want it to be him. I'll never forget him. Edgar seemed tired. I promised I'd write to them. I know I won't keep the promise, so I kissed them again.

François and Françoise told me that I'd done a lot for their daughter and I was a 'splendid young lady'. I tried not to show it (I mean, 'splendid young ladies' don't cry), but I was touched.

Louise was hanging back slightly, waiting her turn. She

was keeping it under control, but her eyes looked so sad. She gave me a kiss on each cheek then, in a quavering little voice, she said, 'It was great meeting you, you slag.'

I gave her a big hug and added her as a friend on Facebook.

Louis handed me an envelope. I didn't open it in front of him, but I knew what was inside it. I kissed his forehead and whispered, 'Thank you, little poet.' He went bright red and chuckled.

I went over to Julien and Noah, who were saying their goodbyes to Mum and Lily.

Lily whispered something in Noah's ear, then she planted a kiss on his cheek and hurried off to the rest of the group.

Mum was trying to smile. I couldn't hear what Julien was saying to her, but I spotted their hands half touching. The campervan-whisperer promised me we'd see each other again soon. They don't live far away and Lily's planning to go and play with Noah. It didn't feel right to give him a hug, so I just said that was nice and left them there, privately thinking that I was actually going to miss his lumberjack shirts.

They all waved exaggeratedly as we headed off to Oslo. Mum dissolved into tears. So did Lily. So did I.

Anna

I don't want to go home. I want to do a U-turn, head back to the North Cape and start the trip again, but the envelope is nearly empty. We've got to take off our fancy dress and get back into everyday clothes.

Chloe tries to comfort us by saying we shouldn't be sad but happy because we've had such good times. Lily says life really is stingy for shooting by so quickly. I don't say anything. Chloe's basically right, and I'm trying to be light-hearted, but nostalgia's already leaning hard on my shoulders. I'm sure the three of us will have plenty more happy times, but we'll never have these times again: the ones I've just shared with seventeen-year-old Chloe and twelve-year-old Lily. They're unique experiences, unlike anything before or after. And as of now, they're just memories. I've tried to press the pause button several times, but it didn't work. I'll never get enough of them.

As an excuse to have a two-day extension, I've dredged up what I remembered of an article I once read about a park in Oslo.

After four hours on the road going over our reminiscences, we reach Oslo early in the afternoon. It takes another hour to find somewhere to park.

'It was better with Julien around,' Chloe says.

I avoid the temptation to agree with her.

'Is this the Vigelandsparken?' Lily asks as we go through the gate.

'It is indeed.'

We're walking along the path, pausing here and there to admire the art. The park is dotted with huge Gustav Vigeland sculptures of naked men, women and children.

'It's amazing!' Chloe exclaims. 'They look so real.'

She's right. Their faces are expressive and their bodies realistic. The sculptures represent scenes from everyday life, some funny, some poignant, like the one of an old man holding his frail wife in his arms; the couple welcoming their child into the world; the woman consoling another woman with a hand on her head; the two old women, one with a hand over her mouth as if she's forgotten something; and the three people forming the wheel of life. Each sculpture exudes emotion, but Lily, Chloe and I are immersed in emotions, too. A mother holding her baby with outstretched arms, her face lit up with joy. A mother consoling a crying child who has her arms over her face. But more than any of the others, the mother walking with her hair streaming behind her, pressing her child's body to her face, and the child's arms around her neck, his head resting on hers. We come to a halt when we see it. The girls don't say anything, but I think we're feeling the same thing. This woman's strength, her concern, her love for her child, the bond they have, which is indissoluble, come what may. The bond between a mother and her child, between the mother who will love that child more than anyone else and the child who will be her greatest love.

We go back to the campervan later after eating smoked herring in Oslo's port and wandering through the busy streets trying and failing to muster a feeling of cheerfulness. The sky has darkened to match our mood and is now spitting, forcing us to hurry along. By the time we get back we're soaked, and we've only just changed when a violent thunderstorm erupts.

The three of us huddle together in the bed. I don't hear the thunder rumbling or the rain thrashing on the roof and I don't see the lightning. Instead, I feel Lily's feet moving and Chloe's breath against my neck. I smell vanilla in their hair and feel the warmth of them against me. I'm aware of my arms going numb under their weight and my heart surging with happiness.

I think I know now, we don't need to chase any more stars – they're right here.

The Chloe Chronicles

We got up early, planning to visit more of Oslo. We
hadn't had much sleep because the storm had gone on
for a long time.

'I hope you're proud of yourself, Mum,' Lily said suddenly over breakfast.

'Proud of what?'

'Well, because there was a thunderstorm and it was
just the three of us and you didn't even have a panic
attack.'

Mum didn't say anything, but it was obvious she was
proud, too.

We were about to leave the van when the phone rang.
Mum picked up, but I couldn't work out who she was
talking to. It wasn't someone she knew well – she was
using her slightly posy voice – but it wasn't someone she
disliked either.

'That was your headmaster,' she said when she hung
up. 'We need to talk.'

So we talked. Monsieur Martin had reminded her that
my first exam was in three days' time, and he wanted to
check that I hadn't changed my mind. She's asked me

about this several times during the trip, and I've stuck to my decision. What's the point? The only thing that made me waver slightly was that I wanted to please Mum. But that wasn't enough of a reason.

'You're right,' she agreed. 'That's not enough of a reason. You must do things for yourself.'

'Right . . . and, for me personally, I can't see the point in taking these exams.'

She smiled.

'It would probably make it easier for you to get work in Australia.'

'What?'

'You sit your exams, and then you're off – that's the deal.'

'But, how do you . . . what? Did Diego dob me in?'

She didn't say it was him, but her smile didn't deny it.

'Well, I won't be going,' I announced.

'Chloe, there's no way you can sacrifice your dreams for me. I don't need you, I just need to know you're happy, even if that means you're the other side of the world. And anyway, I've always wanted to see the Great Barrier Reef. How about you, Lily?'

'And kangaroos! And koalas! When are you leaving?'

'We're going to take care of all that,' Mum said. 'But you're going to sit your exams first. We've got two days to get home. We can't waste a minute.'

I didn't have time to think and, suddenly, there we were on the ferry taking us away from Norway. I kept my eyes pinned on that beautiful country until it was lost in the haze. I wanted to give it the goodbye it deserved.

Once I was inside I went straight on to the phone so that I didn't have to face up to my thoughts. There was a new message from Kevin.

'Hi, when r u back?'

I tilted the screen so Mum couldn't see it and pinged off my answer: 'Hey! I'll be back the day after tomorrow. Why?'

His reply came straight back: 'I'd really like to c u, can I come over to yours?'

I thought about it for several minutes. I thought about things Mum had said, things Diego had said, the way Kevin looked at me, Louis's poems, Lily's diary, Kevin's hands, and I said yes.

Lily

13 June

Dear Marcel

The trip's over. We're almost in Germany, Mum's driving the whole time and we're hardly stopping at all – we need to get back in time for Chloe's exams.

I'm really really really really sad, you know. I'm not saying I don't like our life at home, but it wasn't the same. Mum was always at work, my sister never talked to me and spent the whole time in her room, and plus, I had to go to school. I really hope things are going to be different – Mum's promised she won't do evening shifts any more and Chloe's changed. And that's a relief. She was definitely on a downward spiralizer.

The hardest part was saying goodbye to Noah. I really miss him already. He didn't talk, but I still understood everything he said to me. I know he understood me, too. I told him he was the best person I'd met in the whole of my long life and I gave him a kiss. He didn't back away and I get the feeling he smiled. But I'm going to stop talking about him because my eyes are dissolving.

I remember when his dad told us he was different. Well, he was wrong. Noah's not different, he's better.

Mum asked if I was looking forward to going back to school. There's only three weeks left because, after that, the older kids have got their exams. I thought about it for a while and said yes. If I stay at home, I'll have to kill time and I don't like violence.

I'll be off then, Marcel, I want to watch the scenery go by.

Lily xx

PS You're almost finished, but I'll never abandon you.

Anna

It's strange coming home but not feeling at home. The apartment's cloaked in darkness and feels hot. I close the door behind us, and the silence is palpable. No wind blowing, no birds singing, no engines running.

'What do we do now?' Lily asks.

'We open the shutters.'

We go round opening all the windows to let in the air and start shuttling backwards and forwards between the parking space and the apartment, which gradually fills with bags, souvenirs, food and life. The trolls I bought in Lofoten find their place above the TV straight away. Lily lines up her pebbles on the rug in the living room.

The letterbox is full and I put its contents on to the table without opening it. Chloe goes off to her room to revise. But comes back three minutes later to settle on the sofa. I look at our suitcases, all waiting to be emptied, and sit down next to her.

'Do you need any help?'

'No, it's fine. But I'm a bit hungry.'

Ten minutes later I've cooked some pasta and there's scalded water all over the hob – I've got so used to my little electric hob. We open a tin of herring and eat in silence, sitting on the floor around the coffee table in the living room.

We go to bed early. Chloe has a philosophy exam in the morning and Lily's going back to school.

Lily's nose and eyes are all I can see above the duvet.

'Aren't you hot?' I ask.

'Yes, but it reminds me of being there.'

I give her a kiss on the forehead and wish her goodnight.

'Could you leave the door open please, Mum?'

Chloe's lying on her stomach, lost in her revision notes.

'You should get some sleep.'

'I'm going to read it through once more, then I'll switch the light off, I promise.'

'Goodnight, my big girl.'

'Goodnight, Mum.'

My throat feels horribly tight as I head to my bedroom. There's a whole corridor and the living room between us – I won't hear their breathing tonight. The bed feels enormous and I curl up right over to one side.

I've almost surrendered to sleep when I hear padding footsteps. My bedroom door opens and Lily's outline appears. Then Chloe's. I shift to the middle of the bed and open my arms. Lily's on my left and Chloe on my right, snuggled right up to me. Now we can sleep.

The Chloe Chronicles

I had stomach ache. Mum had gone to get bread and fruit and had made a nice breakfast, but I couldn't eat a thing. She slipped a banana into my bag.

I took the bus with Lily: I sat with Karim and Ines, and she sat with Clelia. Her school's before mine and she blew me a kiss before she got off.

It felt weird being back – my head wasn't really there yet. I looked closely at all those people I've come such a long way with but don't really know. The tall, dark-haired boy with his Star Wars T-shirt and his baseball cap down over his ears; the shy-looking girl with the glasses; and the one who never stops smiling and keeps changing her hairstyle. Would I get on with them if we'd done a road trip together? Would we have realised we have lots in common? Do we often let possible friendships pass us by?

Dad had texted me to say he was thinking of me and keeping his fingers crossed. I thanked him and sent a kiss.

'Aha, back from the dead!' someone said.

My whole class was waiting for me outside and they gathered around me in a circle.

'So what was it like?'

'Did you really go to the North Pole?'

'Did you see any polar bears?'

'Why did you run away like that?'

I gave them brief replies and showed them a few pictures, although they didn't seem to take it in properly. I listened as they told me about their plans, the courses they hoped to do at uni, their hopes for the future, and I felt for the first time that we weren't just children in grown-up clothing. We were there now. It was time to spread our wings.

'Can we think without other people?'

That was the subject of the essay. Mum had said, 'Definitely not,' Lily had thought absolutely, yes . . . luckily, I had some arguments to support my answer.

I made a detour via the bakery on the way home. Kevin was putting pastries into the oven, and we smiled at each other. His hair was different; it looked nice. We'll be seeing each other soon.

Mum was waiting for me at home with lots of information about Australia. She'd found an organisation that handles visa applications, identifies host families until you have accommodation, lists colleges that offer English classes and can also find casual work for you. I just need to be eighteen – and that's next month.

'It's the working holiday visa you mentioned,' she said.

'You go on an English course, you work to pay your way and you can travel. You can even move from city to city as much as you like.'

'And I can stay a year?'

She nodded.

Lily was next to us, doing her homework. When she saw that I'd eaten both ends of the baguette she flew into a terrible rage.

'You took the best bits!'

I didn't say anything, but she hadn't finished with me.

'You only ever think about yourself! You're so selfish!'

'Oh, come on, give me a break. It's only bread.'

'Calm down, girls,' Mum said firmly.

'It's not me,' I said. 'Lily's the one who's up on her high horse.'

'I haven't got any horses, I was just saying you're really selfish, and that's what I think!'

She went off to her room and slammed the door loudly, just in case we didn't know how she felt. Mum shrugged her shoulders.

'I hope nothing happened to her at school.'

I went to find Lily in her room . . . but it took me a while because she was in her wardrobe, sitting between a coat and a dress.

'What are you doing in there?' I asked.

'Nothing.'

'Do you want to talk?'

'No.'

'Do you want me to leave you alone?'

'No.'

'Well, what do you want?'

'I don't want you to go.'

Lily

17 June

Dear Marcel,

I hope you're okay. I'm all right but not all right all at the same time.

Mum still hasn't unpacked the suitcases – they're all over the place. She says she doesn't have time, but I say she doesn't want to do it because, once she does, we'll really, definitely, totally be home.

We went to take the camper back to Pops, and he was pleased to see us – specially because there wasn't a single scratch on it.

They wanted to hear everything, and we told them pretty much everything (but we'd all agreed not to tell them about Mathias the rat – I wouldn't tell anyone that, even if they put corkscrews on my thumbs). They liked the trolls we gave them, but they really weren't into the fermented herring. We showed them loads of photos on Chloe's phone. There were even videos of waterfalls but, tbh, I don't see the point because it's nothing like the real thing. It's like watching someone eat – it always makes you hungry.

On the subject of food, Granny Jeannette had made waffles for us, and I ate four, one with sugar, one with jam, one with chocolate and one with all three, but afterwards it was back-payment time from my stomach. Just as well the waffles weren't good – otherwise, I dread to think . . .

Chloe talked about Australia, and I'm starting to get used to the idea (mind you, I'm hoping she'll be attacked by a crocodile and come home straight away). Even with a leg missing, she'd still be my sister.

I like going to my grandparents', but I also like leaving their house, because I never feel quite right there. I think it's because of their big brown furniture and Jeannette's wool-craft pictures. The one in the living room is of a dog. You should see it's face – like it ran into a window (several times). And don't even mention the big clock that goes tick-tock and all the doilies. Basically, it feels like being in a house from the Middle Ages, and they are *not* middle aged. I hope I don't get old when I'm old.

Have you noticed I'm having to write really small? It's coz I don't want to finish you and you've

only got a few pages left. Maybe it would be better
if I only put the consonants?
  Keep smiling, Marcel
  Lily xx

PS I won't put a PS today to save space.

Anna

Monsieur Fox arrives bang on time with his briefcase and his spray-on smile.

'Hello, Madame Moulineau,' he says, offering his hand to shake. 'Is your daughter here?'

I smile privately, remembering the reception Lily gave him.

'No, don't worry, she isn't.'

We sit in the living room, and he takes out several files and spreads them over the coffee table.

'As I explained on the phone, because the bank has blocked your direct debits, your debts are mounting up. Do you have a solution, Madame Moulineau?'

I applied for about ten jobs yesterday, in various fields: cleaning, care work, secretarial. One cleaning company called me back and the young woman told me they were interested in me for cleaning private homes. The hours were flexible, I could choose to work full- or part-time and it paid the minimum wage. I'm going for a trial tomorrow – thoroughly cleaning one room and doing some ironing   but she assured me this was just a formality.

I thought it over. With that job, I'd be earning less than at the restaurant, but I did have a solution so I grabbed my phone and called before I changed my mind.

'Mathias, it's Anna.'

'Hi, Anna! How are you?'

His voice was bright and cheerful, as if we were old friends, as if nothing had happened.

'I'm fine. You do know that I've always tried to understand you, I've never wanted to be hard on you or to make you pay for anything, I—'

'Okaaaay, this isn't sounding good . . .'

His voice sounded more clipped now. I swallowed hard. Even on the far side of the country, even seven years later, I was frightened his fist could reach me.

'Mathias, you know I'm really struggling to make ends meet. I can't cope any more. I've never asked you for anything, I knew you weren't working and it was tough for you, too, and I didn't want to add to your problems, but apparently you've got a good income now so . . .'

He gave a sort of snigger. It certainly didn't sound like a laugh.

'Your little trip's cleaned you out so you want to come and leech off me, do you?'

I paused for a moment. What was I expecting?

'You know this money isn't for me, Mathias. You're their father. You need to help support them, even though you don't live with them. I could have asked a judge to force you to make payments right from the start, but—'

'How much?' he interrupted.

'I think maybe . . .'

'Chloe's old enough now – she can work – but I'll give you something for Lily. I'll look into it and let you know.'

An hour later he messaged me saying he'd give me two hundred euros a month and, in exchange, he wanted to come and see them from time to time. I agreed, on condition that I was around for his visits.

Monsieur Fox gives a little cough, tearing me away from my thoughts. He's waiting for my reply.

'I can't pay everything back at once, as you'd like me to, but I'll commit to starting my monthly payments again and I can give you a hundred euros a month towards the debts.'

He heaves a big sigh.

'Madame Moulineau, I've kept my client waiting for three months now with promises that you would clear the debt.'

'I know, but that's the best I can offer.'

'That puts me in a very awkward position . . .'

'I'm really sorry.'

'Well,' he says briskly, getting to his feet, 'we'll have to start proceedings to get an injunction to make you pay. I'm sorry I ever trusted you.'

'I promise I'll be true to my word. I'll make all my monthly payments on time. I'm sure you'll be able to persuade your client that a guaranteed payment is the best solution – even if it does take a long time.'

He ignores me and heads for the door. The time has come to use the secret weapon Françoise supplied me with.

'Monsieur Fox, I've asked a solicitor for advice, and she explained that, given my income and my outgoings, I could apply to the Bank of France for a debt burden moratorium, the application would be accepted and my debts would be frozen until my circumstances improve. I don't want to resort to that – I took out this loan and I intend to repay it – but you must have faith in me.'

He leans on the door handle without a word . . . then turns round.

'Can I ask you something?' he says.

'Of course.'

'We were meant to have a meeting nearly three months ago, when you claimed you had the necessary funds to pay off your debt in its entirety, but you cancelled the meeting. It wasn't true, was it?'

'It was. I really did have the money.'

'Well then, I don't understand. Why didn't you use the opportunity to get rid of this debt?'

I think about how best to formulate my reply, but it pops out of its own accord, 'Because I used it to do something more important.'

Lily

20 June

Dear Marcel,

  I hope you can read this. In the end, I decided against writing just the consonants, it would be too hard to understand, so I'm writing teeny-tiny.

  I just wanted to say I'm really happy. I went to Clelia's house this afternoon. Her dad asked if I'd seen any Vikings and then went back to his old friend the TV, so we were free to play with the rats. It turns out Prattle and Drat have had more babies while I was away and Clelia kept one for me coz she knows me so well.

  You wouldn't believe what a fight I had getting Mum to agree. Luckily, I've got more than one violin to my bow and I managed to get her to see that it really really really matters. Fine, I had to promise he'll never come out of my bedroom when she's at home, but I'm sure she'll get used to him with time. I'd like to make you guess what I've called him, but we haven't got room for that so I'll just tell you: he's called Rat-a-tat-tat. Actually, he's walking over the right-hand page at the moment, so I hope you two get along okay. Oh, btw, Chloe called Diego and Edgar to find out how it went when they got back. We kept their secret till the very end, but we wanted to hear what happened. It turns out that, because of their bank card and the campervan's GPS, everyone knew where they were, and they didn't even need to search for them. In the end, the director didn't file a complaint, but he doesn't want them in his retirement home. They'll have to find somewhere else and, apparently, it won't be easy for them to stay together. I tell you, Marcel, I'm glad I use my mum's anti-wrinkle cream, coz it means I'll never grow old.

Okay, I need to go to bed, I've got school tomorrow (I'm going to try sleeping in my own bed tonight). I'm really glad because things are going well with Juliette and Manon – they're acting like I don't exist.

Lily xx

PS Rat-a-tat-tat says sorry, he didn't do it on purpose (the wee, I mean).

Anna

My grandmother is sitting in her armchair, near the window. She's been waiting for us. She was glad I brought my visit forward by a day so the girls could come with me. One day less in her diary of loneliness. I give her a big hug and her cheeks feel cool against mine. Lily kisses her and hands her a small black stone.

'Here, Nanny. I brought this home from North Cape for you.'

Nanny is touched, stroking the pebble as if it were a diamond. Chloe takes her hand and whispers something in her ear.

'I didn't do anything special,' Nanny replies very quietly.

'But you did, Nanny!' I say. 'You did a lot.'

She brushes away any credit with a modest flick of her hand and turns our attention to the biscuits on the trolley.

'Help yourselves. Madame Duport's granddaughter made them.'

'No, thanks,' Chloe says. 'I'm trying to be careful – I've put on ten kilometres.'

'And it suits you very well. You look much better than the last time I saw you.'

Lily agrees with a nod of her head as she bites into her biscuit. She puts it straight back down, her face twisting into a grimace.

'Are these concrete biscuits or something? I nearly lost all my teeth.'

'Well, they were good last week,' Nanny says in amazement. 'Anyway, tell me everything! I have such wonderful memories of Norway. Did you like it?'

I let the girls talk. My grandmother already knows how I feel – I've been calling her once a week. The three of them compare their experiences and their reactions to things, which were almost identical, despite the sixty years between them.

'What was your favourite thing?'

'That's hard,' Chloe replies. 'I loved so many things . . . Maybe the northern lights. Or Preikestolen. No, no, I know! My favourite thing was the three of us being together.'

'Well, my favourite thing was the whales,' Lily announces.

Nanny throws her head back and laughs, and the girls join her. I watch them, savouring how lucky I am to be with three of the women without whom I wouldn't be who I am. There's one woman missing, but she's in all of us.

*

We stay till it's time for her supper, which is served in the dining room.

'I'll be back next week, Nanny,' I promise as I kiss her goodbye.

'Me, too!' Lily cries. 'But throw away those biscuits, they're dangerous.'

'I'll come, too,' Chloe says.

My grandmother's over the moon. She keeps her eyes pinned on us till we've left the room. The girls go ahead of me and I'm about to close the door when I hear her calling me back very quietly. I turn around and see a conspiratorial twinkle in her eye.

'So, have you heard from him?' she whispers.

'I was actually planning to call him now.'

'Are you going to say anything?'

'I don't know yet.'

She rubs her hands. Under her wrinkles, she's a ten-year-old. I stick out my tongue at her and close the door.

Five rings. I'm about to hang up when he answers.

'Hi, Anna!'

'Hi, Julien, how are you?'

Lily

25 June

My dear dear dear dear Marcel,

This is the last time I'll be writing in you, and
I'm really sad. I feel like you've been here forever,
and now I've got to leave you coz you're full up. I
shouldn't have done such big writing at the
beginning, I should have talked to you more spare
roomingly. That'll teach me.

Anyway, first I'll tell you the latest gossip, then
I'll say a proper goodbye.

First of all, I'm really happy because I'm going to
see Noah this weekend. My mum called his father,
who thinks it's a great idea for us to get together.
I'm a bit worried he won't recognise me, but I'll
whisper songs to him, like when we slept outside –
that should bring back memories. I personally can't
wait to see him, coz I've had a good look at school
but there's no one else like Noah.

Seeing as we're talking about school, it was
amazing. The twins haven't forgotten about me.

They were just waiting for the right time. They spotted me in the changing rooms by the gym when I was getting changed (I had my trousers round my ankles). Juliette called out that I was a snitch and, thanks to me, her sister had been excluded from school for three days, and Manon said it would have been better if I hadn't come back. I said I didn't have anything to say to them, that you can't mix chalk and cheesecakes, but that made them laugh and they just carried on making fun of me. Everyone was watching, but no one did anything about it. The twins said I needed to stop being such a show-off and that I'm a fart-face, specially with my short hair, and my mum should have chucked me down the toilet. When it came to that bit, I told them they shouldn't talk about my mum, but they kept going, they said she's fat and she's poor, and it made my eyes sting. I almost said that their mum's so short her face smells as bad as her feet, but I suddenly remembered what Françoise taught me: reply to their nastiness with a compliment.

I looked at Manon, who was busy saying all this horrible stuff to me, and I gave her a big smile and thanked her. She asked me what for and I said I was really touched by her kindness and the planet could do with more people like her. Everyone laughed, which made her even more angry. Her sister screamed that I'm completely mad and I said – very softly and sweetly – that she was pretty, specially when she smiled. Well, that shut her up. I wish you'd seen her! Everyone else fell about the place laughing, the twins muttered a few more insults and then went off to do something else. Okay, they did start up again in Maths, it's not going to stop just like that – got to be realistic – but I now know how to deal with it. I swear to you, Marcel, if anyone ever gives them a brain scan, they're in for some surprises.

Anyway, I hope you're proud of me. Either way, I'm proud of you, and I've really enjoyed spending four months of my life with you. Four important months.

I'm really going to miss you, but I'm not abandoning you, it's just I won't be able to talk to you any more. I'll keep you forever – you'll even be there when I'm in an old people's home like Nanny. You really are the best diary ever. I'll never forget you. Thank you for everything, my darling Marcel.

Lily x

PS I love you.

The Chloe Chronicles

Mum was working all day, for the first time since she started the cleaning job. The agency's already found her quite a few contracts and she thinks she'll soon be working full-time. Lily was at Clelia's house for the day.

I got up late, something I hadn't done for a long time. The stress of exams is wearing off now that it's all over. I went to get some photocopies for my visa application and then came home to get ready.

I straightened my hair because I know he likes it like that. I put on an LBD, heels and red lipstick. He was late, but he brought some pastries.

'Hi, Chloe.'

'Hi, Kevin, come in!'

He looked at the wall in the corridor, which we've covered with pictures from our road trip. He didn't look very relaxed, and I didn't feel it either. My legs were shaking.

'It looks nice.'

'It was amazing. Would you like something to drink?'

'What have you got?'

'Water.'

'A glass of water, then.'

We sat on the sofa and he put a hand on my thigh.

'It's really good to see you,' I said. 'And I'm so sorry about my mum . . .'

'Yeah, she really took the piss.'

'I know. Are you angry with me?'

'A bit. But you know what to do if you want me to forgive you . . .'

He pressed himself up against me and kissed me. His hand eased up under my dress. He smelled of warm bread.

'Do you want to stay here, or shall we go to your room?' he asked.

'I'd rather go to my room.'

He followed me, and I'd hardly shut the door before he started kissing me furiously. He flung my dress off and I took off his jeans, then he stroked my back and unhooked my bra. I pulled off his T-shirt and he groaned. He ran his mouth all over my neck and I let him grope my breasts while I took off his boxers. I pushed him on to the bed and he waited for me there with feverish eyes. He took my hand and pulled me to him.

'Come here,' he said.

'Wait, I've got a little surprise.'

He smiled eagerly and I slipped out of the room and shut myself in the bathroom. I ran back out moments later, screaming.

'Quick, Kevin! Quick, get out, there's a fire, the flames are huge, we need to get out!'

He popped out of the bed like an ejected CD and scrabbled around for his clothes.

'Quiiiiiiick!' I yelled, pulling his arm. 'We're going to burn! Who gives a stuff about your clothes!'

I dragged him into the corridor, still screaming, and I'd hardly opened the door before he was racing down the stairs. It took him a good two flights to get it. He came back up, trying to cover himself with his hands.

'Count yourself lucky,' I said with a smile. 'I left you a sock.'

I locked the door and called Louise to tell her all about it.

Anna

Lily absolutely insists on knocking on the door. After about twelve knocks, it opens and standing behind it is Julien. His smile sets mine off.

Lily says hello as she glances around to find Noah.

'He's in the living room. Come in!'

My daughter races inside and I'm left there, facing Julien. He doesn't give me a chance to hesitate before giving me a kiss on the lips and leading me into his apartment.

Lily is sitting next to Noah, who's rocking backwards and forwards.

'Noah, it's Lily. Do you recognise me? Do you remember, we went to Sweden and Finland and Norway? I used to come and see you in your campervan and we played with your top?'

The child doesn't react but keeps staring at the nature programme on TV. Lily gets up, puts her hand in her pocket and takes out the luminous yoyo she asked me buy on the way over. Without paying any attention to Noah – who sneaks a glance at her – she starts to play with it.

'Come on, let's leave them to it,' Julien whispers, leading me out of the room.

We sit on either side of a small green table on the balcony outside the kitchen.

'It's good to see you,' he says.

'You, too.'

'It's been hard without you. I've got into some bad habits.'

I smile, and he puts his hand on mine.

'I love you, Anna,' he says quietly.

My heart beats harder, as it does every time he says those words.

'And I love you, too. With all my heart.'

He strokes my hand.

'Do you think it's time to tell them?'

'I think so. My grandmother can't bear it any longer – she wants to know how they'll react.'

'Do you think they'll take it well?'

'I'm sure they will. I think they really like you. Well, Chloe might ask you to get rid of your shirts!'

He laughs.

'Do you know what day it is?'

'Of course I know.'

'Happy anniversary, my love.'

'Happy anniversary, my darling. A year already . . .'

Two Months Earlier

Anna

5 April

I knew Julien would be there when we reached the site in Hamburg. I struggled not to laugh when I saw the look on his face. I was fighting with the campervan's toilet unit.

'Anna? What on earth are you doing here?' he asked with a huge smile.

'Careful – my girls are watching out of the window. I took your advice – we needed to get away. And I thought it was a great opportunity to surprise you.'

'You have no idea how much I want to kiss you.'

Julien used to be head chef at L'Auberge Blanche, and we worked together for five years. I liked him – a great tall, friendly man, always ready to make a joke in the middle of a busy shift – but we'd never taken the time to get to know each other properly. Until the November morning when he came to work and the smile had gone out of his eyes. His wife had just left them – Noah and him – and he was devastated. I saw something of myself in the state he was in; my own family had been blown

341

apart two years earlier. With time, with a bit of confiding here and a shared silence there, we became friends. Our wounds brought us together, our damaged surfaces were drawn to each other like Velcro. He would help me clean the restaurant and I'd help him tidy the kitchen. We'd put the world to rights as we worked and our conversations often went on after closing time.

Three years ago, Julien left his job to look after Noah full-time, and I felt so empty that I started to think he was more than a friend. But I was already desperately short of time I couldn't possibly get into a relationship. Not to mention the armour I'd put up around myself, armour I wasn't ready to take off. I didn't even know if he felt the same.

We stayed in touch from a distance. He travelled with his son, I struggled with my girls, we'd message each other every now and again. Then he came to have supper in the restaurant last year . . . and I dropped three plates during that shift. I was in quite a dither. He stayed on after closing time and the easy closeness between us was there straight away. Like in the old days, he walked me back to my car and wished me goodnight before shutting the door. Except this time it wasn't my cheek he kissed.

Over the next few months we saw each other occasionally and spoke on the phone a lot. I wanted to devote all my free time to my girls, which didn't leave us with much, but we made the most of what little time we had. It didn't take long for me to throw off my armour. Julien was not

Mathias. He respected me and didn't try to get me to think like him; he listened to me and took pleasure in knowing I was happy. He left the last square of chocolate for me. When I was with him I didn't have to think about every word I said, I didn't back away the minute he raised an arm to take a book from a shelf or swat a fly. When I was with him I felt good.

When he told me he was going on another road trip with Noah I envied him. He suggested I went with him, saying that it would be a good opportunity to introduce our children, but it was a crazy idea. And then the reasons to go started outweighing the reasons not to. I didn't want to be part of the group. Following from a distance so I wasn't alone in an unknown country, fine; knowing Julien wasn't far away in case there was a problem, yes; but the plan was to spend time with Chloe and Lily, not to go off on a package holiday. The girls didn't give me a choice.

So we set off on the journey that would change our lives.

Two Months Later

The Chloe Chronicles

I know I haven't written anything for a long time, but I had a good excuse: I've been getting ready to leave.

It's the big day. In three hours, I'll be on a plane to my new life.

Mum won't leave me alone for a minute. She's trying not to show that she's sad, but she tells me she's happy a bit too often, so I'm starting to have my doubts. I think she'd have been happier if I'd failed my exams so we had to cancel the whole thing.

Lily isn't even trying to pretend – she's cried pretty much the volume of the Norwegian Sea since this morning.

If I'd gone last year, it would probably have been easier to leave them. Right now, it feels like we're being separated when we've only just found each other. Life at home has been much nicer the last few weeks. During the day Lily goes to the leisure centre and Mum works. I make the most of having the apartment to myself, writing, texting Louise, getting my stuff ready and hanging out with Ines but making sure I never go past the bakery. Then Mum, Lily and I have dinner together and watch a film every evening. When I put it like that it sounds like an ad on TV, but don't worry, there are still times I have to resist the urge to yell in Mum's face and throw Lily down the rubbish chute. Then I just have to remember how far away they'll be for the next year and that averts the crisis. When the end's in sight, you get on with what really matters.

Dad called this morning to wish me a good trip. I promised to go and see him when I get back. A year should be time enough to prepare for that.

Kevin sent me insulting texts for a few days but then got bored of it. Since then, there's been Malo, who waited two weeks before I invited him into my bedroom, and Sami, who didn't wait. I'm gradually making progress. As Lily would say, Rome wasn't built in a day-care centre.

'Are you ready, sweetheart?'

Mum is standing in the doorway to my bedroom. It's time to go. I glance at my room one last time and close the door on my teenage life.

'A year will fly by,' she says brightly, as if to convince herself.

'We can Skype each other.'

Lily nods and says, 'Yes, and if we get rich, we can come over. I hope we get to see koalas and kangaroos.'

Noah and Julien are waiting in the car. I'm glad they're coming to the airport with us – I daren't think what it would be like if Mum and Lily had to drive home on their own. I'm glad they're here, full stop. I couldn't hope to leave Mum and Lily in better company. Lumberjack shirts are underrated.

'I've got good news,' Julien says as he opens the boot of the car. 'Clara just called while she was shopping for the baby. She's managed to find room for Diego and Edgar in the retirement home where she and Greg work. They'll be sharing a studio, and they're over the moon. Biarritz isn't that far away – we could even go and see them.'

Mum's smile changes; it's now real for the first time today. Cheered by this happy outcome for the two olds, I sit by the window in the back, looking out over this scenery I know by heart. Mum slides her arm around her seat and strokes my leg. I take her hand and squeeze it. I'm going to miss you, Mummum.

I'm scared, of course. Given that I have a thing about loneliness, it's going to be tricky being on the far side of the world and not knowing anyone. But I feel ready. I have this constant need to be loved, and I don't think I'll ever shake it off, but on the other hand, I no longer have a need for approval. My own opinion should be enough for me from now on.

I want to thank all of you from the bottom of my heart for being there these last few months. Your comments and support have done a lot for me. Even though we don't know each other, you've helped me grow up. I've realised that there are lots of us feeling the same things and, even more importantly, that it doesn't matter if we don't.

It's time I said goodbye. I'm going to stop writing about my life and start living it.

I'll leave the blog online in case it's useful for someone going through the turbulent conditions they call the teenage years.

And who knows? We might meet for real one day without even knowing. In Sydney, Toulouse or somewhere else.

Lots of love
Chloe xx

Lily

25 August

Dear Josiane,

I'm Lily, and I'm twelve years old. I used to have
a diary called Marcel, but he's finished. At first I
didn't want to replace him, I was worried he'd be
upset, but I found you all on your own on the shelf
and heard you calling to me. When I introduced
you he seemed to really like you.

Btw, you're called Josiane because you're square,
the same shape as Josiane's chin (she's the lady in
the canteen).

Anyway, that's enough talking – this is a serious
moment. We're on the way to the airport. My
sister's flying off to Sydney, in Australia. On the
internet it says that's 17,000 kilometres away as the
crow flies, but I'm not sure how they know that.
Maybe they gave the crow an extra-long ruler so he
could measure it. Basically, my sister's going to be a
long way away. But I hope we still stay on the same
demi-wave length. Okay, so we haven't stopped

arguing (I mean, what do you expect? My sister's often wrong and I'm often right, so there's bound to be trouble), but I really love her.

We're in Julien's car because it's bigger and we could all get in. Noah's next to me, looking out at the road. He's holding the soft round pebble I gave him – he takes it everywhere. I was so happy when Mum said she and Julien were together! We see them nearly every weekend. We go for walks in the woods or by the lake, and sometimes we do nothing, and that's nice, too. I'd really like it if we lived together, but Mum says you have to take your time and do things well. I don't really get that, because you can still do things badly even if you do take time, but it looks like she's made up her mind. So, for now, I'll make the most of being in a little family, until we get to be a bigger one. Noah's like my brother now, except our kidneys aren't compatible. I'm learning a lot from him, you know. Before, if people said I was different, I didn't like it much, it felt like I was in a game of 'spot the odd one out'. But now I hope I'm always different. I never want to be like everyone else. It's stupid to be someone else when you can be yourself.

Okay, Josiane, I'll leave you for now. I'd rather spend some time with my sister while she's still here.

Lily xx

PS I can't take this heat any more. I left the
fridge door open last night to cool things down.
My mum wasn't toooooooo pleased with that,
I can tell you.

Anna

It's time for Chloe to go through Security. Julien and Noah have said their goodbyes and left us on our own. I'm smiling, pretending my heart doesn't feel as if it's being trodden underfoot.

Eighteen years ago, this creature just forty-nine centimetres long was laid on my chest and it immediately filled my whole world. The moment my daughter first cried I started dreading the day she would leave. One metre and five centimetres later, that day has come. I hope I'll manage to keep going without falling into the terrible void she leaves behind.

I stroke her cheek, my tiny baby's cheek, and she checks no one sees me do it.

'It's going to be wonderful, sweetheart.'

'I know,' she says, wiping a tear that's escaped. 'But I'm going to miss you both.'

Lily throws herself into her sister's arms, hugs her tight and then pulls away almost immediately.

'Here, it's a lucky charm,' she whispers, slipping a pebble into Chloe's hand. 'I got it from the car park on the estate so you'll have a little bit of home with you.'

My little Tom Thumb of love.

Chloe strokes the pebble and puts it in her pocket, then tilts her chin towards Julien and Noah.

'They'll fill the gap I leave behind – it'll be fine!'

'No one can fill the gap you leave, Chloe.'

'No, seriously! After a year, you must be kind of fond of him!' she says, laughing.

He's watching me anxiously from where he's standing. He knows this is agony for me.

I remember the moment we officially told our children we were together. The girls made me say it three times. They were convinced it was a joke. They thought back over our trip and, every time they remember a clue, they gave a shriek. Once they were over the initial surprise, they insisted they'd guessed but hadn't said anything so as not to ruin our fun.

'You really should go through now, sweetheart,' I say eventually. 'You need to leave plenty of time.'

Chloe looks right into my eyes, and I can see a mixture of apprehension and determination in hers. She flings her arms around my neck and hugs me with all her might. Lily's little arms reach around the two of us and we stay like that for several seconds, charging ourselves up with each other's love.

'I'm so proud of who you've become, my darling,' I tell her.

'It's thanks to you, Mum.'

She slowly breaks away from our hug, wipes her cheeks,

slips something into my hand and then walks away. I watch her until her tear-clouded figure disappears around the corner and then I look at what she's given me.

It's a photo, a selfie of the three of us at Vigelands-parken in Oslo. Behind us is the statue we all loved of a mother carrying her child, hugged against her face. Lily's sticking her tongue out, Chloe's deliberately squinting and I'm roaring with laughter.

Our trip didn't change a thing. When we got home the bills were still there, and so were all the problems, I didn't have a job, Lily had enemies and Chloe demons. Things hadn't changed. But we had.

Even 17,000 kilometres apart we'll be together.

Even when my daughters are fifty years old we'll be together.

We have something that will never die.

We're a family.

Acknowledgements

A reader recently asked me to thank my nearest and dearest for letting me write. I was deeply touched because, like her, I believe that I can only tell these stories, I can only feel these emotions and put them into words, because of the people closest to me.

My acknowledgements are usually about contributions to the book in question. This time they're about the contributions to my life.

Because we're all aboard the same bus as it trundles forward inexorably . . .

There's no question that the first thank you should come to you, my dear mother. I came on board the bus forty years ago, and you were waiting for me there. Thank you for giving me so much. Thank you for keeping us on track, despite the twists and turns, the accidents and breakdowns. Thank you for teaching me to look out of the window and see how beautiful it is out there. Thank you for leaving the biggest space on your seat for us. Thank you for allowing us to travel without leaving home. Thank you for making the three of us a family and for knowing when to let go our hands while still waiting behind us, just in case. I couldn't wish for a better mother than you.

Thank you, Marie. Apparently, a few days before you were born, I announced that I would never love you. How wrong I was . . . Thank you for joining us on the bus and for becoming my hairless younger sister. Thank you for being so sensitive, funny, generous, whingeing and ever-present. The fact you have no idea what a beautiful person you are makes you even more beautiful. Thank you for being the one who cherishes all these memories with me.

Thank you to my son. When you can read, you might well find these words a bit soppy. I can't help it, every time I think of you my blood turns to honey. You changed everything the day you got on the bus. The sky got bluer, the scenery more resplendent and my emotions stronger. Everything had a meaning now. I think, even if you weren't my son, I'd love you with all my heart. You're funny, kind, attentive, cuddly, empathetic, sensitive and, most of all, you like sleeping in in the morning. I hope this will be a long journey.

Thank you, A. You didn't stay on the bus very long, but it feels as if you're still here. Since you left, I've had something less, but I've also had something more. I know how to look at the world. I know how to make the most of things. I know how to feel. I hope you're proud of me.

Thank you, my love. You're the most kind-hearted person I know, thank you for choosing me to make this journey by your side. I'm struggling to remember what it was like before you. Thank you for laughing at my not-always-funny jokes, thank you for understanding me even when you can't, thank you for listening to me talk about my characters as if they were real without calling in the men in white coats, thank you for your ideas and support, thank you for being happy just to see me happy, thank you for being the husband you are and the father you are. When I was little, I thought Barbie's Ken was the ideal man. But you don't even need a ju-jitsu hold to wipe the floor with him.

Thank you, Granny and Grandpa, for never being far away, for your door being always open, and your hearts, too. Thank you for cooking me lovely things when I'm in my intensive writing phases. Thank you for taking part in this adventure with such joy. Thank you, Dad, for being so proud. Thank you, Mimi, for being the most fun aunt in the world. Thank you, Yanis, Lily, Gil, Céline, Guy, Anna, Antoine, Arthur, Claudine, Marc, Gilbert, Simone, Carole and everyone else in the family – I love you.

Thank you to Clara Climent, for your reader's comments, which help me fly, and for being my friend for such a long time (old girl). Thank you to Gaëlle Bredeville, my kitten, for your friendship, for reading my work, for your enthusiasm, your madness and your tajines (when's the next one?). Thank you to Serena Giuliano Laktaf, Sophie Henrionnet and Cynthia Bavarde for becoming so invaluable, thank you for your kindness, the laughter we've shared and for being on the bus. Thank you to Constance Trapenard for making me feel like the funniest and most insightful person on the planet. Thank you to Baptiste Beaulieu for your lovely words and your friendship; it's great knowing you're there and so similar. Thank you to Gavin's Clemente Ruiz for the photos of buttocks, your friendship and the *Guides du routard* travel guides, which really helped me. Thank you to Camille Anseaume for being who you are and for the friendship you give me (even when you do nick my Basquella chocolate spread). Thank you to Marie Vareille for your detailed and perceptive reading, your valuable advice and our chats.

Thank you to the teams at Fayard for giving me the opportunity to write what I like and then liking it, too, thank you for helping with my books with so much enthusiasm. Thank you to Alexandrine Duhin: over the years you've become more than my editor. Thank you to Sophie de Closets for your little notes – about the manuscript or not – because I find them very touching. Thank you to Jérôme Laissus, Éléonore Delair, Martine Thibet, Katy Fenech, Laurent Bertail, Pauline-Gertrude Faure, Valentine Baud, Carole Saudjaud, Ariane Foubert, Anna Lindlom, Lily Salter, Véronique Héron, Sandrine Paccher, Marie Lafitte and Marie-Félicia Mayonove.

Thank you to the teams at Livre de Poche for your energy and kindness, and in particular to my dear Audrey Petit, the wonderful Véronique Cardi and the lovely Sylvie Navellou, Anne Bouissy, Florence Mas and Jean-Marie Saubesty.

Thank you to my dear France Thiabault – at last a

chance to publicise you! my publicist, for going to so much trouble to spread the word about my books.

Thank you, dear booksellers. During signings, I'm always moved by your passion and your eagerness to find *the* right book for each reader. It means a lot to us, knowing that our stories are in your hands.

Thank you to the teams of reps for being the first messengers and for putting so much enthusiasm and fervour into championing my books.

Thank you to the bloggers for sharing your reading experiences so passionately. I'm often touched, struck and energised by the things you say about my books. With the things you say about other books, my bank manager is much less appreciative.

A special thank you to Fabien, alias the slam poet Grand Corps Malade, for kindly agreeing to give me your title 'We'll Still Have That'. A different title was chosen in the end, but I was touched by this offer. As I always am by your work.

Lastly, just this once, I'll end with you, my dear readers. Don't they say we keep the best till last?

The readers who write to me at length, the ones who come to meet me, those who read me discreetly, those who lend my books to their loved ones, those who pop me under the Christmas tree, those who come up to me in the street, those who recommend my books to their patients, those who send me photos, those who laugh at my flights of fancy on Instagram, those who stumble across my books by chance, those who read my blog, too, those already waiting for the next book, those who comment on social media, those who read passages to their partners, those who underline passages, those who fold over the corners of pages, those who reread books several times, those who tell me who they are, those who cry on the Métro, those who burst out laughing at my work, those who read my words in retirement homes, those who get together in clubs, those who have my book stolen on a beach, those who send me their regional specialities, those who introduce their students to my stories, those who are planning to read me soon, those who are helped through difficult times by my words, those who want to go and visit Biarritz, those who are no longer afraid of growing old, those who read together, those who text each other about my books, them and so many others . . .

When my first book was published I thought it would sell forty copies, all of them bought by my mother. But I didn't mind: I'd realised my childhood dream.

A few years later, I've had four books published and I get wonderful messages from people every day (my mother promises they're not from her). Even my childhood dream wasn't that good.

Thank you, all of you, for this fantastic adventure, thank you for reading me and encouraging me, thank you for your messages, your smiles, your tears and your secrets. Thank you for sitting down next to the little girl on the bus with a head full of dreams. The journey's magical with you.